Fun with Dirk and Bree

ALICE KAHN

POSEIDON PRESS

New York London Toronto Sydney Tokyo Singapore

Poseidon Press

Simon & Schuster Building

Rockefeller Center

1230 Avenue of the Americas
New York, New York 10020

POSEIDON PRESS is a registered trademark
of Simon & Schuster Inc.

POSEIDON PRESS colophon is a trademark
of Simon & Schuster Inc.

Designed by Chris Welch
Manufactured in the United States of America

10 9 8 7 6 5 4 3 2 1

Library of Congress Cataloging-in-Publication Data
Kahn, Alice, date
Fun with Dirk and Bree / Alice Kahn.
p.   cm.
I. Title.
PS3561.A3635F86   1991
813'.54—dc20   91-19844
                                                                CIP

ISBN 0-671-69151-1

We are grateful for permission to quote from the following:

"Heart" words and music by Richard Adler and Jerry Ross. Copyright © 1955,
copyright renewed © 1983 by Richard Adler Music and J & J Ross Company.
Rights administered by Songwriter's Guild of America. All Rights Reserved. International Copyright secured. Used by permission.

"That's When Your Heartaches Begin" words and music by Fisher-Raskin &
Brown. International copyright renewed © 1952 by Fisher Music Corporation. All
Rights Reserved. International Copyright Secured. Used by permission.

"Love on a Two Way Street" words and music by Sylvia Robinson and Bert
Keyes. Copyright © 1968 by Gambi Music, Inc. All Rights Reserved. International Copyright Secured. Used by permission.

*For Eddie
and all those who avoided the trend
toward total integrityectomy.*

Fun with Dirk and Bree

1

They were not long, the days of wine and yuppies. We consumed things and were consumed by them. It was a time to make money; it was a time to think opportunity would always leave a message on the machine. Some realized their dreams and some had recurring nightmares. But did we get what we deserved?

Do we ever really get what we deserve? I mean outside of those two hours of free-falling ecstasy when you realize a deal is going to happen. Two great hours until it hits you: you're going to have to do the work.

Sure, we feel rewarded when someone says "I love you." I've only heard it from four or five people—two of whom were my parents and, at first, I didn't believe them. They had to get back to me on that.

Oh yeah, I forgot about sex. It's easy to forget about those thirty seconds of actual ecstasy, because you can hardly have a career and sex at the same time.

But most people I know, and I mean even people getting paid in like the high seventies, don't feel they're getting what they deserve. Even people with health insurance feel gypped. Even people with dental. I think that's why I always watch award shows.

On awards shows, you have an endless parade of famous people doing their impressions of real people finally getting what they deserve. So after I made my screenplay deal, the two hours of ecstasy were spent imagining the awards ceremony.

I imagined Dan Rather presenting the award to me, even though I know Dan Rather doesn't do the Academy Awards. Although a lot of people hate him, I've always had a thing for Dan, ever since I read in *Good Housekeeping* that he'd done heroin for a story in the fifties. I thought there was a little film over his eyes that separated him from the other anchors, a little something that said: Mine eyes have seen the glory.

And he's got those tight lips that always appear to be smirking. "In Charleston, another man, another semiautomatic weapon, another third-grade class . . ." Smirk. Smirk.

Mmm. I just love those tight little lips. What's the frequency, Dan?

And I just love the way he says "cap-sue-el" instead of capsul. "Today in the Middle East, the President took a cap-sue-el of Tylenol laced with LSD." Smirk. Smirk.

But in my dreams, my wonderful dreams, I wipe that smirk off his face and see him opening the envelope, and from out of that slit in his straight mouth, I hear my name: "Laura Gloriana."

And then, of course, because this is fantasy play-by-play, as the camera shows me kissing my boyfriend Russ before making my way to the proscenium, lifting up the bodice on my red strapless sequined job, we hear Dan saying, "Gloriana, a first-time screenwriter, has taken the Oscar for her monumental saga 'Perfect Love,' a cap-sue-el of our times. 'Perfect Love,' based on a series of articles Gloriana wrote for *Lifestyle, A Magazine* and developed from the actual love story of an actual couple."

On the way up, I stop to kiss Mia and Woody. I wink at Dustin. As I walk across the stage I see Bruce and Demi stand up. Soon everyone is standing. They're cheering "Bravo." They're chanting "Au-thor, au-thor." They're yelling "We love you."

Marlon Brando is in the front row mouthing, "You are great."

I rush up to Dan. He places those absent lips on mine. The statue is still warm where his fist embraced it. I am so composed I whisper, "Later," in his ear.

"I'd like to thank . . ." I hear myself saying. I'm a little bird flying over a cartoon bubble above my head, and the bubble says: "I'd like to thank . . ."

"I don't know what I did to deserve this, but there are so many people I'd like to thank that I'm sure I'll leave somebody out. First of all, I'd like to thank whatever Supreme Intelligence may be guiding the universe, be it God, Buddha, or just a potted plant. I'd like to thank my boyfriend Russ Nelman for putting up with my moods, my parking tickets, my writer's and menstrual cramps, my repetitive stress injury, and the fact that I can't come unless the TV is on. I'd like to thank everyone who worked on this picture—Steven, Syd, Lew— everyone at Sigalawinkie Productions. I'd like to thank the crew, the best crew a writer could have to work with, particularly Marilyn at Just the Fax on Fourth Street. I'd like to thank my parents, Lenore and Harry Gurvitz. Lenore is no longer with us, and I only wish she were alive to see this day. Harry is finishing a difficult life at the Kai Kapu on the beautiful island of Hawaii, and I know he is watching. Even if you are not cognizant of what is going on around you, Daddy, I hope you know I love you. And please, please don't think I changed my name because I didn't want people to think I was Jewish. I changed it to get attention. And I'd also like to thank the Jewish People.

"But most of all, I'd like to thank two people without whom this entire project would never have been possible. Those people are Dirk and Bree. When they first shared their life with me and let me record it for *Lifestyle, A Magazine,* I don't think any of us ever dreamed things would go this far. From the series that began in the early eighties with 'Dirk and Bree, an American YUPle,' to my book *Dirk and Bree and Baby Makes Three,* they have opened up their mouths, their home, and have shared their most intimate thoughts with me and millions of readers. I don't know why they did it, but I love them for it."

I hold up the statue and say, "Dirk and Bree, this is for you."

2

I wasn't there when the dream ended. I saw it on television. I hadn't planned to watch. In fact, I considered watching talk shows, watching any daytime TV, a sign of depression. I had only turned the TV on as background noise, to drown out the sound of a neighbor's leaf blower.

Dirk would later describe the scene in the greenroom, which, by the way, was actually painted beige. Bree looked cool as she poured herself a glass of white zinfandel from the buffet; he called out from across the room, where he was seated between the zookeeper and another couple, "Make mine a double, Bree."

While Bree filled his wineglass he watched the monitor, seeing what I could see at home. As Del Warfield was finishing up the low-cal whipped cream segment with Richard Simmons, Dirk and Bree clinked glasses and toasted each other. She gave him a little kiss on the cheek, a kiss like Gorbachev saying farewell to Boris Yeltsin.

Chuck "Just call me Chuck" Chernoff, one of Del Warfield's segment producers, came up and touched each of them on the shoulder and said, "You're on, kids. Just be yourselves. It's cool."

On the screen, Del Warfield was saying, "We're broadcasting live from California, where so many trends start. Today we're going to hear from experts as well as couples who've experienced the latest California craze. Today on 'What's Hot and What's Not,' Dirk Miller and Bree Wellington are here to talk about their Caring Divorce. Caring Divorce . . . next on the Del Warfield show."

"Oh shit." I turned off the computer and ran to the TV, hoping—praying—it was some other Dirk Miller and Bree Wellington.

During a Nightengale douche commercial, I turned my phone ringer to off and my answering machine volume to low.

After the damsel with the douche marched off my screen, Del bounded onto the stage. The audience burst into applause as she walked on, over the driving drumbeat sounds of the Del Warfield theme song.

"Welcome back. Today we're talking about Caring Divorce. Can you separate and still be friends? Can you give up the marriage but not the love? In a minute we'll be talking to Dirk Miller and Bree Wellington, a couple who are in the process of doing just that. Jane Fonda and Tom Hayden could not be here, but Betty Slovitch and Rick Halsey, who got their caring divorce three years ago, are here to tell us how it's working out. We'll also meet zoo director Frank Owsely and a very special guest, Cheetah Rivera—the new baby cheetah!"

The audience applauded like trained dogs.

"But first, Dirk and Bree, welcome to the Del Warfield show."

"Thank you, Del, a pleasure to be here," said Bree, who looked predictably stunning in a turquoise silk blouse and a simple but very short black skirt. I could tell she was holding her knees together for dear life—no crotch shots on network TV.

"Hi, Del." Dirk smiled and waved, the cuffs of his gray sports coat pushed up to the elbows.

"Now, when did you two first realize you were going to get a caring divorce?"

"Well, it really started three months ago, but I think I can speak for Bree and myself when I say that once we decided to get a divorce, it was going to be a caring one."

Applause.

"Dirk and Bree, anyone who's read *Lifestyle, A Magazine* in the past decade probably knows who you are. But let me fill in those members of the audience who may not be familiar with your story. You were essentially the first known yuppies."

Applause.

"Yes, in a series of articles about new lifestyles, writer Laura Gloriana coined the term 'yuppies' to describe you—"

"Actually, I think I used the word and she picked up on it," said Dirk.

"No, honey," said Bree, turning to him. "Don't you remember when she asked us, 'Aren't you just hippies turned consumer junkies?' and I said to her, 'We're not hippies. We're not junkies. We're yuppies.'"

"With all due respect, Bree, I remember quite distinctly saying, 'Yuppies, young urban professionals, are what we are and who we market to.' "

I cannot believe this. First they decide to get a divorce and now they were grabbing my claim to fame.

"I thought it was Bob Greene who made it up," said Del, looking into the camera and then turning to them. "Dirk and Bree, what made you decide to let a reporter and then a TV crew come into your home, explore your lifestyle and invade your privacy?"

"It was Bree's idea," said Dirk as Bree said, "Dirk wanted it."

He smiled, but I could see that he was getting a little exasperated. "I never wanted it. You were the one who brought Laurie Glory into the house—"

"Laurie Glory?" Del asked excitedly.

I sat absolutely motionless, frozen.

"Yeah," Dirk said, "she used us, you know. She made a career of us. It was Bree's decision to let her come in and make us the laughingstock of the entire country."

What betrayal!

"My decision? Ha! That's a laugh," Bree said, deadly serious.

The audience laughed and clapped as Bree spun around to face him.

"Dirk, you were the one who said the publicity would be good for Recovery, Inc."

"Whoa!" said Del. "What's Recovery, Inc.?"

"I'm glad you asked me that, Del," Dirk said. "Recovery, Inc., is the most successful substance abuse program in the country. As president of this chain of treatment centers, I'm proud to say that our franchises report an overall success rate of seventy-eight percent. Now," he said, looking directly at the camera, "You can just say no to recidivism."

What an asshole!

"Excuse me, Dirk," said Del. "We're going to take a moment to hear from our sponsor, the good people at Golden Spa Cuisine, who will show you how you can have your pasta with pesto and still show your legs with gusto. Then . . . Caring Divorce, on today's Del Warfield show."

I sat numb, panting, watching a woman in a bathing suit eat a plate of pasta without getting a ripple in her thigh or a basil leaf in her teeth.

Then the Del music started and Del's face filled the screen.

"So, Dirk and Bree, how will you remain friends as your marriage disintegrates, as your world is collapsing around you?"

"Well, I think the key here is being open and sharing our feelings. As we say at Recovery, Inc., 'If you can't let it out, you'll end up taking it in.' "

Dirk paused as if he'd said something worth pausing for.

"You know, Dirk, if we had ever had time to talk, we might not have needed a divorce." The camera was closing in on Bree.

"But no-o-o-o," Bree continued, opening into a full Belushi. "You were always at your computer pretending to work, while I know you were in fact e-mailing love letters to your electronic slut!"

The audience gasped and booed. I wondered, was Dirk on the LoveNet?

"What slut?" Dirk said. "I was getting more love from my computer network than I was getting from my fancy lawyer wife."

Del, like a bullfighter's assistant, attempted to drive in one lance. "Dirk, are you saying that your wife's career had something to do with your divorce?"

"I'm saying I was home with the baby, trying to run a business, trying to raise a child, and even trying to make a decent dinner . . ."

Bree stood up. "Maria was watching the baby. You were fooling around on the computer. The Mobile Gourmet was making us dinner. And I gave up a thriving law practice for you . . ."

The audience began clapping. More people were booing. Women yelled "Yeah! Yeah!" and grown men hissed.

Dirk stood up and faced Bree. "Nobody made you do anything. Your career was going nowhere. The baby and I were just an excuse for your own inadequacies."

Suddenly, Bree reached forward to the large mauve vase of artificial flowers on the coffee table in Del Warfield's fake living room. With one forward thrust, she smashed it into Dirk's face.

Del Warfield placed her strong arms in a half nelson around Bree Wellington's petite shoulders and pulled her back. We got a close-up of Dirk's bloody, rearranged face.

3

I watched the whole episode in horror. My career flashed before my eyes. My dollhouse was collapsing in front of me. I couldn't believe Dirk and Bree could do this to me.

I made them a household word—at least in certain households of affluent college-educated nonsavers between the ages of twenty-five and forty-five. There wasn't a party Dirk and Bree could go to without someone saying, "I saw you on television" or, "I read about you in *Lifestyle*" or, "I read the

book." Now we were on the brink of Dirk and Bree, The
Movie. And they had to go and ruin everything.

You're probably wondering, does anything real ever happen
in my life, or am I just talk, talk, talk? I've wondered as much
myself, especially after a long hard day of slaving over a hot
disk drive. As much as I tried to treat Dirk and Bree as a
work of fiction—"the Dirk and Bree property" my agent called
them—the reality of Dirk and Bree had finally exploded in
my face, just as the nineties nuked the eighties.

Some people think you can tell the history of our times in
terms of war, but I think it can also be found in life's trivial
details—like what year you bought what machine. For a typ-
ical middle-class person, that history might resemble my own:

1981—Blow-dryer
1983—Coffee/espresso machine
1985—VCR
1986—Computer
1988—Answering machine
1990—Modem; Salad shooter

I decided to draw a line in the sand at the personal fax
machine. There was really only one machine I used to propel
myself toward that odd kind of notoriety some people call
success. As my friend Mai Blender liked to say, "Dirk and
Bree were your vehicle."

When I revved up the Dirk and Bree project, one of the
first things I wanted to know was what machines they had
and what machines they wanted. By 1983, Bree had an answering machine, Dirk had an Apple II, and they had a state-
of-the-art—now obsolete—Beta VCR. I shocked them back
then when I told them that I didn't have any of these things
and added, a bit smugly, that I had no intention of acquiring
them. It shows you how little I understood about the way the
decade was going. In '83, I still thought it was politically
correct not to want too many material possessions. In '83, I
still cared about being P.C.

"You're just a maintainer-striver," Bree said to me during our first formal interview. I don't need my notes or a tape to remember that day.

I can still picture the way her green eyes slowly blinked as she stared at me from her white woven Haitian sofa, surrounded by mauve and teal throw pillows. Don't ask me why, but those eyes inspired as much awe as envy. We were sitting in the living area of the Bay Gauche condo she and Dirk had bought that year. I was trying to figure out what Bree was attempting to communicate with her hairdo. Back then, her red hair was cropped short—not the conservative pageboy she now wears. It was in a mod, almost punkish style that contrasted sharply with the padded-shoulder suits she wore to work. I decided her hairdo was meant to hint at the Victoria's Secret lingerie hidden just below the proper surface.

At first, I hated her. She was so beautiful. And she was smart. She loved to talk in that demographers' lingo she picked up at the Stanford Futures Institute while she was in law school down on the farm.

She told me that I was not the first person who had studied her. In fact, she was the subject of a video made at SFI called "Women Achiever-Leaders: A Force Among Young Professionals." She also revealed, right in front of Dirk, that she had had an affair with the SFI scientist who conducted the study, and that in several of the preliminary interviews she was videotaped naked! They, of course, were not used in the final report on Baby Boomer Consumer-Loomers prepared for the ad agency of Doyle Skully Cachet & Schkutzum—the legendary study that many say paved the way for the electronics explosion.

When Bree and the research scientist broke up—she dumped him, Dirk let me know that—Bree demanded the cassettes. They still had them, and: would I like to see them?

Bree made popcorn first. She used a hot-air popper because Bree watched her intake and output like an orderly. I think it was the first time I was ever served Perrier. I have that in my notes from the first interview: *Bree walks over to the*

*kitchen area and gets out this sleek green bottle and these tall
oversized goblets and fills each with some of a water from
France called Perrier. Dirk sets up the tape on a videocassette
recorder which they have attached to their TV. Dirk—male-
model handsome, square jaw, conservative short blondish-
brown hair, but dark haunting eyes, slightly ethnic nose and
lips—Al Pacino goes to Yale.*

While she was out of the room Dirk started talking about
their relationship, revealing his lower-middle-class origins,
which he regarded as a shameful secret. Dirk thought Bree
was above him.

"I bet you wonder what she sees in me. I used to wonder
that too. But I'm an achiever and an achiever-worshiper, and
Bree needs to be both an equal and an icon. It's a perfect
match. And why not? I used a computer stimulation to test
our relationship."

He said "stimulation." Really—I have it on tape.

I had no idea what to make of the high-tech kinkiness going
on. I hadn't yet placed my toe in that virtual reality of the
computer, which would become a true addiction for Dirk. As
Joe M.B.A. normal as he looked, Dirk was a man of many
secrets and many addictions.

When Bree walked in and handed me the Perrier and popcorn, I didn't even notice the little line of cocaine Dirk was
inhaling. This was before hip coke became underclass crack.
I was so naive I thought his animation during the tape showing
was merely a response to Bree's video exhibitionism.

As we sat there munching and talking we watched a naked
Bree sitting in a stylized chrome chair in a sun-filled office
somewhere in Palo Alto, California, saying, "I was born in
Milwaukee, Wisconsin, in 1953 to prosperous but ambitious
parents. Much was expected of me because even though we
lived in a large mansion, always filled with antiques and fresh-
cut flowers, my father often came home smelling like a brewery. In fact, he owned a brewery."

Dirk started laughing insanely. Later, I would try to explain
to my boyfriend Jeremy how weird this scene was. Of course,

I kept the bizarre details out of the story I wrote. I wanted the readers to see Dirk and Bree as kind of cartoon characters. "The Yuppies," I would call the series, and I thought it should be a fun read. But in the flesh—the actual flesh, in Bree's case—all their weirdness made Dirk and Bree slightly frightening.

It was always Bree, much more than Dirk, who defined "yuppie." Yuppies were basically women; women in business suits, posing like young urban drag queens, inherently made a mockery of male professionals. New sensitive men like Dirk were basically what we used to call "women."

On the screen, Bree, whose breasts were—I couldn't help noticing—all erect nipple, was saying, "My father owned the Wellington-Babs Brewing Company, and I was named Barbara Wellington. They called me Babs. And I suspect some of my desire to achieve grew out of the fact that I was horribly ashamed that I was called by the name of a beer. Some of my school friends would sing the Babs commercial as I walked by, 'Babs, Babs, Milwaukee's Best Beer—Babs, Babs, Milwaukee's Best Beer . . .' When I was twelve and won the figure skating finals, I could hear that song even though my winning piece was to 'Norwegian Wood.' "

Dirk suddenly dropped his hand in my lap. Never one for subtlety, I screamed, "Hey!"

"Sorry, sorry, I thought you had the popcorn," he said, flashing me a blinding smile.

Bree thrust the bowl onto his lap. He held it up so I could see it.

"We found this art deco bowl at a flea market in Carmel last summer . . ." he said, oh so casually. On the screen, Bree was saying, "I won a scholarship to Radcliffe with my essay on how drafting women could help end the war in Vietnam." The scientist who was videotaping her at this point went in for an art shot of Bree's crotch that filled the entire screen.

Bree suddenly got up and ran to the bathroom. I could hear her vomiting. Dirk inappropriately laughed again.

"Popcorn allergy," he said.

I decided not to probe too deeply in future interviews with Dirk and Bree. I was looking for some laughs for a lifestyle rag, not a study of the psychopathology of modern life.

On the way home, I spaced out on the Bay Bridge listening to my tape of the interview with Dirk and Bree. It was the first of some fifty interviews I would conduct over the next seven years, at their Bay Gauche condo and, later, after their daughter Rachel was born, at their house at Quail Glen. I feared that it was pure voyeurism, but it was also symbiotic—the Watcher had found the Watch-mes.

Maybe I'm being too psychological about it now, a bad habit from one too many therapy sessions. Maybe it had been economic all along, our *campagne à trois*. All three of us started making money as the eighties bloomed, and the mutually attention-grabbing articles in *Lifestyle* certainly contributed to our success.

I decided one thing, though. After what they had willingly shared with me in the first interview, if Dirk and Bree had anything to hide, I didn't want to see it.

4

Not half an hour after I had turned off the disaster on the Del Warfield show, I got a call from Slow-go Rosenbloom, my Hollywood agent.

"Well, have you scraped your ego off the wall, sweetheart?" He could say the worst things in the cheeriest voice you ever heard.

"I have to tell you the deal is off," he continued.

This wasn't getting any better, and the thought of an accelerating downward spiral didn't cheer me up. In half an hour I had lost fifty up front, fifty on delivery, and seventy-five plus points if the movie gets made. Where would I be by this time next week?

"How can the deal be off?" I screamed into the phone, picturing Slow-go on his orange Naugahyde couch. He'd decorated his whole office with the fifties motel furniture he collected. He was probably sitting there reading a script and getting Rolfed while he was sending me to sleep in People's Park.

"Darling, publicity like you got today, you don't need. The whole mystique of compatibility has been shot. That was our thing here—that marriage can work, can be romantic, can be adult entertainment. That was the value of the Dirk and Bree property. We might be able to still do the dolls, though. With boxing gloves."

"But you're supposed to be my agent. You're supposed to do something."

"Honey, if I thought I could save this deal, I'd be over giving Lew Shnorman a blow job right now, while his hideous Selma looked on. It's undone. It's dead. You know, careers run hot and cold. I won't say you'll never work in this town again, but you might need a new identity."

"Like what?" I said, forgetting that sarcasm was spoken here, thinking there might be some career left to career-salvage.

"Like a Southeast Asian who's good with computer hardware."

That Rosenbloom sense of humor—totally devoid of comfort.

"Slow-go, do me a favor," I said, feeling close to the edge. "Go fuck yourself."

"Kiddo, I know how you feel, but no one wants a divorce movie. No one wants to dig up the bodies of Kramer versus Kramer. We want funny. We want sexy monogamy. Your mistake was using real people. It's hard to get creative control on real life."

"Unless you're God."

"Ri-i-i-iight. Oops! There's Danielle Steel on the phone.

Look, I'll try Lew again. Maybe we can tell him it was just a
ploy on Dirk and Bree's part to get a cut. Talk to them. Find
out what they want. Gotta run!"

What *they* want? What about me? What did I ever get out
of it? Did I even get a life?

Only ten years ago I had been a marginally employed free-
lance writer cum retired social worker cum maîtresse d' cum
anything to support my journalism habit. Now I had a New
York agent, a Hollywood agent, and even a licensing agent.
There was talk of Dirk and Bree dolls. There was talk of "Dirk
and Bree on Childcare" videos.

The shocks were hitting me one after another. Why didn't
they tell me they were getting a divorce? Why didn't they
call me? I could've done "Dirk and Bree on Caring Divorce."
Why didn't they let me know?

And what about that tone? What about calling me Laurie
Glory? I knew some people called me that behind my back.
I knew there were other writers who were jealous. There was
the ongoing controversy over who made up the Y-word. Who
did Dirk and Bree think they were kidding?

I actually thought Dirk and Bree liked me. Dirk used to
flirt with me all the time. Right in front of Bree. How was I
to know it was the cocaine talking?

By now, I even liked them. Oh sure, at first I thought Bree
was cold and vain. If I were as pretty as she is, I would be
too—not that some people don't think I'm pretty. Thirty-two
consecutive boyfriends can't all be wrong. I do have that dark
and perky look—like Winona Ryder on steroids. And I do
have a not-too-big nose and thick black hair, which looks good
short or long—the way I wear it now, in kind of a forties
glamour-gal retro style. The thing is, I have never really *felt*
pretty, and I think men like that about me; they sense my
vulnerability, which is the very last thing I want anyone to
sense.

Yes, at first I did think Dirk was an egotistical schmuck.
He was really much better when he was off drugs, and so
much better when you got to know him off drugs. I remember

one story about going with him to his health club, "Dirk Talks About Bree in the Sauna." We were sitting there sweating— I was lying on the bottom bench, Dirk was sitting on the top one—and he told me about the time his father lost his job at a shoe store. His family had to eat mustard sandwiches for two months until his dad "got back on his feet again." Dirk looked down at me and started laughing, then added, "I swore I would never be poor again." He leaned over the top shelf and said, "Laura, this is all off the record. Never write that I was poor."

It was the first time I'd felt the undercurrent that seems to run between Dirk and me—a mixture of lust and disgust on my part, a bit of flirtation and arrogance on his. I didn't use any of it because my stories weren't about Dirk the person, they were about Dirk the symbol.

I knew this was the inherent problem with journalism— having to deal with pain-in-the-ass real people. I should have gone into fiction. Or real estate. But for better or worse, I was stuck with them.

Who? Dirk and Bree.

What? The first North American yuppies.

Where? San Francisco Bay.

When? Near the end of the millennium.

Why? I wanted attention. I wanted to make a hit on Broadway. I wanted to be a credit to my parents. When I wanted to lose weight, I went on the Dirk and Bree diet: every time I started to crave food, I'd write about Dirk and Bree. I thought there was something there. The generic couple for the generic age. Our satire, our selves.

5

Without the glamour, would Russ be totally turned off? It was his house, his view, his deck, his dreck. In one week I'd be out of there.

I could tell he liked having a girlfriend whose name was known. He always made a point of introducing me as Laura Gloriana—not Laurie, not Laura Gurvitz. And even if everyone was on a first-name basis, it was always, "Jan and Tom, this is my friend, Laura Gloriana."

Among his friends, who were all doctors or lawyers or brokers, a writer was glamorous, something they'd be if they weren't busy making money. You could see Russ's blue eyes light up when some entrepreneur in his party clothes, his woven shirt and his bolo tie, would say, "Not *the* Laura Gloriana?"

I looked up at the photo of Russ and me and a cardboard Jose Canseco on the mantelpiece. It was taken at the A's opener, our first real date, six months ago—the day I decided to move in with him. Pretty pathetic to be thirty-seven and in need of housing and love. Russ was ready for a live-in. In the two years since he'd divorced his wife, he'd had about six girlfriends, but they seemed to have been there only for the sex. Of course, what were we other than sex, exercise, food, and videos?

But if my career was over, what did I have that would appeal to him? I'd have to move.

I'd live in a hotel. I'd withdraw my savings—how much did I have anyhow?—for a down payment on a tiny house in East Oakland. I'd miss the mortgage payments by the end of the year. I'd be foreclosed. I'd have a garage sale and take my last three hundred dollars and live in my car. "We're all just one disaster away from being homeless" was writ large among the samplers for our times.

Russ came home. He threw his keys down on the dining room table and went straight for the mail. He looked wasted. I suppose he had no idea what I'd been through. "How was your day?" I asked him, hoping to hear nothing more than, "Fine, and yours?" but what I got instead was . . .

"Really bad. I had two hernias, a hemorrhoidectomy, three follow-ups, a breast lump I referred out, and then right at three o'clock, what should come in but a damn teenager with an appendix. I am beat. Forget the bike ride. Let's just eat."

The thought occurred to me: What if he wasn't really a surgeon but some weird guy with an imagination? With his dark, curly hair and blue eyes and chin dimple, he even looked a little like Tony Curtis in *The Great Imposter*. But you know, you've got to trust somebody. Especially a doctor with a bed-side manner like Russ's.

I followed him as he went into his office, the small alcove off our bedroom, to check his phone messages. He stood there passively listening to a bunch of reports from various nurses at the hospital and only shifted his feet when a message from his ex-wife said that the check had not arrived yet. I watched from outside the little stucco archway as he took off his hospital clothes—his unbloody afternoon-rounds surgery greens. Everything came off but his beeper.

The beeper was what defined him. He was a surgeon, a respected authority, and yet he was also a puppet, a remote-controlled robot, a man held hostage by Mrs. Garcia's burst stitches or Miss Shabbaz's internal bleeding or Professor Lamb's retrograde ejaculation. I knew what he wanted most from me was escape, entertainment, a respite from the visions of bloody organs that dominated his consciousness. He let me define our time together, as long as he didn't have to think and be decisive. He was not one of those doctors who enjoyed playing God. My friend Mai Blender once said about Russ, "Tyrant in the operating room, pussy-whipped at home."

He put on jeans and a T-shirt and immediately reattached his beeper. Be fun, I told myself, be a fun gal, but I had this stuff bottled up ready to uncork when he came home.

"Sorry if you had a bad day, but you won't believe what happened to me."

"Do you think we could eat first and share the misery later? Just this once."

I wanted to say, "You uncaring oaf," but I realized I did complain a lot about little things, and he had no way of knowing this was really the Big One. Well, not cancer big, or death big, or endangered species big, but it was kind of a career Chernobyl.

I decided not to say anything. That was our style—no confrontations. I went to the kitchen and started boiling water and took down a jar of pasta from the shelf. It was a toss-up between the spinach seashells and the white spirals. I also had some tortellini frozen in the fridge. Russ always said the tortellini were little belly buttons, and I figured if the last thing he did was an annoying abdominal surgery, I'd better go with the seashells.

I cut up some tomatoes, garlic, zucchini, and onions. I thought I'd stir-fry them for pasta primavera and maybe have a salad and some bread and cheese. I liked cooking, but couldn't really stand to do it when I was writing an article. There's only so much creative energy in this world. Of course, with Dirk and Bree, who needed to create? Every word was quotable. You just had to punctuate for irony.

He'd looked bad in that last, long close-up on Del's show. All you could see was Dirk standing there, dazed and bleeding, his nose scrunched leftward. And Bree. Jeez, in seconds Bree went from a lifetime as a passive-aggressive to an aggressive-aggressive. All on national television. Didn't they have any shame?

I was thinking about Dirk's nose and dicing a tomato, when the phone rang. I listened as our new message began. First, two bars of "Don't Hang Up," then: "Hi, you have reached Laura and Russ. We can't answer now. Guess what we're doing? We'll get back to you as soon as possible if you leave your name, your number, and your exact weight."

"Very funny. Laura, it's Dirk. I'm in Kaiser Hospital. I just had an emergency nose job. Did you hear about Bree going nuts? I want to talk to you about it. Don't believe anything she says. Before the show, she decided we would blame everything on you. Now you know which one of us is really crazy. Laura, it's like the three faces of Eve. The two slices of Bree. Call me at home tomorrow. I'll give you a story that will define the New Male Resurgence. New Male Resurgence . . . I like that. They gave me Demerol. You know, I love drugs. Why did we stop using them? I love you, too, Laura. Bye."

I decided to chop some more garlic, maybe add some wine. Maybe I should take some Demerol. Poor Dirk.

"Did you hear that?" Russ said, coming into the kitchen and rubbing up to me with a fierce erection.

"Is that a zucchini in your pocket, or are you glad to see me?" I wondered if just the thought of Dirk coming on to me was enough to take him from zero to eight in sixty seconds.

"Forget dinner," he said as his hands moved around me and grabbed my breasts.

"Whoa! Hold it," I said, taking his hands off. "I can't just change channels like that. I'm chopping garlic, I'm thinking about what happened today. I'm a little distracted."

He was wearing his old tight jeans—which I've always thought brought out the best in a man's crotch—and he started hugging me, conversant, nonchalant, and ready to shoot. "What happened, Laurie?" he asked with the compassion of a man who needs a woman.

I dropped the garlic and took his hand, and walking him to the bedroom, I began to tell him the saga of Dirk and Bree dumping me and each other on Del Warfield.

We fooled around on the bed. He knew better than to grab my breasts and now he teased me, slowly walking his fingers around my nipples until they responded. *An American in Paris* was on the TV. Gene Kelly was dancing with Leslie Caron down by the Seine.

"She broke his nose?" he said. "Who did the surgery? I think Sam Cohen was on tonight. He studied at Cedars Sinai with Marvin Freeman, who did Michael Jackson's fourth nose. Do you think Dirk can sneeze and moonwalk now?"

"Why is this funny?" I asked as I got up to turn on the news and then lay on my back on the bed. I unzipped the fly on his classic Levi's jeans.

"It's funny," he said, lifting up my Basta Pasta T-shirt, pulling down my spandex bicycle shorts, and unhooking the snap front of my Sweet Nothin' bra, "because the Rockies may tumble, Gibraltar may crumble, and we can still do this." He started kissing my nipples, sweet little wet kisses. We didn't need to use a condom. Russ had himself tested for HIV almost every week, but I could still have a little Gloriana. In fact, I thought as I reached over to get my diaphragm, I could still write in this or any other town. I could just go back to being plain old Laurie Gurvitz, child of the swamps.

I heard the phone machine go off. It was Bree. She was in no mood for jokes. "I just got released on my own recognizance. I was searched by a disgusting lady cop. I want to know what part you played in all this, Laura. I smell your manipulations."

"I smell garlic," Russ said, and I realized that he was going to smell like garlic too. Penis primavera.

He had to recover what Bree's interruption had cost us. He hovered over me, tempting me with his garlic-smelling monster. When I was good and ready—how could he know these things so well, was it a medical secret?—he pushed on. And in. I was extremely distracted now but I probably wouldn't come. Although maybe. Mmmmm.

"Today, trash-and-slash television took another victim when a wife lunged out at her husband during the taping of the Del Warfield show," said Dan Rather on the TV.

Just before Russ's beeper went off, I came.

Smirk. Smirk.

6

Russ left for work, as usual, by 6 a.m. I knew he would stop at the Oakland Y and do a little swim and weights before his first gallbladder. I would usually get to work on My Incredibly Hot Career, but now I had to face my meltdown.

I got up and looked out the window. I could see some fog behind the Golden Gate, but I couldn't tell if it was coming or going.

The house, a tiny white stucco gem squeezed into a sloping lot in the Berkeley hills, was where Russ moved when he split from his ex-wife, Nan. He had an aging hippie do the gardening on Mondays, and a part-time therapist cleaned the house on Wednesdays. All I had to do was live.

Not so easy to do when things were as out of control as they seemed to be now. I needed the illusion of control. I remember when I had a bumper sticker on my car that said: "Women Take Control!" Like a lot of people I knew, I paid too much attention to bumper stickers and not enough to where I was going.

I had to figure out how to get Dirk and Bree back together. Fast. We were all so close to realizing our dreams. . . . Yet I really had no idea what kept people together. My own track record was based on one simple rule of relationships: If it's broke, don't fix it.

Of course, I could try to write about something else. But all I'd known for the past seven years were Dirkness and Breedom. I clicked on my computer and thought: Write, write, write. Since this wasn't going to happen, I did what I usually do when I can't face something—I logged onto the LoveNet. I usually went to my computer network when I

wanted to waste time. It didn't turn you into a zombie the
way watching TV did. It was interactive. It made you an interactive zombie.

Through my modem, I could get on the LoveNet and look
at the list of topics.

1. Common Fantasies
2. Uncommon Fantasies
3. For Gays Only
4. For Lesbians Only
5. For Macintosh Users Only
6. Disease Update
7. Sex and Sexism
8. The First Time
9. Pen Pals
10. Tantric Sex
11. Are There Aphrodisiacs?
12. Your On-line Impotence Therapist
13. Celebrity Sex Fantasies
14. The Joy of Sex Toys
15. Yoko Onanism
16. Why Don't We Do It in La Jolla?—Great Places To
    Go and Come
17. Your Aging Gonads
18. Readin', 'Ritin', and 'Roticism
19. New Uses for Your Mouse

I decided to go right to number thirteen, celebrity fantasies.
They were listed by personality, and next to each name was
the number of entries: Ellen Barkin 135. Michelle Pfeiffer
112. Cher 107. Meryl Streep 89. Jack Nicholson 35. Bart
Simpson 5. Tina Turner 97. Dustin Hoffman 14. Tom Cruise
23. George Bush 4. Barbara Bush 31. Roseanne Barr 43. Donald Trump 12. Andy Garcia 47. Eddie Murphy 34.

There was not a single listing for Dan Rather, although
there were thirty-two for Barbara Walters. I was about to

open up Dan for fantasy but then I thought: What is it I'm doing here?

With a flick of the mouse, I was out of there. Rather than wasting my time writing about Dan and me on the LoveNet, I ought to be writing a screenplay. It might be better than trying to save my Dirk and Bree project. I typed: " 'The Ghostlover—My Life with Dan Rather,' by Laura Gurvitz." And stared at the screen.

That was too difficult, so I decided to play with another machine. This is the beauty of machines. You can play, fast-forward, and rewind with just a touch of your finger. Out of tape, out of mind. And you can erase.

I went to the phone machine. There were eight calls, frozen in time—my time. Dirk again . . . he was at his current home, a rented room in the Marina District. Bree again . . . was I afraid to face her? My friend Mai Blender . . . did I see what happened? Sean from *Lifestyle* . . . did I see what happened? Caryn, my book editor . . . did I see what happened? The Kai Kapu staff nurse: Your Dad is getting worse. Dad. Is getting worse. *Worse.* Phyllis, my New York agent . . . did I hear what happened? And of course, Chuck Chernoff.

"Laura Gloriana, Chuck Chernoff from the Del Warfield show. I assume you've heard that your people turned nasty here on the show yesterday. Our ratings were outta sight. We'd like to do a follow-up show as soon as possible and we'd love it if you'd join us. Can you call us in Chicago at 312 555-ZING ASAP?"

I wasn't sure what I wanted to do first—talk to Bree, call Dirk, or call one of my agents or editors. Of course, what I should do is call the nurse in Hawaii. Dad was getting worse. But when I tried to dial, I couldn't move. I just couldn't face it. The phone rang and this time I picked it up. Sometimes you just need to hear someone live.

"Laura, it's Mai. My God, I can't believe it. You know they arrested Bree. Dirk spent the night in Kaiser Hospital. Rachel Whoopi watched the whole thing and Maria said she was crying, 'My mommy hates my daddy.' But what are we going to do for you? You want to have lunch?"

"I don't know, Mai. I'm kind of in shock. I mean, they did sort of blame me."

"Laura, is that you? I thought I was getting your machine. Don't say another word. Meet me at Chez Panache at noon. You need focaccia therapy. Poor baby."

Leave it to Mai to have some sympathy for me. I didn't think anybody would. Although in a way, it was Mai's fault as much as mine. It was Mai who first got me and Bree together, and that started the whole yuppie ball rolling.

It was in early 1983. The big bull market was roaring and something was happening, and I knew what it was. Didn't I, Mr. Jones?

Even though nobody I knew would actually admit to being in the stock market, there was clearly some kind of shift. People seemed less shiftless. Everyone was getting a job or a husband or a child. Everyone was getting a life. I don't know where it started, but everyone began saying: Get a life.

Herpes was everywhere, AIDS was just starting, and we all seemed to be settling down. Maybe it was because we were getting older. Maybe it was because everyone stopped taking drugs. Or maybe it was just that money was the new drug—the one we hadn't tried. Our parents' drug—insofar as we acknowledged that we had parents and that they got high.

I had written three articles for *Lifestyle* at that time: one about how to meet people while jogging, another about how to write a personals ad, and one about how to find your G-spot. The G-spot really put me on the map. I got dozens of letters from women telling me the most incredible stories that always ended with the plaintive question: Is that it? Is that it? Eureka! Have I found it?

Looking back on '83 seems strange now. Like a car commercial.

It was a time of G-spots and short curly hair. Jeans were out and suits were in. We listened to Lionel Richie and Thriller and ate pasta instead of noodles. We bought word and food processors. Relive those days in the new Ford Yuppie—the car that brings back the eighties.

It could happen, you know. The nostalgia turnaround is

speeding up. It may already be dated. What's hot and what's snot.

It's funny how the eighties self-destructed right on time, when the decade ended, unlike the sixties, which lasted until 1974 at least. Mai and I are old friends from the sixties. We met in the Women's Collective when we were working on a booklet called "Gynecology as Torture." Mai was going to the Psychology Institute to get her M.F.C.C., which we always called her Mother Fuckin' Crazy Counselor certificate. I was drifting between college and wanting to save the world. I had come to school in Berkeley to major in World Saving.

I call Mai whenever I want a sixties fix; I know she'll always be there. Around 1983, when my stories were starting to show up in *Lifestyle*, Mai kept calling me with ideas. And so it was Mai who called me up to point out Bree's ad in *Lifestyle*. Everyone was starting to read *Lifestyle* then. It looked like the underground press, and the politics were like the underground press, but what everyone was looking at were the futon ads, the electronics ads, and most of all the personals.

There, in between "Young urban professional male, early 30s, into jogging, wine, and sharing, seeks female companion for quiet walks on noisy beaches" and "Male Ph.D. seeks Well-Hung Stud for same-sex seminars," was an unusual one. A lonely Bree Wellington had placed this ad:

"Woman with great job and great boyfriend seeks quality women friends for coffee, hiking, and chatting. No time to make friends. Please write Bree c/o this paper. No complainers or crazies, please."

Now, to get back to the origin of my problem, I tried to rewind the tape of my relationship with Dirk and Bree and replay that first meeting with her. What I remember most was how intense Bree seemed, how lonely. The ad was not a casual thing.

We had lunch at some trendy food place—I think it was Thai. Bree actually stood up and shook my hand when I came in. This seemed like such an oddly formal thing for a woman to do with another woman. That's Bree, a funny mixture of formal and informal, traditional and new, obedient and pioneering. Bree seemed like someone who would have attended her debutante cotillion on acid. She was, and still is, such a knockout that I think it must be very confusing to her that the same good looks that take her so far with men create such distance with women.

We talked a lot about Dirk during lunch. They had been together about a year then, had just bought the condo together. She wanted to talk about him. I wanted to hear more about what kind of response she was getting to her ad. I didn't actually tell her that I planned to write about her ad looking for friends, and I guess she thought I was looking for friends too. Maybe I was.

If she hinted at Dirk's drug problem, I didn't pick up on it. I really didn't want to see any problems then. I was thinking from the start about how Dirk and Bree could be an updated *I Love Lucy*. Bree used the words "intimacy" and "commitment" enough to make me think she was the archetypical modern woman, a woman who talks about relationships too much.

When she spoke about her feelings—about being depressed because she and Dirk weren't really connecting, about feeling isolated as one of only three women at her law firm who weren't clerical, about the fact that her mother had always sided with her father and never had any independence when Bree was growing up—I just changed the subject as quickly as I could. I have a habit of changing subjects and jobs and boyfriends.

I told myself that I didn't want to hear about Bree's problems because some of them wouldn't fit in with the satirical intent of my story. Now I think it was more that I just can't stand those kinds of serious personal discussions. Unless they're about me. Which is why you *pay* a therapist to listen to you talk, right?

What I remember most about our first meeting was that when we were standing outside the restaurant, Bree thanked me and said, "I hope we can meet again soon." At that point,

I swear, I thought she was going to cry. It made me uncomfortable, and all I could think about was: how am I going to get my story?

"Actually, I was wondering if I could come to your place sometime," I told her.

She had an almost girlish look on her face. "Oh, that would be great," she said.

"Do you think we could set up an appointment?" I asked, getting out my little black book. "I'd like to interview you and Dirk together for a story I'm doing on yuppies."

"Yuppies?" she said, and her formality returned. "You want to interview me and Dirk? What are yuppies?"

"Well, they're young, urban professionals. People who eat croissants. People who buy, you know, stuff, status symbols . . ."

"Jerks?" she said.

"Oh no, no. Cultural leaders."

She didn't buy it.

"Of course. Call my secretary and she'll make an appointment for you. Go ahead, write about me. Tell my story."

She handed me her business card, shook my hand, and headed for her car. Then she stopped and turned around. "I drive a BMW," she said. "I suppose you think that's amusing."

7

Russ Nelman was kind enough to let me make an office in one of the bedrooms in the modest but well-kept house where he kept me. In the office, I had files with clippings of all my old stories. I went to the file labeled *Girl Meets Bree*. There was the story, torn from the Relationships pages of *Lifestyle*. Around the time everyone was telling me to get a life, I heard a little voice say: Hey, get a lifestyle.

My lifestyle was to go out and meet people and write about them. I didn't think it was a big deal, but people started getting pissed. They didn't know I was a writer, they'd say later. Look, I didn't know either.

But Bree was different. "Go ahead, write about me, Laura. Tell my story," she said. And I did just that. Her story, my way.

I found the yellowed clipping. *Lifestyle* was printed on newspaper back then, not those oversized slick, glossy pages they use today. The title was in that funny kind of print that looks like pasted-together letters, like what a killer uses to send notes to a kidnap victim's parents. Now, of course, they use that fancy script that looks like Leona Helmsley's signature. Everything was simpler then. Everything is always simpler then. The date was May 10, 1983—before the Gary Hart, Jim Bakker, Jimmy Swaggart, Ollie North, Fawn Hall, Jim Wright, Tawana Brawley, Barney Frank, Zsa Zsa Gabor, Ivan Boesky, Charles Stuart, Michael Milken, Marion Barry, Charles Keating, Donald Trump, Neil Bush, and Milli Vanilli scandals. It was an era when everyone seemed to be vying for his fifteen minutes of defamation.

I found the story. I wanted to see how the truth, as documented in my story, matched my recollection of our somewhat awkward and slightly painful first meeting.

A GIRL CALLED BREE: FRIENDSHIP IN OUR TIMES
By Laura Gloriana, Staff Writer

Staff writer, that was a laugh. I was getting thirty bucks a story and the right to use the staff bathroom.

She's young, she's urban, she's happening. She's got red hair, green eyes, and a 24-inch waist. She's got an old man who's rich and a young man named Dirk. She's a lawyer with a real estate specialty in the offices of Sharkey, Sharkey and Goniff. She's got a new condo in the upscale Bay Gauche development. She's got a Cuis-

*inart and a portfolio. But she doesn't have a friend in
the world.*

*Her name is Barbara "Bree" Wellington. We are talk-
ing over a light lunch of blackened crawdads and apricot
gumbo at Mammie's, the hot hot new restaurant in
Berkeley's Gourmet Ghetto. Here, where the counter-
culture is becoming the counter culture, where the bar-
ricades of garbage can lids have been replaced with the
wheels of Brie, where the marijuana lids have been replaced with the Dom Perignon bottles, we investigate her
search for chums. We are talking about finding friends.
Once, we would have talked about overthrowing the
establishment. Now we talk about getting established in
our field.*

*"I'm in a great job. I have a great relationship. But
sometimes I just want a girlfriend," she says. There is
loneliness in her voice. There is poignancy in her breath.
And I dare not tell her there is collard green on her
teeth.*

*I know what she means. I have an OK job—the glam-
orous world of Lifestyle reporting. I have an OK relationship, although my boyfriend found my vibrator
today and told me he was worried about being replaced
by a machine. But I, too, sometimes long for the kind of
friends you had in high school. Someone to yak on the
phone with. Someone to shop for clothes with. Someone
to cut men to pieces with.*

*What made Wellington turn to the personals when she
was looking for Ms. Goodfriend Bar? She says that
whenever she called up anyone she used to know, they
were with their boyfriends or looking for a boyfriend or
looking for a better boyfriend; or they were too busy
looking for a job, working on a job, or looking for a
better job.*

*So far the response to her ad has been spotty. One
person wrote, "Who do you think you are, Miss Oh So
Perfect! I am one of those crazies who need not respond*

to your ad for a sane friend. If you want sane friends, why don't you move to the suburbs?"

Another person wrote, "You've got a great boyfriend, huh? What's her name? If you want to try it before you buy it, call me, Mona 'Butch' Butler."

One letter Bree did respond to was from a woman who said she was a lawyer and had a great relationship and wanted to meet for coffee. They got together, and it turned out to be a woman in Bree's office who lives in the same condo complex and belongs to the same health club and—get this—she and Bree were wearing the same tweed jackets. "But I don't know," said Bree, "she seemed kind of shallow."

That's life in the big urban environment. Will Bree Wellington find friendship, or will she just have to shop alone? I'll be following up on this and other stories in the weeks to come. Let me know what you think. I can use all the support I can get. My boyfriend is absolutely no help on this or anything else. Once he's done, he's done. My orgasm means absolutely nothing to him.

And so, I'm outta here.

Well, I have to admit, even I was shocked by how different the tone is from my memory of the event. I really am an artist, I guess, because the whole thing bears so little resemblance to the truth. My memory was a better tape recorder than my pen.

When I look back on this piece, as I look back on other items in the Gloriana oeuvre, I simply cannot remember what was going on in my head as I wrote it. All I can remember is who it offended and whether I cared. I was just devastated by the letters I got from lesbians calling me everything from a fascist to a closet sadomasochist. Bree told me she generally liked the piece, although she was really sad that the kind of shallow woman in her office never spoke to her again. My boyfriend of six months took it very badly and moved out within a week. Still, I got the apartment, and Bree and I became friends. Maybe I was not the sort of friend Bree was really looking for, but she took what she could get. Oh, so did I.

We both got the attention and notoriety we craved. She got more clients than she could handle and I got a health plan and fifty bucks a story, but only if they were typed.

I put the folder away and went to the phone to call Bree. In my humbled state, I allowed a tiny bit of guilt over my strange relationship with Dirk and Bree to penetrate my consciousness. To be honest, I always felt flattered when Dirk seemed to be flirting with me, as he had done on the phone last night. Now maybe it was just the Demerol talking but if they were really splitting—who knows?

Not that I wasn't happy with Russ Nelman. Russ Nelman was in a way the boyfriend jackpot. He was a doctor, which meant the world to my dad when I told him about Russ and me. Although in his most recent confusion, my dad seemed to think I was living with an undertaker. "Hold a button when his car goes by," my father told me on the phone. It was some kind of Old World superstition. Whenever we passed a cemetery when I was a kid, Harry would tell me to hold a button. You can hold a lot of buttons in Brooklyn, where we lived until I was five and we moved to Teaneck. And now, just thinking about Harry, I grabbed the button on top of my sweater. Because even if Harry only had about thirty percent left in this world, I didn't want him to check out just yet. There was nothing to connect me to my life before California but Harry. It was as if I had just hatched in my twenties and all that previous stuff was another incarnation.

When I finally called Bree, she wasn't home or maybe she was call-screening. "Hi, you have reached the home of Bree Wellington and Rachel Whoopi Wellington-Miller. We're not home now but you can leave a message. If you wish to reach Dirk Miller, that's your problem."

"Bree, it's Laura. Let's talk. Let's work on it. Our relationship is too important and too long-standing to throw out the window. I'm sorry for what is happening to you, Bree. I'm here for you."

I'm *here* for you. God, what a bitch. I'll say anything.

It was almost lunchtime. I hadn't gotten a thing done. I was feeling lost, and sometimes when I felt lost, I tried to think of something to do for Russ. You know, besides being a doctor—a surgeon yet—he had so many other great qualities. He was flexible. He could get married or whatever. He could have children or whatever. As long as he came once a day and got his exercise, he was happy. He was a simple man and not given to the extremes of a Dirk Miller.

You could do almost nothing to piss him off. Believe me, I've tried. I think he puts so much into cutting people up and sewing them back together that he can't take anything else very seriously. There's not a person on earth I would rather have touch my pancreas than Russ Nelman. But I'm not so sure I want to marry him.

Actually, I first met him when he was playing doctor. I would never go to a man doctor unless my life depended on it. But around eight months ago Carol, my nurse practitioner, found a lump in my right breast—my favorite extra-sensitive touch-me-there one.

I was absolutely terrified. To die before Harry? It was unbelievable. And of course, my career was hot then too.

So I went to Russ Nelman and he touched me there. He was so reassuring. He said he didn't think it was anything, but he wanted to "follow my breast" for a while.

I came to him once a week for a month. He would slowly and meticulously walk his fingers clockwise around my right breast. During the second month, he started following both breasts, clockwise and counterclockwise. After another full month of urging, I persuaded him to follow up below the waist. He swore he'd never done anything like that before. Thank God, the door had a lock. You know those green surgery suits with the little V-neck? You could see Russ's thick black hair in the V. I never really cared for men's chest hair before, but I just had to get my hands on him. As I've said, in my mind he wasn't really a doctor but Tony Curtis playing a doctor in *The Great Imposter*, a movie Harry and Lenore took me to Radio City to see.

I made Russ get on the table and use the stirrups. It was kind of funny. I was wearing a paper gown backward and stood at the foot of the examining table. When I got up on the stair, I was just the right height. I'm five four and Russ is six two. He was making such wonderful little ecstasy noises I thought someone was going to knock and ask, "Are you OK in there?"

OK? It was great. Although I didn't come, I did get very, very excited. Unfortunately, there was no TV in the examining room.

That's all right—the whole thing was covered by my health plan.

8

A still rain started falling just before noon. I couldn't tell if this was the end of the drought or the start of a flood. In California, it's always one or the other. I was glad to see it because we needed rain, but I was also annoyed by any inconvenience from the climate. If you couldn't count on perfect weather around here, what could you count on?

I especially hated this kind of misty stuff. It always made me think of some dumb guy's voice, coming from the back of a rock concert, yelling at the rain, "Git it on!"

Mai Blender was standing at the entrance of the restaurant dressed in the politically correct uniform: a woven Guatemalan peasant shirt, black 100% cotton drawstring pants, and, even in the rain, huarache sandals. Around her neck, she wore a string of glass beads that had an African pendant on it, the kind they sell at the flea market and that all the black teenagers are wearing. Her gray hair was still in the bangs she'd always worn, but it was shorter now, cut in a pageboy. It had hung down the length of her back when I met her in

1969. Her hair was blond then and her blue eyes full of fire. Every cliché of the sixties and seventies could be found in the Mai Blender Nostalgia Museum, and yet it was comforting today. The fire could still be ignited, especially on your behalf. Unlike my chain of hired friends—my therapists—Mai seemed to really have sympathy for me even when I hated myself. I wondered if she was as sympathetic to the paid clients in her practice.

We had barely been seated when the waitress—there but for the grace of journalism go I—came to tell us about the specials. "We have a Lakeland Ranch beef stew. Lakeland Ranch raises cattle without any chemicals, steroids, antibiotics, or any adulterants whatsoever. The stew includes tomatoes from antique vines that once belonged to Jack London. There are new potatoes in the stew. We also have a salad of True Wind Farm baby lettuces. Are you ready to order, or would you like some more time and/or a glass of wine?"

"We'll have two glasses of the Binge Creek cabernet," said Mai.

"Is she kidding?" I asked Mai after the waitress left.

"I can't tell," Mai said. "Last week when I was in here, she had a Veal Liberation pin on."

The glasses came quickly and I downed mine. I can't imagine drinking or using drugs for any reason other than escape. All I wanted at this point was to be able to change the channel. One afternoon glass is enough for me. I mean, enough to get me drunk. And drunkenness was what I wanted. Thank God, I wasn't alcoholic. That could get expensive.

"How's Rod?" I asked her.

"Hard up for cash, as usual."

Her husband, Rod Rodriguez, is a carpenter now, but he was the first Hispanic to get an engineering degree from MIT. He had worked at Bechtel for a while and there were rumors that once, as an engineer on a nuclear power plant, he had built a defect into the design that plagued the utility company for years. No one could ever prove it, but even the rumor that he was a corporate saboteur made him very sexy to Mai.

It also made him permanently unemployable as an engineer.

She took out some photos of her kids. Mai's son, Che, is now at MIT and is supposed to be some kind of computer whiz. I suppose one of these days he'll end up slipping in a virus somewhere and Mai will be proud of him. Che is her son with her first husband, Neil Blender, a guy that Bree once had an affair with.

Che was about six when Rod moved in with Mai, and that's when Mai had Shoshona. Shoshona was a beautiful little girl. Mai showed me her high school freshman pictures. "Shoshona gets all A's and is planning to try out for cheerleading. That's how she rebels against me—I think it's great. I tried to get her to come with me to the Dead shows, but she called the Deadheads 'the grateful brain-dead.' Pretty creative for fourteen."

We ordered salads, and the waitress brought them along with whole wheat focaccia. We were mercifully spared the history of the wheat.

"So what do you plan to do about your Dirk and Bree problem?" Mai asked. "Are you going to write about it?"

I hadn't really considered that option, but I began to see the headline—"An Open Letter to Dirk and Bree"—even as we spoke. There had to be some way to save this marriage. And, incidentally, my movie deal.

"Well, what can I do? I think Bree would say I've done enough."

"Oh, Bree doesn't have a clue what she wants. That's how she ended up with Dirk. I've always thought he was a colossal jerk, but she never listened to me. I wonder how she's stood it this long. Now, though, I think they need to patch things up. Rachel Whoopi is at a fragile age. After seeing her parents fight like that on TV, I think she needs to see them get it together or she'll never trust anyone again. I know one thing that will throw Dirk and Bree back into each other's arms."

"What's that?" I asked, halfway into glass number two. I was beginning to see double. Two Mais. Two gray pageboys, four blue eyes, two strings of beads with African pendants, two handwoven Guatemalan shirts with thirty embroidered peasants dancing on them.

"People like Dirk and Bree are driven by acquisition. And fear of losing what they've got. If you can impress upon them that divorce could actually mean the loss of love, then they won't get divorced. As long as they believe this caring divorce bullshit, they'll go through with it. Personally, I believe caring divorce is the stupidest idea since open marriage. Remember, Neil Blender and I had an open marriage."

"So what can I do about anything?" At that moment, I had the feeling that keeping my head from falling to the table was the most I was capable of.

"Well, who is Dirk insanely jealous of? Neil, right? Remember that Bree almost split up with Dirk for Neil. Bring Neil back in her life and you'll bring out the competitor in Dirk. He would rather die than lose Bree to Neil Blender."

This was all getting too complicated for me and Mai could tell I wasn't listening, but she said one more thing which woke me up.

"There *is* another approach you could take," she suggested. "You could start up with Dirk and drive Bree insane."

I had this sudden urge to run out of the restaurant. I often got this urge when I was out with people, but I knew I wasn't supposed to act on it. This time, the alcohol had obviously loosened up my inhibitions. I remembered the meter. "Mai, I've got to go. I can't get another ticket. They'll throw me in jail." I walked out.

Mai would have to understand. If she didn't, then she wouldn't be Mai, and who wanted anyone *like* Mai who wasn't Mai?

My Toyota was parked up the street and the meter maid was giving me a ticket. I thought of pleading my case to her, but the fact that I already had fifty tickets might not make her more sympathetic. Should I tell her that I had a date tomorrow for a court hearing to answer why I hadn't responded to repeated warnings on the tickets? Should I refer her to my attorney, Bree Wellington, Esquire?

Then I imagined getting in a big fight with the meter maid
and slapping her. I'd end up in jail for sure. Maybe jail was
the place for a criminal like me.

I knew that all I cared about was getting Dirk and Bree
back together for my own selfish reasons. I envy people who
can convince themselves that they are doing things for others
that also just happen to benefit them. In some way, I also
love to feel guilty. Harry always said, "Guilt is what keeps us
human."

And Dad was getting worse.

I didn't want to face the maid, so I walked up to Peet's
Coffees and got a pound of Colombian and a free cup of coffee.
I was doing my part to help change the Colombian economy.
The coffee cut the double vision but not the uninhibited de-
spair I felt.

I got in the car, but instead of going home I headed toward
the Richmond Bridge and over to Marin. I held my breath
as long as I could passing the Chevron refinery. They say the
cancer cluster around here has nothing to do with the Chevron smokestacks. Sure, and I'll have a PCB sandwich on DDT
bread.

The sun broke through the clouds, throwing beams on San
Quentin. It looked beautiful, a medieval castle where happy
knights jousted in the courtyard. We're all in a kind of prison,
I thought, only this one isn't a metaphor.

I went north up 101, and in half an hour's time I found
myself driving around Quail Glen, trying to find which Lane
or Court or Way was Dirk and Bree's. Although I had been
here at least twenty or thirty times since Dirk and Bree and
baby Rachel moved in, the uniformity of the architecture and
the landscape disoriented me. I'd see something I thought
was a landmark, like the house with the statue of a goddess
in front, and then when I hit a dead end, I'd realize it was a
false goddess, a trickster, there to drive me astray, a lawn
goddess that was bought on sale at Smith & Hawken.

In the front yard of one of the houses I passed, two little
boys jousted with nerf lances. There were children or evi-

dence of children everywhere at Quail Glen. Swings on trees, scooters on lawns, and orderly playgrounds in every little subdevelopment. The whole suburban nightmare. Why were people I once knew as young and exciting moving out here?

I should know the answer. Dirk and Bree went over it when I did the piece "Dirk and Bree on Abandoning the Urban." Of course, the answer was simple: a grassy lawn, good day care and schools, other children, and less crime. But in the piece, I had tried to find more complex sociopolitical meaning. Meaning that Bree took offense at and that Dirk would have also if he were as sharp as she is.

At the time, I personally took offense at the idea of their moving to the suburbs, or "a more rural atmosphere," as they preferred to call it. As long as they lived in a condo in the city, the fact that they were married and had a kid did not make them all that different from most of the single people I knew. In fact, their lifestyle was almost identical to the gay couple who lived in the condo next door to them, except that Dirk and Bree didn't eat as well and their furniture was less valuable. I viewed their move to Quail Glen as a sellout and Bree knew it. She called me on it.

After the piece came out, she said I had no understanding of what it was like to be responsible for any life other than my own. Rather than "an act of selfish acquisition"—which is how she said I described it, although I would never use such a leaden phrase—the purchase of the home was an attempt to give up the convenience of the city so her daughter could have a better, safer life. "The trouble with you," Bree said, "is that you're still so busy raising yourself you can't even imagine having a child."

Oh, that hurt all right, hit me close to where I live, which, at the time, was a rent-controlled mother-in-law apartment not far from the Oakland condo Dirk and Bree sold. After that conversation, I really went out of my way to portray Dirk and Bree as self-indulgent consumers. And once, when I was over there trying to interview them and I complained that Rachel Whoopi's "terrible twos" tantrums were too disruptive, Bree

said, "You just don't get it, do you? You can't just turn her
off. You have to cope with it."

A week later, they got their first au pair, Anya. And when
I wrote, "Yuppies hire au pair girls to pretend that it's still
the sixties, and that they are living in a collective—the Me
First Liberation Army," Bree left a screaming message on my
machine. "Laura, this is like the pot calling the kettle selfish.
Who, I ask you, who is really the selfish one?" Fortunately,
it was on my machine and I was able to erase it. And while
I thought I had also erased the unease it caused me, here it
was again rewinding and rewinding in my mind. Who is really
the selfish one?

Conceding that I was totally lost, I stopped in front of The
Inn at Quail Glen to look at my map. I was on the corner of
Serendipity Lane and Blue Jay Way. Dirk and Bree lived on
Costa del Sol, although we were far from any water. Their
street was just off Serendipity, second right, around the corner
from Prosperity.

I rang the bell and Maria came to the door. She'd been
Dirk and Bree's au pair for two years now. I'm not sure if she
knew who I was. I'm not sure if she spoke any English. I'm
not even sure if she was legal.

Maria stood back and I came in. Bree walked up to me and
glared. She didn't say a word. Rachel Whoopi came skipping
up and said, "Hi, Laura. Hi, Laura. Did you bring me a bear
or something?"

Once, I brought her a little brown musical bear, like the
bear I'd had when I was a kid. Mine played Brahms's
"Lullaby." Hers played "It's a Small World After All."

"No, sorry Rachel, no bear this time." It had been at least
a year since I'd brought the bear—a fourth of her life ago,
and she still hadn't forgotten.

"I have a new kitten from my mommy. Want to see it?"

"Maria, why don't you take Rachel to feed Meowski and
we'll come see him later," said Bree, cool, composed, and
slightly tense.

We sat down on the wicker chairs in the solarium. The
room smelled of violet and lavender from several well-placed

bowls of $7.50-a-scoop English potpourri. Outside the window, I could see Rachel's new redwood play structure and several expensive yard benches, as well as Bree's aging beamer. If the yard was *Sunset* magazine, then the sunny room was *Metropolitan Home*, the Country Quaint issue. The wicker chairs and settee were covered in pink and blue material with geese on it. There were statues of geese on the floor behind a big blue and white oval hooked rug and on the pine table in the corner. I could hear the interior decorator saying, "I see geese here. How do you feel about geese as a concept?"

Boy, I really couldn't stop it, could I? The snide view of Dirk and Bree was all I'd known for the last seven years. I could do it in my sleep. Was I good for nothing else? Now, if they split, what was I going to do?

"Bree . . ."

"Laura, don't say anything. I'm in the process of considering my options. Dirk has the right to file for battery, and he's talking to his lawyer. One option includes you. There is the issue of invasion of privacy."

"Bree. Bree, listen, I know how you feel."

"Laura, you can't possibly know how I feel. You've never been a parent. You've never been married. You've never owned a home. All you know is watching other people. You're a voyeur, that's all."

"Bree, I know you're hurting and you want to hurt back, but listen to me—"

Just then, we heard the phone ring. Bree let the machine answer it, and I could hear the message. "Bree, this is Neil. My service gave me the message that you called, and I'm glad you did. I'll fly up tonight if you want. What do you think? Call me, baby."

Bree looked puzzled. "That's really strange. I never called him." And then, as if she'd reached the same conclusion that Mai Blender had obviously reached about the effect on Dirk of Neil being back in the picture, she said, "I suppose you'll tell Dirk all about this?"

I wasn't sure whether or not I should tell her that I hadn't spoken to Dirk. Dirk and I had always had a strange relationship. I would think he was flirting with me, and then, if I called him on it in any way, he would act as if I were the vamp. At their fourth-anniversary party, when Bree was pregnant with Rachel, he came into the kitchen where I was pouring fresh raspberries over the chocolate decadence. He stood about an inch from me and said, "You don't know how decadent I can be."

I was sure he was going to kiss me and I felt myself getting excited. He had a kind of insane Dennis Quaid sparkle in his eye, and I knew he was off cocaine by then. Just a week before, I had done "Dirk and Bree on Money, the Drug for the Eighties." He was so close I could inhale the Glenfiddich on his breath. Bree walked into the room and Dirk said, "Honey, Laura is coming on to me again."

Bree paled for a minute, looking even more beautiful in a green velvet maternity dress, then started laughing. "Get back in here," she said to him. "The potential investors are getting restless."

Now I was staring at the blank eye of a stuffed goose. I pressed the stop button and this old tape came to an abrupt halt.

"Have you talked to Dirk since the Del Warfield show?" I asked her.

"Only through lawyers and doctors. He's going to be OK. He'll finally get the nose he's always wanted. I'm sorry it had to be this way, though. It would have been better if it were elective surgery."

"So you don't know about the rest of it?" I said.

The worst part of this whole thing is that I was completely sober by now. I have no way of explaining what happened next, except that Mai always seems to have some kind of power over me. If Mai had decided to slip Neil Blender into the mix as a teaser for Dirk, then I was obliged to be Mai's zombie and slip myself in as Bree bait.

"What rest of it?" asked Bree.

I looked to see if there was a vase on her wicker coffee

table. "Dirk and I are going to get married as soon as your divorce is final," I said. "I'll let myself out."

I peeled down Costa del Sol, did a two-wheel turn around Prosperity, and took Serendipity back to 101 without looking back or doubting for a moment that I had done the right thing. Journalism ethics were for who-what-why-when-and-how bozos. I was beyond journalism or ethics. I was a performance artist.

9

As San Quentin came back into view I wondered just what crime I'd committed. I felt guilty. Was there something in Mai's magic pendant that had caused me to deceive Bree? Was I actually attracted to Dirk? Was it God punishing me for once claiming to be Sicilian on Rosh Hashanah? It must have been that I'd voted for Dukakis. Could I have actually done something to deserve this?

Two days ago I was on top of the world. I've been there before. The this-is-really-it syndrome, where you become convinced that you have it made. That you will never have to grovel again. That no cruel people can ever reach you with their cruel words again. That rejection is just a memory. That you will stay beautiful, and you will stay thin. You will never question why you didn't have that baby or marry that guy. You will never again regret that you didn't get into Stanford or that your dad wasn't a big corporate executive or that you weren't born blond. You believe that all the petty little denials that make you who you are never existed. That is the fantasy.

Now, in no time at all, I had lost my $150,000-at-least deal and I seemed to be entering some new level of complete dishonesty with Bree. And Dad. Dad was getting worse and I was immobilized.

I imagined the guilt police booking me, fingerprinting me, and taking my photo head-on and profile. They would think: Cute nose for a Jewish girl, and then they would begin writing on my sheet. Name: Gurvitz, Laura Beth. Alias: Laura Gloriana. Age: 37. Address: 712 Grizzly Peak, Berkeley. Status: Single. Modus Operandi: Journalist. And finally: "You get a phone call to your lawyer."

In Richmond, past the refineries, I pulled off the freeway and drove through one of the poorest neighborhoods. I got stuck behind a huge semitruck outside a funeral home. It said, "Evergreen Casket Company" on the truck. Here is a recession-proof business, I thought. I pulled up to a parking lot filled with cars and people. None of them were women, but there were a lot of people and a phone booth. I went up to the phone and called Bree.

"Bree, what I said about Dirk and me before, well, I was kind of kidding. I don't know why I did it. You don't think Dirk could ever love anyone but you, do you?"

"Laura, I don't know what to believe anymore, but if you and Dirk are fooling around, then I guess he's been one busy little bee."

"Why?" I asked. I noticed some guys outside passing around a bottle of wine cooler.

"Every time I turn on the computer, something called the LoveNet clicks in and there's another message in Dirk's e-mail for Big Boy from Hot Mama. Listen, whatever you and Dirk are up to, I just hope it didn't start until we separated."

"Bree, I didn't even know you separated until the Del Warfield show. We aren't up to anything. He's devoted to you," I said, watching one man outside give another a little plastic bag.

"Well, I don't know what I did to you to make you want to play games with me like that. Look, I'm on my way to the airport to pick up Neil Blender. Make sure Dirk knows. See you in court," she said, and hung up.

See you in court? What did that mean in this context? I had always counted on Bree's lack of irony, but maybe she just played at having an irony deficiency when it suited her. Maybe Bree was playing with *my* head now.

Then I remembered, tomorrow is my hearing in traffic court for the fifty tickets I had forgotten to pay. They were mostly parking tickets, but Bree had said they could actually arrest me for them or, more likely, hit me with a huge fine. She had agreed to come represent me and help work out a settlement. My fate was in her hands now in more ways than one.

A man started rapping on the phone booth door, a wild-eyed man with a grocery cart full of crushed beer cans and a machete holster on his hip—not the kind you want to upset. As I was walking back to my car a teenager approached me and said, "Jewel?"

"No, journalist," I said, and I got in, locked all the doors, and headed home.

A pile of messages were waiting on the machine. Dirk wanted to know where the hell I was. Neil Blender wanted to talk to me. Neil Blender? Me? Russ wanted to tell me he had an emergency and would be really late. Mai wanted to brainstorm. Sean, from *Lifestyle*, wanted to talk about my doing a story on the Dirk and Bree breakup.

I knew that it was time to do what I had been putting off doing—call Hawaii and find out what shape poor Harry was in. Under all of my guilt about Dirk and Bree was this even greater guilt that I could hardly name, my father. When I allowed myself to think, even for one minute, that Harry might be in pain, unhappy, or suffering, I went into this litany: What could I do even if I were there? I can't give up my life for him; he's old and will have to die someday; he's comfortable where he is; he's getting the best possible attention; he's too out of it to notice I'm not there.

Still, I could not face the reality of my father's condition. "Look at your pattern," Becky, my last therapist, had said. "You put things off and put them off until they become uncontrollable."

I called Dirk. He said he was in a lot of pain and had used

up his Demerol. Did I know where he could get any? "Do they still make ludes?" he asked. "Hey, remember ludes? You know, if all else fails, I can go down to one of the Recovery, Inc., centers and see if the sample pills on the display tray are real."

He was really out of it, so I thought I'd ask him. "Dirk, what do you really think of me? I need to know."

"What do you mean, think? As a person? As a writer? As a writer, I really respect you."

"I mean, more like as a woman."

It was as close as I'd gotten to confronting him since our interview in the sauna. At the time, in our bathing suits and in that sweaty spaced-out, overheated state, I'd asked him if he was flirting with me. I was in between boyfriends then, and looking for whatever signs of interest I could read. He had told me that if Bree ever caught him flirting, she'd kill the woman. I said that Bree always seemed far too cool and refined to imagine that way. And he said, "You don't know what Bree can be like when someone tries to share her toys."

Odd, I thought then, that he would accept that role. I wrote in the story "Dirk Talks About Bree in the Sauna":

> *Madonna has her boy toys and Dirk is Bree's Bree toy. But then Dirk gets to access Bree's Bree bucks. So we're right back to the question of the decade: Who is using whom?*

"What do I think of you as a woman? You *would* ask me that now," Dirk said in a slightly slurred Demerol accent. "I don't know. I guess sometimes I think you would do anything to anyone to advance your career and other times I feel you are a clever, assertive woman who knows how to capitalize on an opportunity. I hoped to profit from that cleverness. Why else would I have gone along with the whole thing—the articles, the book, the screenplay?"

"You know, of course, that the screenplay is off. Unless Neil Blender works something out with Bree."

"What's that cheap opportunist got to do with it?"

"He's coming to town to be with Bree now that she's available."

"Whoever said she was available? And I thought he was seeing Cher."

"Cher? What Cher?"

"*The* Cher. Bree told me that. She said Cher created a new perfume for him—Kneel by Cher, Share the Fantasy. I don't know—something like that. I'm getting confused."

He sounded like he was tripping on drugs. I told him I would come see him.

"Bring some APC with codeine, OK?"

I realized now that the whole cycle would begin again with Dirk. His recovery. His re-recovery. I remember him saying, "My recovery was the major event in my life. It's the center around which everything else is maintained." That's in my story "Dirk and Bree on Dirk's Addiction."

Drugs have made a mess out of the twentieth century. All we've achieved has gone down the drain—not just of addiction but the drain of recovery. Ask Dirk Miller, who says that it takes all of his energy to stay in recovery. Constant self-monitoring, constant motivation, constant effort.

And, says his partner, Bree Wellington, "It takes constant support. It's as if I've become addicted to helping him recover."

My, my, it's getting very confusing, isn't it? It almost makes you want to say: And so, I'm outta here.

Not one of my favorite pieces, and I got a lot of angry letters from all kinds of adult children telling me what an insensitive writer I was. And I was.

Talking to Dirk was exhausting. He was out of control. My life was out of control. And my dad was getting worse. I just couldn't call Harry now. It would have to be in the morning.

I picked up the remote control and got in bed with a pint of chocolate frozen yogurt.

"This is Dan Rather for '48 Hours in Jewel Town.' Jewel, the new synthetic drug being manufactured in quiet suburban houses and sold cheaply by kids as young as six, threatens this country as no drug ever has. Due to its ease of distribution and manufacture, authorities believe that jewel will make the crack epidemic of the eighties look minor. Jewel—the designer drug for the nineties. You'll find out why when we return with 48 Hours."

Oh, Dan, if we had only dreamed of where this was going to lead, we would have lowered our consciousness to the basement back in the sixties. You wouldn't have done smack and I'd have married Larry.

When Russ got home around ten that night, I was already sound asleep. I sat up in bed and said, "You won't believe what happened to me today."

"Laura, I love you, but you're the biggest complainer in the world. You're always imagining disasters. I suppose that's part of your job, and you're certainly good at it. I had a strange night myself, but this really happened. Around eight o'clock, your Dirk shows up at my office and says I've got to help him. He wanted me to get him some Demerol. He said if I didn't he was going to steal you away, that you were crazy about him and were trying to seduce him. Anyway, he was really weird and looked like such a mess—someone did a sloppy job wrapping that bandage around his face—that I had to talk to him for a long time. I don't usually see people like that except when the anesthesia's wearing off. I thought of giving him some Thorazine, but I ended up taking him out for a couple beers instead. He calmed down and I drove him home. He's still in love with Bree, although I think the nose thing made him wonder."

Russ got in bed and started spooning up to me. I really was not in the mood. I once saw Dr. Ruth on TV addressing this very situation. She says you're not supposed to reject a man out of hand. "Vy let that beautiful erection go to vaste?"

I was taking the matter in hand when Dirk began screaming on my answering machine. "Pick it up, Laura. Damn it!"

I put down Russ, got out of bed, and picked up the phone. Dirk was drunk and really raving. "Why didn't you come? You said you would. What is your game?"

I told him that I had never said I was coming that night. I promised that I would come see him the next day.

"I called Bree tonight and told her I wanted to talk. I told her I wasn't going to press charges for the nose, even though my lawyer once got the largest award for a nose in California history. She said she had to go—someone was there. We got into a little guessing game. I got it in eighteen questions. Balding and lives in Santa Monica was the giveaway. Look, I want you to find out why Neil Blender is here and what is going on."

I was in no mood to argue, and besides, you don't argue with a drunken man with a large nose bandage. And yes, I did want to find out what was going on. It had been at least forty-eight hours since I had a clue.

10

I took a meeting with Neil Blender the next morning. I use the verb advisedly. Neil was more Hollywood than thou. Hollywood is really too far east. Neil was even more Coast Highway than thou. He French-kissed me as soon as I met him. I'm talking full frontal tonguity—just like that. Here's my tongue, what's your hurry?

I hardly knew what to say. "I'm Laura," I said awkwardly.

"I know," he said.

For the first ten minutes of our meeting, I tried to imagine what I could do to get even for that oral violation. I went so far as to consider grabbing him by the *cojones* but, just my luck, he'd find that erotic.

It was weird because I knew a lot about Neil Blender even though I'd never actually met him. I'd been hearing about him for twenty years from Mai, who never had a good word to say about her first husband. In fact, she used his name like a curse. If she stepped in some dog poop or banged her head on a cabinet, she would yell, "Neil Blender!" instead of "Oh shit!"

I guess Neil knew a lot about me too. "Scone and a latte, right?" he said when the waitress came. It could have been a random guess, but it happened to be my favorite breakfast.

I considered saying, "So you really like it when the woman is on top." I knew that from Mai, but I didn't want to mix it up with him. There is nothing more intimidating to a ballsy woman than a ballsy man—unless it's a woman with four kids who insists she is, and appears to be, totally happy.

We were at an outdoor cafe in San Francisco on a crisp but sunny morning. A little cold to be eating outside, but it was the kind of morning that if you woke up to it in New York, you might be tempted to scream out, "Thank you, Jesus." Even if you were Jewish.

"See that woman over there," he said, nodding towards a Dianne Wiest clone in Lizwear. "She's carrying his child." He pointed to a homeless guy who was going through the garbage can in front of the cafe.

"How do you know this?" I asked him.

"I don't," he said. "But this, baby, is how screenplays are born."

Was there any talking to this guy? Was it worth it to mention that I was not his or anyone else's baby? Except for Harry Gurvitz, the once proud Formica king who now lay dying in a palm-surrounded paradise he would probably never see again.

Neil was a throwback to 1966, when men were men and women were chicks. He was so manly he didn't even bother with anti-balding cream. There was no stopping the relentless surge of his testosterone. My God, the man was actually wearing a gold chain.

"I like that dress you're wearing. Women should wear stripes more, a reminder of curves."

"So you're a screenwriter?" I said.

"It's a living. It's an art form that gives you two chances to express yourself—the art of the spiel and the art of the deal. You've got to be one part Nathanael West, one part Babaloo Mandel, and one part Donald Trump. I do OK."

I thought of that old expression "it's better to keep your mouth shut and not admit that you don't know who Babaloo Mandel is than open your mouth and admit you're a fool."

"What have you done?" I asked, knowing it was a fair and very specific question in the Neil Blender universe.

Just then, the waitress set down my scone and latte, along with his huevos rancheros. Beans for breakfast. Fortunately, we were eating outside. Neil was definitely one of those so-secure-I-can-fart-anywhere people.

"I did a version of 'Batman,' although I never got any credit. I'm working on 'Batman II' now. I've done a couple made-for-TV movies. The last one was 'A Scream in the Nursery,' based on that weird preschool teacher in New England. Maybe you saw it. We had Loni Anderson as the teacher. We originally wrote it for Roseanne Barr, but she got too big. No pun intended."

Now, should I tell him that there was actually egg on his face, or just enjoy the moment? Before I could decide, that enormous tongue, that tongue which like his reputation preceded Neil Blender, came rolling out, licking everything in its path.

"Has there been enough work to keep you in *huevos*," I asked, perhaps a little too archly.

"Oh, *huevos y mucho dinero*. It's not the stuff that gets made that makes you. It's the dozens of jobs that never get out of development. I've probably made half a million dollars in the past couple years on undone deals. *C'est la guerre*. *Comprende*, baby?"

"You mean you can actually live in LA on products that never materialize?"

"They don't call it the marketplace of ideas for nothing. A lot of it is just that—platonic. Now you see it, now you don't."

I wasn't at all sure what he meant by that, but Neil was the kind of person who created an aura of hipness and to question him was to reveal your own unhipness. With Neil you were either on the bus or you were nowhere. Of course, that's where the bus was headed, but you couldn't talk to the driver and you'd better have even change. Dig?

"So you turned that trial of the preschool teacher into prime-time television?"

"Reality-based is very big right now. That's why your Dirk and Bree property sold."

He *knew* about my Dirk and Bree deal. I only found out a few days ago myself. Not too long before I found out I lost it. How could he know about that? I was beginning to more than loathe Neil Blender.

"Oh, the West Side of Los Angeles is the smallest little gossipy town around," he said as he wiped up some egg on his plate with a tortilla. "The Dirk and Bree deal is a classic example of a property being sold because the story was in the media. Now, of course, you're faced with the problem of the story self-destructing in the media. But I think we can work around that."

We? Did he say we? What you mean *we*, white man?

"There are several things that would make it easy for us to collaborate," he elaborated as he unfurled that tongue to scoop up some salsa way down south near his chin. "Of course, I prefer not to work with someone without previous screen credit or experience, but you make up for that by having other writing and a certain amount of name recognition. After Del Warfield I think more people will know you than just the yuppies and DINKs and boomers and quality-time parents who read those gloss-and-floss-style magazines. That was a million dollars in publicity you got there. It made Dirk-and-Bree a household word. And you too. But I won't say what that word is."

"Well, obviously, Mr. Blender," I said, "you've got it all worked out. But why would I want to share my deal with you?"

The homeless man had now left the garbage and was spare-changing the woman who was carrying his baby. She was trying to ignore him.

"What deal?" he said. "I know Lew Shnorman pulled out when he saw the Warfield fiasco. Nobody wants too much reality in the reality base. But I think the whole thing can be salvaged and I'm interested in helping you."

"Well, excuse me for looking a gift horse in the tongue," I said—slip of the tongue intentional—"but why are you being so terribly generous?"

"I like that. I like that sarcasm. I respect sarcasm in a woman. My first wife was a real queen of sarcasm. Oh, you know Mai, don't you? See, that's why it's going to be so easy for us to work together. We both know Mai. We both know Bree. We both know Dirk—insofar as there's anything there. And we're both represented by Rosenbloom Associates."

That's how he became the man who knew too much. That big mouth Slow-go had told him everything.

"So, basically, you're just moving in for a piece of my action," I said, and felt like spitting in his face.

"Hold on, baby. You're forgetting one thing. You ain't got no action. That's your first problem here. And without me, you aren't going to get any. I guarantee it."

"You know, I could report you to the Guild for this. I've got my script registered."

"Oh, you could report me to the Guild. You could report me to Dirk. You could report me to your readers. But if you want to do business, you're going to need me. See, for openers, I can help you solve this little problem of Dirk and Bree interruptus."

"How?"

"You know how. Once Dirk finds out that Bree and I are back together, he'll want more than a caring divorce. He'll want a caring piece of ass."

Great. Now this crude scumbag and I had actually reached

the same conclusion. "But are you? I mean, are you and Bree back together?"

"Not really," he said, wiping up the last drop of yolk with the very last bit of tortilla. "But the illusion of it will be just as good. Suppose we arrange for you to bring Dirk to a certain location where I will be looking domestic with Bree. Say, the Monterey Market, tomorrow, around noon. Your being with Dirk would be even more perfect. Plant the seed in Bree's mind, as if it's not planted there already."

But I still didn't see, I told him, how we could overcome what he appropriately termed the Warfield Fiasco. My script was all about a couple of yuppies settling down and raising a family—a light, romantic domestic comedy. Lucy never broke Desi's nose.

Neil countered that we—and he used "we" the way a too eager first date does in planning your life together—could make that a turning point in the script. "We do our rewrite around surviving the divorce threat. Your script—nothing personal—is funny, but it lacks a certain tension."

In for a penny, in for a pound. I asked him, "OK, what exactly is it *you* want? Or, should I say, how much?"

The Dianne Wiest look-alike handed the homeless man a pile of change. He tipped his cap and left.

"Never let it be said that Neil Blender isn't an honorable man. I want no part of the money that was promised you. All I'm asking for is an equal amount from the producer and a share in the screen credit. I'm certainly willing to put in some work on the script. I mean, I am known as one of the best punch-up artists in the business."

"But if Shnorman's out, who on earth would be willing to pay that kind of money? Who has it?"

"Oh, lots of people," he said, laying down his shiny gold credit card with his own photo on it next to the bill. "Cher for one."

"Cher?"

"Yes. I happen to know that she is interested in this property."

"Then it's true that you're having an affair with Cher?"

"Let's put it this way. I can count on one hand the women I've met once who could resist me. And I've met Cher more than once. I've only met you once, but the day is just beginning."

He actually put his hand on my knee at that point and I actually slapped him. "Good reflexes," he chuckled.

I began to think the guy was just total bullshit. A bullshit castle out of bullshit sand.

"Are you telling me that Cher wants to play Bree?"

"I'm telling you that Cher is looking for a stretch. She wants to play Bree *and* Dirk."

So I began to realize we might have a deal here. No one could make this up.

11

Technically, I could go to jail for being a ticket junkie. Bree had warned me to look good and act responsible in traffic court. So I had an incredibly difficult time trying to decide what to wear. Bree is someone who knows these things, but I was still learning. Nothing in *Cosmo* on this—"Treat Yourself to Something Sexy for Court." Nothing in *New Woman* either—"Over 35 and Still Looking Good on the Way to Jail." And of course, *Lifestyle* was no help. They had never considered the Traffic Violator Lifestyle.

Trying to figure out what to wear always brought up the bitterness I felt at losing my mom, even after twenty years. She died when I was seventeen. I think I spent an extra ten years mourning her, which might explain why I still felt as if I were in my late twenties and always on the verge of growing up. To have a husband and children would be to break from the life I knew as Laura, the girl who lost her mom. Dirk and Bree were the closest I had come to having kids.

Whenever I feel like a fashion illiterate, I remember the day my mom took me to Lord & Taylor on Fifth Avenue and bought me a brand-new dress for my piano recital—a story I've told many times, to every boyfriend and every therapist I've had. The dress was pink dotted Swiss with a pink satin sash. I wore my hair in a high ponytail with a matching pink ribbon that my mom made from the material she had cut from the dress when she hemmed it. She didn't sew all that often, so I saw it as an extreme act of love. Since she died I've had lots of time to reflect on how no one would ever sew for me or cook for me or care for me the way Lenore did. Except for boyfriends, who can be very maternal when love is new, which is why I have never been without one for more than a couple months in my entire adult life. And probably why we always split after a year or so.

I've had stupid boyfriends, brilliant boyfriends, doting boyfriends, and briefly an abusive boyfriend. He only slapped me once, but that was enough for me. Somehow I've never had the boyfriend I wanted to spend my life with. Russ Nelman is as good as it gets. He regularly says, "Hey, if you really want to, we can get married." But that's not how I imagined it, and I've been imagining it for a long time.

I went back to Lord & Taylor just after my mom died to look for my graduation dress. I was standing in the Junior Dress department and all of a sudden, I started crying. I must have known then that whatever happened—even if I got married and had kids, a possibility I have never ruled out—I would still feel a little alone for the rest of my life. I would always be a motherless child.

I ended up wearing my little purple velvet miniskirt and a see-through blouse to graduation, and afterward, my friends and I went to this park we called Itchy-coo Park and smoked grass all night. I really gave Harry a hard time. Something he didn't need then and had never deserved.

Two years later, I spent a summer working at Lord & Taylor

to pay for an abortion that was still illegal back then. I had borrowed the money from my boyfriend Larry, who would eventually become a completely straight, boring IBM drone who supported the war in Vietnam. He was 4-F, because of his asthma, so he didn't have to go. I worked in the men's leather section at Lord & Taylor selling wallets and cigarette cases and other items on commission. Larry would come over on his lunchtime and caress the leather and say dirty things to me.

I had no respect for myself that summer. After the abortion, I felt kind of hollowed out. Not that it wasn't the right thing to do at the time.

It was weird to think that if I hadn't done it, I might have a kid in college. Over the years, I have sometimes thought about how old my kid would be and what it would be like. I've never gotten pregnant again—I've been really scrupulous about birth control—and I sometimes wonder if I can. When my friends had babies—especially Dirk and Bree—I almost felt that they were doing it to spite me, to flaunt the fact that they can have babies and I can't. Even though, and here's the really crazy part, I don't know that I can't. These are the kinds of things women like to torture themselves with, not because they feel guilty about having an abortion but because they feel guilty about succeeding in life. You know—the survivor syndrome.

The abortion itself was one of the worst things I have ever experienced. I try not to think about it, except to remember that I wore a white dress with black polka dots—don't ask me why. Someone said the baby was only the size of a dot and it was just like removing one dot from my dress. Whatever that meant, I never wore polka dots again.

There haven't been that many special occasions in my life since then—I mean times when I bought a dress thinking it had to be perfect for the occasion. I always imagined myself wearing a suit to my wedding, maybe even a pantsuit like young Katharine Hepburn would have wowed them with. You know that movie where she's a career gal and she marries

Spencer Tracy the sportswriter and they almost break up, even though they're in love, because they never have time to be together? Didn't she get married in a suit in that movie? *Woman of the Year*—that's the one. A suit, right? Maybe even a pantsuit. In the forties yet.

Was that really Dirk and Bree's problem? That they never had time to be together? It occurred to me that I had no idea why they were actually breaking up, and I wondered if even they knew. Something about Bree being jealous of Dirk's computer. Something about not really talking. Isn't that what couples always say when they break up, that they weren't really talking? What do they do all day? I was missing something here, although perhaps I was being too rational about it. I have a talent for being rational about other people's lives and irrational about my own. That's probably the reason I never got married. Why would anyone get married? And then, why would they break up? I hadn't a clue.

And of course, why would anyone have a baby? On one hand, love and companionship. On the other, ruin your life and lose your freedom. Was I crazy, or was the latter not a more compelling argument against marriage, children, or anything else you couldn't get out of in a minute by saying those two little words: I quit?

I've said 'em to boyfriends and I've said 'em to bosses, and I was as free as the hawks that fly by Russ Nelman's picture window when you look at Russ Nelman's panoramic view of San Francisco from the living room of Russ Nelman's house.

I've told all of these stories over and over to my therapists. My mother's death. My abortion. My first serious boyfriend, Larry. My hippie youth. My birth fantasies, marriage fantasies, arrest-and-imprisonment fantasies. My Dirk and Bree envy. They, the United Therapists of America, always say the same things: slow down, get into the feeling, you're being too glib. Hey, glib was my living.

I picked out stripes that morning to wear to my hearing, not to show my curves to Neil Blender. I already knew what to wear to a graduation and a piano recital and an abortion and a wedding should I have one. I thought of all the Barbies that guided little girls to appropriate fashion: Fun in the Sun Barbie, Dream Date with Ken Barbie, Getting Aborted Barbie, Traffic Violator Barbie.

Stripes to my hearing. Aren't we all in a kind of metaphorical prison? And now, Ms. Laura Gurvitz originally of Brooklyn, New York, how would you like to try for the real thing?

12

The offices of *Lifestyle, A Magazine* had been redone in sea foam green. The Southwest stuff from a few years ago had been replaced by heartland stuff—wheat sculpture; Shaker furniture; bent-hickory benches; bent-willow chairs; prairie-style furniture; paintings of flat, flat fields of barley, corn, and wheat; etchings of foxes, grouses, and groundhogs. The more unnatural the people at *Lifestyle* became, the more they memorialized nature around the office.

The offices were in San Francisco now, so I decided to stop by and drop off my latest before I went to court. When I first started writing for *Lifestyle*, the whole thing was put together in a little office near the docks in Oakland, where the advertisers were afraid to come. Sean Garrison had a brilliant idea when he took *Lifestyle* national. The plan had been to create a kind of hip *USA Today*, with color, graphics, glossy pages, and . . . political correctness. It was a perfect read for the once left-leaning, mind-expanding youth now trying to raise families and incomes while lowering their consciousness and cholesterol.

I stayed with it for a variety of reasons. *Lifestyle* still showed more concern for the homeless and the environment than the dailies did. And the people who worked there had more frequent orgasms in more interesting ways than the corporate journalists. Sean Garrison now paid me a grand for a piece—when he paid me. If I could come up with three a month, I could make an almost respectable salary.

Sean came out to greet me at the receptionist's desk. The receptionist, an efficient-looking man wearing a Butthole Surfers T-shirt and a ponytail, was trying to explain to a woman that they didn't take ads that advocated violence. We walked back through the computers and typesetters and potted jacarandas to Sean's office, which had a view of the bay. Before he sat down at the Big Desk, he made me an espresso from his own little machine. "Laura, I've never seen you in stripes before. You look ready for jail."

Little did he know, until I told him, that I had so many tickets I was afraid I would end up there. "I have a hearing today on the whole mess. Bree is supposed to be there to advise me as my lawyer—if she still shows up. We've had a falling out since the Warfield Fiasco."

It was now already a historic event. The Battle of Bull Run. The Gulf of Tonkin Resolution. Operation Desert Storm. The Warfield Fiasco.

"You know," he said, "that would make such a great story. Your fantasies about life in prison interspersed with a mock-news-style report of your hearing. We could tie it in with Bree. Finally see her as a professional—put the *p* back in yuppie kinda thing. I'll talk to Monique in graphics. We could do the reporter stuff in boldface and the fantasy in eighteen-point italics. Jay could do some wonderful sketches and—"

"Sean, it's my life. It's real. Let me live it before you start doing the layout on it, OK?"

I handed him the piece I had written and sat watching him as he read it. I tried not to care as his composed face twitched into a smile or his head nodded, ever so slightly, "yes" approval or "no" incredulity. He pored over the document sipping his espresso, about to drip some Italian Roast on my piece. Why do editors always hold coffee cups over your work? Drip lightly, for you drip on my dreams.

AN OPEN LETTER TO DIRK AND BREE

Dear Guys,

I'd like to say: Gloriana made you and Gloriana can break you. But even back in Sicily, my people knew that no one makes an offer someone can't refuse.

So I make this offer to you. Sit down. Talk to each other. If you still love each other, then get back to where you once belonged. Why? For each other and for your child.

Nobody should stay together just for the kids' sake. But why have a caring divorce when you can have a cockamamie marriage? It's cheaper, it's convenient, and from a sexual point of view, it's certainly safer.

If I were your daughter, I might put it this way: Mommy, Daddy, I want you to live together the way people do on my favorite TV shows, the ones I get in rerun on the blurry channel. I want to be in the Brady Bunch but without all those other brothers and sisters hogging the attention. I want you to be Lucy and Desi, but I don't want you to ever leave the show. I want you to be like Mr. and Mrs. Huxtable, but I know you'll always be white. You can't help that. Anyway, I don't want My Two Dads or Kate or Allie or the Who's the Boss? guy to raise me. I want a mommy and daddy if they can just stand to be together. OK?

If I were your real estate agent, I might put it this way: Why not get divorced? It will get you further into a market that's about to turn around and go up, up, up. Look, you can take a second mortgage on the house. Bree and the kid can stay there. Using the refi funds, Dirk can get a great condo in a fabulous location location location. Either way, I can't lose. Don't stagnate. The condo market is heating up again. I'm even willing to cut my fee by two percent, but only if I get an exclusive on the Quail Glen house.

Now, who would you trust, your agent or your kid?

Think it over, Dirk and Bree. Which deal feels right?

The other night I was in bed making love with my boyfriend—we have a caring nonmarriage—and I suddenly sat up and thought about you. My boyfriend got really mad and said, "I wish Dirk and Bree would just go fuck themselves." And I thought: What a great idea!

So here's my offer: If you do decide to get back together, Lifestyle will pay for a second honeymoon at the Pacific Farm, the new family retreat on the Mendocino coast. We'll photograph it all for our Reunions issue. A Family Reunion—all expenses paid. You can liquidate your psychological debt now.

And so, I'm outta here.

"Laura, this is great."

"It is?"

"I love the tie-in with the Reunions issue. Do you think you could get them to close on this November first? That's the closing date for advertising for the issue."

"Sean, I don't know what's going to happen next. I could end up in jail on some kind of fluke. Maybe Bree will want to put me there."

And without a moment's hesitation, he said, "Now that would be the story opportunity of a lifetime. I'll give you fifteen hundred for any story you send me from jail."

"Speaking of money, I'd like my check."

"Laura, I want to ask you to wait on that. We're expanding into special regional issues—*Lifestyle, A Weekly Magazine for San Francisco; Lifestyle, A Weekly Magazine for Chicago*; and so on. We may be opening up a new monthly publication—*Demeanor*. I know that you would want to expand your readership with us, so I'm asking you to just hold on a month through the launch."

I wanted to launch him into the firmament right then and there. Where was an eject button when you needed one? But I had a rendezvous with the City of Berkeley Traffic Court. Maybe I'd be critiquing the interiors of San Quentin. Was that a state or a federal facility? Or just someone's weird idea of a bed-and-breakfast?

Sean knew he had me by the ovaries. First of all, he does have a lock on my demographic group. Second of all, he doesn't care if you miss deadlines or ramble on. And besides, you can't say "fuck" in the dailies.

13

Driving back across the Bay Bridge, trying to think about where my life was going, I realized: I had no idea. I was on my way to face the music as a traffic violator. Was I a people violator, too?

Was I in cohoots with Neil Blender, flirting with Dirk, or manipulating them both? Was I Bree's friend or client or biographer or tormentor? Even I didn't know. If I was flirting with Dirk, is it because I'm afraid of getting too close to Russ, or because I needed another notch on my ego?

I was living with the perfect man, in my late thirties, and I still didn't know if I wanted to get married or have a baby. This man was supporting me and I wasn't even objecting. I was saving enough money so I could move out if I wanted to. It was as if keeping my options open was the only thing that mattered.

Once, I made fun of Dirk and Bree for being "culturally promiscuous." At least they had made some kind of commitment to each other. They had at least had the baby, even if the whole thing didn't seem to be working out for the best.

Oh God, I don't want to go back to a therapist again. I don't want to sit across from another sympathetic woman dangling her Birkenstocks and offering her Kleenex. How many sessions and how many Ph.D.s and M.A.s and M.F.C.C.s does it take to put Humpty together again? So my mother died. So I'll always feel bad. So I've got to let go of pain and anger. So I was abused by fate. So. So. So.

I turned on the radio just to turn off my mind. The Beach Boys were singing some stupid song called "Still Cruisin' After All These Years." I liked the Paul Simon song better, "Still Crazy After All These Years," but I wished it weren't my theme song.

Even stupid Beach Boys are better than no Beach Boys. There's some line in the song like, "Baby, you've got a greenhouse effect on me." I'm not kidding. They don't write 'em like that anymore.

Berkeley has an ugly little courthouse, not one befitting its architectural needs although perhaps appropriate to its bureaucratic obsessions. Traffic court is the happening place in Berkeley, the Bulgaria of traffic laws. Every block in the city is littered with traffic signs: Residential Permit Parking Only; Handicapped Parking; No Parking Between Signs; No Parking on the Third Thursday of the Month Between 12:30 and 2:30. I could barely keep track of my periods. How was I supposed to know how many Thursdays were in each month? My favorite sign was: Drug-Free Zone. I thought it meant that if you were drug-free, you could park there. So I just let the tickets pile up. Judging by the wait for a court date, I was not alone.

Architecturally, Berkeley needed a courthouse that made a statement, something like the one in Marin County, one of the weirdest buildings on earth. It's one of the only things Frank Lloyd Wright ever plunked in this part of the world, and I wonder if he was serious. I mean, get real, Frank. A huge, giant pink building that looks like Emperor Ming's winter palace with a big space needle sticking out of it. It's the ultimate only-in-Marin joke. Did Frank know something we didn't know about how it was all going to come down?

Berkeley needed an only-in-Berkeley traffic court—one shaped like a peace sign with the roof ripped off and sitting on the front lawn.

I tried to park near the courthouse, but every space for

miles around was metered or residential-permit parking. I realized I would probably get another ticket if my hearing took more than two hours. Now, you would think that would have stopped me, but it was getting close to the one p.m. court time and I started to panic.

I found my way to the room where I was to "appear" before Judge Bradford Corman. He looked like someone who gave up a promising career as a jazz musician to sit in judgment on poor girls like me. Thank God, he was a man—my counselor looked stunning.

Bree was wearing a lemon-yellow suit with a beige silk blouse and beige heels. No one in the room could possibly take his eyes off her. Especially the smiling man in the back row who happened to be Neil Blender.

"What are you doing here?" I asked him.

"Just watching our investment." He winked. He winks, he grabs, he wears gold chains. He is a man untouched by anything that has happened since 1972, except the inflated salaries of screenwriters.

I approached the Bree before we were to approach the bench. "Look, Bree, I have to know what is going on here. I mean, what can happen to me? And are you my friend or what?"

Bree's eyes lit up. "Well, Laura, that's a fine question coming from you. Let me throw it back at you: Are you *my* friend or what?"

The whole way over, I kept imagining this horrible scenario where Bree deliberately blows the case and I end up doing time because of something I'd written in an article in *Lifestyle* in 1986. Jean Valjean scenes kept playing in my head. Chain gang movies, and those horrible Ida Lupino women's prison movies.

There were even more paranoid scenes embedded in the plot. If Bree actually believed there was something going on between Dirk and me, who knows what the green-eyed monster was capable of. And she did look capable.

"Bree, you won't let them send me to jail . . ."

"Don't worry. I'm a professional and a good one. The main risk is losing your license," Bree said, obviously enjoying the fact that for once she held my fate in her hands. I thought about how she must have felt waiting for *Lifestyle* to appear in its distribution box, waiting to find out what I had done to her.

Judge Bradford Corman was practically drooling when Bree approached the bench. I fully expected him to disrobe on the spot.

The City of Berkeley vs. Laura Gurvitz. I could hardly believe my ears. I, who had worn a Serve the People button in high school, even when it meant my Republican civics teacher would give me a C. I had already gotten into Berkeley. What did I care? Of course, being an adolescent Maoist was nothing to brag about in the post-Tiananmen years.

What actually happened in the matter of the city vs. me was far more tedious and unadaptable to the screen than anything I would have imagined.

"Would you please come up here," the judge told Bree. Sure. Counselor, please come a little closer to the bench. Counselor, please kneel down at the bench. Counselor, please perform fellatio on the bench.

There was a lot of yakking. At one point, when Bree was shaking her head vehemently, Neil Blender started applauding from the back of the room. It was all just so many scenes to him. Of course, it was just so many articles to me—except when it was my ass.

Finally, the judge explained his decision. "While your lack of a previous record suggests innocence . . ." he began, and I expected Neil Blender to pop up with a line about my lack of a previous screen credit.

". . . you ignored fifty tickets and many warnings on this matter. It might have been an innocent mistake, but unfortunately, the courts and the police department are so overburdened at this time that we cannot take time out to function as a collection agency. What I proposed to your lawyer—and she has agreed—is that you bring your financial records to court so that we can decide an appropriate fine. While not the ideal solution, I'm sure you appreciate we are not living in an ideal world. I have detailed the reasoning behind these types of matters in my new book, *The Creative Judiciary*, and I am presenting you with a complimentary copy."

He handed me a book. I couldn't believe it. He handed me not *the* book but *a* book. His book.

"May I confer with my client?" said Bree.

She approached me. "Look, it was the best quick out I could get. Any alternative would have involved more time, legal fees, and fines for you. He was going to slap you with four thousand today. I'm sure when he sees what you're worth, he'll only hit you with half that amount. The warrants alone, without additional penalties, were worth two thousand by now."

"But why do I have to show him my financial records?"

"To keep down the fine. He knows you're a successful writer. He wants to be one too. You have to show him your records to prove how little success is worth in the writing game."

"But Bree, isn't this invasion of privacy, looking at my money? Talk about exposing yourself. Isn't this a violation of something like, say, my civil liberties?"

"Sure it is. And if you want to get the ACLU in on this, that's your right. They might even win. It's a matter of how much time you want to put into it. You could go to the ACLU. You could help them plan your case. You could attend their fund-raisers. You could spend years in a trial. All I'm trying to show is limited financial ability to get him to set a reasonable amount."

I agreed to the whole thing, but producing my financial records would be a problem. Like, what financial records? I usually show up at the tax guy each year with a shopping bag and let him sort out the mess.

Before I left court, the judge approached me. "Ms. Gurvitz, is it true that you are actually the writer Laura Gloriana?" His Honor asked.

"Guilty as charged," I said.

"Well, I am impressed. I've been reading your work in *Lifestyle* for years. It's excellent. And very visible."

I blushed. No writer ever minds being read and appreciated.

"Listen, Ms. Gloriana, I hope you'll enjoy my book as much as I've enjoyed your work. And if you have any questions, don't hesitate to call. In fact, let me give you my home number. I'm going on book tour, but I'd be happy to give you an interview before then. Consider it an exclusive."

As I walked out the door Neil Blender leaned forward and said, "Rosanna Arquette would do her more justice, but Cher's got more clout."

14

On the car radio a woman was saying, "I was always unhappy with my breasts. Then I realized that I could do something about them. I didn't have to be passive."

I knew a lot about my friends. They talked about their needs, their diets, their addictions, their abusive parents, their spiritual quests, and their sexual preferences, but I had no idea what anyone was worth. One's financial situation was the ultimate dirty secret.

The thing is, some people spend and some don't. If I were to guess what someone was worth, it would be more an estimate of their frugality or high-rollerability. How much stuff was enough to satisfy them? That was a need independent of income. Take a guy like Dirk, for example. He is a spender. My guess is that Bree is the saver in that family, and she likes to spend also. I remember in the original Yuppies article I wrote, there was something about their income. In fact, I can still remember most of that article.

Dirk and Bree: An American YUPle

Hey, hey, they're the yuppies. He's Dirk. She's Bree.
Young, urban, professional, and ready to spend on any
new trend. They walk. They talk. They buy. They spend.
    You see them everywhere now. Eating pasta instead
of noodles. Drinking espresso instead of coffee. Buttering
croissants instead of rolls. Riding in BMWs. Jogging for
success. Dirk and Bree do all these things. And they just
bought a new condo at Bay Gauche for $129,500!
    He calls her "Bunnynose." She calls him "Wildthing."
They have sex 3.5 times a week, but because of scheduling
conflicts Bree says she frequently has to "pencil him in."
Overall, their frequency rate is pretty good, and if my
boyfriend finds out about it, he's going to hit the ceiling.
Once, maybe twice a week is the best we can do.

This of course was when I lost my boyfriend Bob, who was
brilliant, handsome, and a nationally recognized expert on
nuclear winter but really inconsiderate in bed. It was also
when I decided to establish my trademark—commenting on
my own sex life in the middle of my articles. That and my
signature line, "And so, I'm outta here," gave me what Sean
Garrison calls "journalistic identity." I knew it was a great
career move and it took a Russ Nelman to be able to put up
with it.

    Dirk and Bree are 32.2 years old. They have a com-
bined education of 39.4 years, a combined weight of 265
pounds, and a combined income of $77,500. This is what
gives them all that disposable income.

As I drove by the toll plaza I thought: What do Dirk and
Bree earn today? She was probably pulling at least a hundred
grand from the law practice before she left at the beginning
of the year. It could have been twice that. And he had fran-
chised at least thirty of his Recovery, Inc., centers in the last

few years. Twenty percent of each franchise at three hundred thou a franchise—that's like—no! Could Dirk have made almost two million dollars?

Dirk was rich. Dirk was really rich. Of course. That was why they were getting a divorce—they were finally rich enough.

From the Bay Bridge, on this fogless October afternoon, I had a clear view of the overbuilt San Francisco skyline and I was thinking about Dirk's wealth. I decided not to get off at Broadway and go through the tunnel. Traffic was light enough to head toward the Golden Gate to get to the Marina District. I wondered what a couple million buys these days besides divorce and a lawyer.

Dirk could afford Quail Glen and not care about the sale of his Bay Gauche condo. He could drive whatever he wanted. He could own almost any machine smaller than a bread box. He couldn't really retire, though, unless he knew exactly what to do with his money. Maybe he did. Dirk might be one of those people who actually gamble in the stock market or sell commodities short or buy frozen orange juice futures.

All of this speculation was my way of avoiding the real issue: What was *I* worth? Where were my financial records? I paid no attention to these kinds of things until forced to. I was Cleopatra, Queen of Denial. One of my therapists, Jan, told me that.

How embarrassing it would be to tell the judge that my boyfriend pays the mortgage, buys the groceries, and pays the gardener and the cleaning person. It wasn't really an intentional thing. I just moved in last March and he already did these things.

I have around twelve thousand saved in Greengrowth, an environmentally-conscious money market account. I pay for my clothes, my car, my gas, my insurance. I get a sort of salary of something like thirty thousand a year from *Lifestyle*, "although you're certainly worth twice that much," Sean Garrison said. I get the Kaiser health plan through *Lifestyle*— even though they deduct a bunch for it, but look how well that worked out for me.

What it all boils down to is: How much do I spend on clothes and did I get a cavity this year? This was the ultimate proof of the fact that I was not a grown-up. When it comes to money, I'm just like a teenager with an allowance, and no doubt, there are many other people out there like me, people who sail through life on a smile and an ATM card. I wasn't the only financial illiterate in town. Why was *I* being called forth for a quiz? It wasn't fair. I had done nothing, absolutely nothing, to deserve this. Nothing other than try to park in the wrong places at the wrong times.

Maybe I should fight. Call the ACLU. Start a Laura Gloriana Defense Fund. Pull out all the stops. I had media contacts. Hey, I *was* media. I could dump on the judge's stupid book. I could take my case to the highest court in the land: the Del Warfield show.

Ron Walden, on the radio, said, "Plastic surgery junkies, people addicted to the knife. Go ahead, caller."

"Yes, Ron, I want to ask Dr. Hemler if they can take the extra tissue from the buttocks and move it to the cheeks?"

I turned off Chestnut onto Dirk's street in the Marina. The people, and even the houses, didn't look real. They looked one-dimensional, like a movie set. This is where I ought to live. I deserved it. It's the best place to live in the city. So safe and clean and pastel.

It was once a family neighborhood of ordinary but immaculate stucco houses with tiny yards and bougainvilleas outside. The large number of cars on the street suggested that there were now mostly adults here. You didn't see any of those bulky plastic tricycles out in front, only an occasional five-hundred dollar mountain bike being pedaled by another thirty-eight-year-old kid in two hundred dollars' worth of gear.

Dirk was staying in one of these houses. It belonged to a friend whom he had met during his coke recovery days. I always wondered whether Dirk was really addicted, or just couldn't stand to be left out of the recovery trend. I often thought Dirk was addicted to what's hot and what's not.

The blue stucco bungalow had an outside gate with a state-of-the-art robot speaker, buzzer, and alarm system. A computerized voice on the motion-sensitive speaker next to the bell said, "Please state your name and your purpose."

"It's me, Dirk—Laura," I said to the black box. It reminded me of the one at the McDonald's drive-through. No answer. I added, "I'll have a Big Mac and a Happy Meal."

Finally, Dirk said, "I'll buzz you in."

I was buzzed.

So was Dirk. When I saw him at the door, I actually gasped. He had such a huge bandage on his face that his mouth stood out like a big bulbous tomato and his eyes looked like two plums. Two big dark, brooding Santa Rosas. Portrait of the abused husband as a salad composed.

Seeing him masked made me consider how very little I actually knew Dirk. Despite hours of interviews, despite the fact that most of my writing for the past seven years had been about him and Bree. Sure, I knew the details that are Dirk. I knew that he grew up the relatively poor kid in the rich town, and spent his childhood in a modest white clapboard house on a main arterial in Highland Park, Illinois. He had two sisters. His father, a former shoe salesman and sporting goods rep and tuxedo rental franchiser, was now living in Chicago and working as a furrier. His mother, before she died four years ago, had been a full-time mother, actually a Jewish mother, but that, like Dirk's humble financial beginnings, was off the record.

He got a scholarship to Williams and studied psychology and English lit. He came to California to get a master's at Berkeley, but dropped out when he and a couple friends started Nature for Sale, a chain of stores selling paintings of rabbits and statues of frogs and other nature things. It was fairly successful, and then they opened a cafe, The Enchanted Organic Forest.

Around the time he was managing the cafe, he met Bree in an aerobics class. It was a Gary Hart fund-raiser—Aerobicize for Peace. It was also around that time that he got involved with coke. After his recovery, he became an expert in addictionology, doing corporate seminars and programs that

he called Rebirth Now Sensitivity Training. It was out of RNST
that he started the Recovery, Inc., chain. He was in the right
place at the right time, but I don't know how hard he worked
to get there.

In 1988, after voting for George McGovern and Jimmy
Carter and Walter Mondale, he voted Republican for the first
time in his life and was part of the baby boomer majority that
elected George Bush.

These were the facts. I knew enough about Dirk to make
an estimate of his net worth, which was more than I could
do for myself. But I had no idea what really made him
tick. All I could think about as I saw him standing there,
with his bandage and his khaki trousers and his blue button-
down shirt, was that it seemed out of character for his shirt
to be unbuttoned, his shoes to be off, and his hair to be
mussed.

He took my hand and held it to his red lips and planted a
kiss on my palm. The bandage was like blackface in reverse,
giving him the appearance of a minstrel with exaggerated
painted lips.

"Dirk, I've had the most incredible day," I said as he
showed me to the neat, almost sterile living room of what had
once been a modest family home. With its high-tech lamps
and white plastic over fiberboard furniture, it looked like an
office. I sat down on a faux-leather sofa. The only cozy thing
in the whole place was the teakettle on the stove. It was the
home of someone who never cooked and only came home to
sleep, someone who was known to direct mail marketers as
Resident.

The faux leather was sticking to my legs. I had decided not
to wear pantyhose with the striped dress. I don't know why.
I was sure that whenever I got up, the couch would screech
off my legs like Velcro—a roar of separation anxiety only
synthetic materials can make.

Dirk was still holding my hand. I thought he had a goofy
smile, but I couldn't really tell with his cheeks hidden. "Dirk,
did you know I had to make a court appearance today? I can't

remember how much I've told anyone. The last few days have been so confusing. But you know Bree was my lawyer."

"Bree was in court today, huh? And was Neil with her?"

"Well, as a matter of fact, Neil was in the courtroom."

"Courting my wife in the courtroom."

He was in kind of a mad Hamlet mode now.

"No, he was just sitting there making remarks. Do you know him?"

"He came by here yesterday. That was the first time I met him, but I've dreamed about him. Before Bree and I got married, he was really trying to snow her, inviting her down to his place in Santa Monica and introducing her to *film* people and such. She eventually made the right choice. It disgusts me that she's seeing him again—although it's hard to hate him, since he did come by and help me out."

I wanted to talk about my court problems and ask Dirk if he thought the agreement to produce my financial records was such a good idea. Russ never let me talk enough about my problems. "I gave at the office," he'd say. I fell in love with him at the office because I thought he had the perfect pickup line: "What seems to be the trouble today, Ms. Gurvitz?"

Dirk wanted to complain too. I often had the feeling that people were competing with me for the gripes microphone. I guess that's why we finally go to therapists, to hog the mike. The annoying thing is that even therapists start telling you their troubles—like, *I'm* paying, now stop that. Del Warfield was cheaper.

Between the bandage and the failed marriage and his disheveled appearance, Dirk seemed to have me beat. I yielded the floor. Besides, I wanted to know just what dear old Neil Blender had done to help Dirk out.

"Well, he brought me my medicine. You know doctors are very tight about Demerol."

"Dirk, you're getting hooked on this stuff."

"Please, Laura," he said, dropping my hand. "Don't tell me about getting hooked. You forget I wrote the book, or at least the pamphlet, on getting hooked. I'm a member of the California Council of Addictionologists. I happen to be in real pain right now. This is the kind of situation that requires a painkiller."

"And Neil Blender brought them to you?"

"Yes."

"Oh, Dirk, don't you see? Neil wants you drugged out and out of the way so he can get Bree."

Dirk thought about it for a long time. Then I realized he was woozy, far more confused than even I was. He'd probably taken enough to knock out a giant. He stretched out on the couch and put his head in my lap. He grabbed me by the shoulders with a strange amount of strength, pulling me forward as if he was trying to get my lips below that bull's-eye in the middle of the bandage. He missed his mouth and banged my face into his nose.

"*Owww.* Shit! Oww," he said, and stood up, grabbing his face.

"Dirk, I think I'd better go." I had no interest in playing nursemaid to this basket case.

"Hot Mama, don't leave me," he said. "Big Boy wants Hot Mama."

This was getting unpleasantly weird. Shades of that first interview—the couch, the popcorn, the drugs, the inappropriate laughter, lies, and videotape. Perhaps the bandage was like a mask, giving him "permission," as the psychologists say, to "act out." I made a move toward the door.

"Dirk, I have no idea what you're talking about."

"Oh, you play it good, you little Macintosh vixen."

"Dirk, listen, I think you need help. You've got a problem with these pills. Read your own pamphlet."

I moved toward the door again and he grabbed me by the collar. When I moved, the buttons popped off the top of my prison-striped dress. He could probably see my Nearly Nude bra, but I didn't care. I had never seen Dirk like this and I assumed it was the drugs. Still, I was curious about the computer reference. Something on the LoveNet? Maybe the same thing Bree was talking about. The whole electronic-slut bit.

He wouldn't let go. "Dirk, cut it out. Look, I want you to meet me at the Monterey Market tomorrow. I'm going to make you lunch and help you get better. Can you drive? I'll call you in the morning and remind you. The Monterey Market at noon."

"After the bandage comes off, OK? Promise me you'll love me after the bandage comes off. Then I'll let you go."

He was slurring. He was swaying. Why did I feel sorry for him? I walked him over to the couch and helped him lie down.

"When the bandage comes off. Now, you go to sleep and I'll see you tomorrow." That seemed to calm him. He was falling asleep.

I knew that he really did need help, but who to call? I didn't want Bree to realize he was falling apart without her. Then they'd never get back together.

On the Bay Bridge again, stuck in traffic, listening to the radio . . .

"I had my cheeks done, my breasts done, my tummy tucked, my thighs sculpted, and my chin moved forward."

"Are you happy with the results?"

I hit scan and stopped for the old Santana song "Black Magic Woman." Mai Blender would know what to do about Dirk. And even if she didn't, she would act as if she did.

15

If God is a vegetable, then the Monterey Market is his temple. You don't pick an apple there; you worship before a Fuji pyramid or a Gravenstein shrine or a McIntosh icon or a Pippin Buddha or golden or red or green Delicious saviour. There are organic lemons and Meyer lemons and tired limes. There are baby zucchini and phallic zucchini, radicchio and radishes, sweet basil and fragrant fennel, enchanted mush-rooms and piles of shiitake. The Monterey Market in North Berkeley is to California cuisine as plasma is to blood. Here where the hungry masses come to adore melons, Dirk and I would accidentally meet Bree and Neil.

Bree was picking through the bargain-priced lettuce mix-ture when she spotted Dirk. She gasped—and it wasn't be-cause I was with him, either. It wasn't just the rubber hose holding up his new nose or the still-bloodshot eyes from the blow and the surgery. It wasn't just the bandage that wrapped his face and made him look like both the hockey mask killer and his victim. It was his disheveled hair. His untucked shirt. And yes, one Reebok and one Nike. I had considered sending him home when I found him like this, but I was already committed to Neil Blender's plan.

Bree herself looked gorgeous even without help from stylish clothes. Her ever tan legs extended from neatly pleated khaki walking shorts. Her slim but toned arms were revealed by a *Kidschool* T-shirt, no doubt hand-painted by Rachel Whoopi. She wore her red hair back in a ponytail, and the turquoise earrings did the trick with her malachite eyes. Looking at Dirk today, Bree must have clearly felt the victor. But where was Neil? He said he would be with Bree.

"Dirk," she said, stuffing her mesclun of lettuce into a bag.

"Bree, don't even say it."

"Say what?" she asked.

"I don't know," he said.

They were careless people, Dirk and Bree. They went around the store talking and squeezing avocados, Bartlett pears, and persimmons until they were too bruised to sell. To their credit, they did better by their child.

"How's R.W. holding up?" he asked.

"Pretty well," she said, grabbing a fistful of figs. "She for-gives me, Dirk. I explained to her that Mommy lost her tem-per, and that was the price Mommy was paying for holding in her emotions for so long. I told her that Mommy would never have hit Daddy if she didn't in fact have strong feelings for him. Feelings that might even still be described as love."

"That's good, Bree. And did you explain that I don't want to see her until my bandage change, because I don't want to look ugly for her?"

"I explained something like that."

"Walk me toward my car. I have something in it that I bought her, and I want you to bring it home."

"OK. Then let's go to my car. I think some of your things are in the trunk."

"Bree, before we go to my car, I think there's something you should know."

"What?"

"I'm renting an Alfa."

Bree left the grocery cart half filled with plastic bags of glowing produce in the middle of a crowded aisle. Dirk took her elbow. It was as if I didn't exist. Bree hadn't said so much as hello to me, despite the fact that I was standing right next to her the whole time. Everyone stopped and stared at them. Even in a place like Berkeley, where people were savvy enough to stay cool around severely disabled people, the crowd had a hard time with a severely disheveled man in the store. A slob picking the garbage is perfectly acceptable, but a disheveled man picking fresh herbs is not.

I followed them through the parking lot to the newly leased Alfa. Dirk opened the trunk and took out a toy dinosaur. "I was going to mail this, but it's better if you give it to Rachel Whoopi and say that I love her."

"Dirk, I really am sorry, and I'm so glad you decided not to litigate me."

"Bree, is it true about you and Neil?"

"You know about Neil? Who told you?"

"Laura."

This was the first time they seemed to remember I was there. Bree still didn't look at me, but Dirk did. She said, "Why doesn't she just e-mail you?" I caught a glint now from those malachite eyes.

"What are you talking about?" I asked.

She addressed him. "Look, Dirk, I've been monitoring your

messages on the LoveNet for the past year. Laura is Big
Mama. She's finally outted herself."

"No, that isn't true," said Dirk, squeezing the green plush
stegosaurus.

"Dirk, listen, I'm willing to try to make this caring divorce
work, but please, please don't play dumb with me." She still
didn't look at me as she added, "I have something to show
you." They walked toward her car.

Neil Blender was sitting behind the wheel of Bree's
beamer. I noticed that the paint was rusting. Neil was smirking his crocodile smirk. Bree went to the trunk and got out
Dirk's laptop computer. He stood there staring at her for a
long time, a dinosaur in one hand, a computer in the other,
and, no doubt, an ache in his heart. Then he placed the laptop
on the ground, dropped the dinosaur, and put his soft hands
on Bree's muscular arms.

A woman waiting for the parking space began honking, but
Dirk and Bree chose not to acknowledge her. A familiar touch
can set off a whole network of memories, and for a moment,
that shared experience must have bound them together.

"Bree, I'm so horny," he said. That seemed to break the
connection for her. She pushed his hands away.

"Do you find me repulsive?" he asked. And then they both
laughed, realizing it was a line from *The Elephant Man*, a
movie they had seen while they were courting. I remembered
that when I interviewed them about their courtship, they said
that they especially liked movies about monsters and ugly
people. Cher's *Mask* was another favorite. Little did they
suspect that the next mask Cher wore might be them.

"Right now, I do find you a bit repulsive."

"Bree, I'm not asking for mercy, just a little bit of what we
once had."

"When we do the follow-up on Del Warfield, I plan to
apologize publicly to you."

"Of course. Those were the terms our lawyers settled on."

"Right," she said, and added, "But I won't be your co-
dependent anymore."

Neil got out of the car, walked over to where they were

standing, put his arm around Bree, and said, "Honey, let's
go home."

Neil Blender, master of scenario, had done his evil deed
with just one spare line of dialogue. Dirk stepped forward as
if to confront his rival and said, "Take your hands off her, you
bastard." But then he remembered. He was nonviolent. And
he was a battered man.

I drove a despondent Dirk up to Russ's house and told him
to rest on the couch while I started a soup. When I came
back to look for him, he was sitting at my computer. He had
called in the LoveNet, but entered his own code word. A
fresh message popped on the screen where I could read it.

> *For: Big Boy*
> *From: Hot Mama*
> *We can shout about it now. Hold on to your hard disk.*
> *I'm only Laura but we can do everything you and Hot*
> *Mama have been dreaming of. Play dumb. I love fantasy.*
> *   Mama Gloriana.*

Before he lost consciousness, Dirk asked if he could make
one more phone call. It was to the place Neil Blender was
staying. I heard him leave a sniveling message apologizing for
being rude and thanking him for getting him the Demerol
when no one else would come through, and could he get him
some more for tomorrow.

I really hated to see a grown boy grovel. What kind of
unholy alliance had I entered into to save my screenplay? I
thought it must be Neil sending that e-mail to Dirk, but he
was with Bree. Who else could be posing as me? All I know
is that Neil Blender comes from that circle of hell that is below
sleazy, and I was sliding in there right alongside him because
without my career, I felt worthless.

16

Ο ne might construe my financial life as evidence that I was somewhere between a sponge, a leech, and a whore, which made me feel a certain pressure to contribute something. I hadn't intended to end up so dependent.

When I thought about how well Russ Nelman handled being a foil in my writing, it made me realize what a prize he was. I'd had at least four boyfriends who said, "One more word about me in print and I walk." My usual response was to write something about how my boyfriend threatened to leave if I wrote about him anymore. But Russ said it really didn't matter to him. He knew it was a joke, a literary device. I don't know—maybe it was also some kind of test I used. If you really love me, you'll let me use you.

I stopped at Andronico's after taking Dirk home, to buy Russ something nice for dinner. When Andronico's was called Park 'n Shop, they were not doing well. So they changed the name, put in track lights, redid everything in gray and white and pink, and started displaying the produce like art. They also installed an in-market deli where you could pick up a quick dinner of celery remoulade, Thai chicken, and agnoli with pesto to go. The basics. In fact, I contributed to the Andronico's turnaround when I wrote a piece for *Lifestyle* called "Great Remoulades of Northern California." It was one of my rare Dirkless and Bree-free pieces. Maybe I could get into food writing.

I wanted to make something special for Russ, so I got a big prime New York steak. Nothing like a bloody piece of meat to please a man. Except for Dirk. Alas, poor Dirk. He once told me he spent a summer on a farm and "bonded" to a cow. After that, he could never eat red meat again. That's in my piece "Dirk and the New Male Sensitivity Movement."

> *Dirk is the quintessential new sensitive male. He refuses all offers of red meat. I guess he's partial to blue steaks with his blue corn tortillas. My own boyfriend loves meat, especially right after sex. His idea of a dream date is to have the steak brought to him in bed immediately afterward. You know, slam, bam, and medium rare, ma'am.*
>
> *And so, I'm outta here.*

As I was getting in line I saw Mai. She was with her daughter, Shoshona, and they looked like two girlfriends giggling about something in their cart. How strange it would be to produce your own little girlfriend. I started to feel jealous and wondered, if my baby had been a girl, if we would have been girlfriends today, or if she would have treated me the way I treated my mother before she got sick.

Shoshona was really a beauty. Prettier than her school picture and already looking more womanly. Like all Californians, she seemed to get the best of the complex gene pool that made her—thick black hair and dark Spanish eyes from her dad, pale skin and a smart mouth from her mom. Mai looked up and when she saw me, gave me a warm hug.

"I come here for the baba ghanouj," she said. "I've been craving Middle Eastern food all year."

Shoshona explained what they were laughing about. "My mom is like all, 'We've got to get healthy organic food.' And then she gets three six-packs of diet Coke to go with it. I mean, diet Coke is hell of poisonous."

I had to admit that I never bought junk food in Berkeley. I couldn't stand the sniffy looks you get from the other people whose carts are filled with jicama and bran and other disgusting things. Like me, everyone must dash to the all-night Safeway in El Cerrito when no one's looking, to get a fix.

"But we're going to have a healthy dinner, Shosh."

"Sure, because Dad's cooking."

"He's making his special *enchiladas verdes*," Mai said, pointing to the bag of tomatillos. "Listen, Laura, why don't you and what's his name . . ."

"Russ?"

"Yeah, why don't the two of you come over for dinner tonight? We could talk about what's been going on. I could meet Russ. I'm sure Rod wouldn't mind, because he likes to make these things in quantity and they never taste as good defrosted or reheated. Why don't you?"

"Yeah," added Shoshona. "Then my friends can come over and she won't be on our case."

"You mean I won't pay attention to the demented things you talk about and do."

"Oh, like I'm really demented next to you, Mom." Then she turned to me and said, "You know what my mom and dad like to do? Rent porno videos. Like these totally gross Debbie's Big Butt movies."

"Shosh . . ."

"Well, you do. Don't try to lie, Mom."

"She has no understanding of what midlife can do to you. So how about it, Laura? Around seven-thirty?"

"Oh, go ahead and change the subject, Mom."

"That would be great, Mai." I said. Since I was already in line, I bought the groceries and thought I'd save them for tomorrow night.

"Good," said Shoshona. "Now Mom'll have to take a bath."

Maybe the teasing showed that they really did trust each other. If I had a daughter, I'd rather she teased me than didn't talk to me, which is what I did to Lenore until the day I came home from school and she said, "I have to tell you. I've got cancer."

"No you don't," I told her, and ran to my room. I remember thinking: Why is she doing this to me? I didn't do anything to deserve it. I locked my room when I went out and I stayed in there all the time when I was home, talking on my pink

Princess phone and listening to my pink portable radio, and
putting up my Pink Floyd posters and lighting incense to cover
up the smell of the stuff my friends and I bought on our
weekend treks to Greenwich Village.

It took her a year to actually die and we did finally talk. I
got a lot of sympathy and I think everyone at Teaneck High
came to the funeral. Harry took it hard and told me I had to
be his wife and daughter now. I guess that's why I went to
college in California. It was as far from responsibility as I
could go.

Harry. I had to call Harry as soon as I got home. Dad is
getting worse.

I floored the Toyota to get it up Marin Street to the top of
the Berkeley hills. It was a war on gravity and the Toyota was
barely winning, but when I got there, I knew, I could look
down and see the world falling away. I'd be safe in Russ
Nelman's nest.

Russ was coming home the other way and we parallel-
parked in the garage. He was happy to go to Mai and Rod's
for dinner, but insisted we had to get in a bike ride first. We
changed into our shorts and rode up Grizzly Peak Boulevard
to Wildcat Canyon Drive. This really was the Wild West.
Maybe the grizzlies and the wildcats hadn't made it, but the
raccoons, the skunks, the deer, and the rattlesnake were staying one step ahead of civilization.

On Wildcat, you could look down at Tilden Park and see
the brown hills begging for more rain. You could hear the
hopeful music of the merry-go-round, a soothing song that
told you that things will spin around for a while and eventually
you'll walk off. What more could you ask?

Russ was far ahead of me. When that man rides, he rides
hard. A real cowboy from out of the West, a native San Fran-
ciscan, who never saw any point to living anywhere else.

As I was pedaling my cares away a couple in top-of-the-
line bike gear rode by going the other way. It was Bree and
Neil—at least I think it was. They both had on helmets and
goggles, so I couldn't tell for sure. She never acknowledged

me and they didn't stop, but I swear he had a triumphant smirk on his face. Of course, why would they be here in Berkeley and not in Quail Glen or San Francisco? Maybe I just had too much Bree on the brain. I'm always thinking I see people I know bike riding here. Once, I was sure I saw Connie Chung. I even followed her up to Inspiration Point, and when I got there I went up to her and said, "Hi, Connie."

And it was a man.

Maybe I just see Bree and Neil coming and going because I can't get my mind off them. Bree and Neil. It was a travesty. It should have been Dirk and Bree. I have always pronounced their names as one word: Dirkenbree. They were, in my mind, the perfect couple. I needed them psychologically as well as professionally. When people break up, they ought to think of more than themselves. They ought to think of the effect it will have on those around them. They ought to do an environmental impact report.

They belonged together—for the kid, for the readers of *Lifestyle*, for the big screen, and for me. I still didn't really understand why they had broken up. Why now, when they were worth so much together? Were we in Scorpio yet?

Ugh. I hated it when I fell back into hippie-think. You can take the drugs out of the girl, but you can't get rid of that hazy thinking.

Russ was waiting for me at Inspiration Point. It was starting to get dark and I wanted to tell him that we'd better turn back quickly. When I came up alongside him, he put his finger over his mouth to say: Quiet. Then he pointed to a treetop just twenty feet away. A great horned owl sat there like a fat cat.

"Boo!" I yelled.

The owl took off, its enormous wings lowering it to some hidden tree below us.

"Laurie, you've got a big mouth," said Russ as he slapped my behind.

"Guess who I just saw?" I asked him.

"Let's see, was it animal, vegetable, or mineral?"

"It was Bree and Neil Blender. Remember, I told you about Neil; he was married to Mai in the sixties and he once had an affair with Bree before she married Dirk. Dirk is jealous—"

"Do you think we could talk about something other than Dirk and Bree? Dirk and Bree. Dirk and Bree. I feel like I know more about them than I do about you. I'm sick of them. What about us?"

This was a shock, even though I knew he had no idea what was going on in my life. Usually I didn't mind, but this was no ordinary week. I needed a man I could talk to. I could talk to Bob, but I couldn't stand to sleep with him. I could talk and sleep with Larry, but I didn't respect his values. Raj was great, but his English sucked. I didn't think Russ really wanted to have those *us* talks.

"Well, sure. We could talk about us. That's really what I want to talk about anyway. What are we going to do if my movie deal falls through?"

"No, no. Wait a minute, Laurie. That's not about us, that's about you. About us is why don't we ever really talk with each other about anything but your work?"

It was true. I thought of Russ as basically a nonverbal guy, a man whose conversations were like an operation. Scalpel. Scissors. Retractor. What's new? Good. Fine. Wanna do it?

"Well, OK. What's on your mind?"

"A lot of things, if you ever cared to ask."

"Of course I care. Tell me about them. I really do want to know what you're thinking about."

We put our bikes down in the grass by a picnic table. He took off his helmet and said, "I'm under a lot of pressure at work right now. Cutting people up is not as easy for me as you may think. Especially when it gets to be like a production line. And these days it's like a production line. I get scared that I'm going to make a mistake. I have already. Do you remember that woman I told you about, the one with the hip?"

The couple I had seen before rode up to the lookout point.

I was watching to see if they would take their helmets off so I could tell if it was really Bree and Neil.

"Look," I said. "It's them. It's Neil and Bree."

"You haven't been listening to me at all. You just can't get off this Dirk and Bree stuff for a minute and pay attention to anyone else."

"But this is different. This is *Neil* and Bree."

Russ slapped on his helmet and got on his bike and rode away. I wanted to stay and see if it was really them, but I got on my bike and tried to catch up with him. Fat chance.

He was lying on the bed watching the news when I got home. He still had his sweaty biker shorts on, so I left mine on too.

"I'm sorry," I said. "I got distracted."

"Forget it," he said. "You're always distracted."

"You're mad at me."

"I'm not."

I knew he was, but I didn't want to press the point. I got up and peeled off the spandex shorts and the black and yellow striped jersey.

"C'mere," he said.

We had time for a quickie during Dan Rather. I wondered if Russ knew about me and Dan, or if we only seemed to find the time between work and dinner so he didn't notice that news time was my time. I wondered when Dirk and Bree had time to do it.

Thinking about Dirk and Bree doing it had an erotic effect on me, and I considered the possibility that they were my own personal porno movie. As Russ was bending over me, I was imagining Dirk with his bandaged face going down on Bree.

When Russ came up to kiss me, I realized that he had eaten onions for lunch. I'm sorry. Onions just spoil it for me. This would be the perfect Scope commercial if only TV were a little gamier.

While Russ was gargling I watched Dan Rather introduce

a story on marriage brokers. They ranged from this rich woman in New York who prepares a computerized report on everything from the potential's teeth to his financial status— maybe she'd just do my financial report—to a Native American healer in Colorado who locks two people in a room for twenty-four hours. No food. No drink. Just two chairs and each other. A kind of Dating Game Wilderness Quest.

Maybe that's what Dirk and Bree needed. Forget Neil "Kiss my gold chain" Blender. Forget me and Dirk. Although, if it took that for me to save their marriage, I'd do it. I imagined, for a minute, Dirk and me together while Bree stood watching in her lemon-yellow suit.

"A little faster," Bree was directing . . .

The smirking face of Dan Rather came on and said, "And that's our report for tonight."

"Hurry!" I yelled to Russ, who was still in the bathroom. "We're going to be late for Mai and Rod's."

The moment was lost. So we got dressed and headed down the hill to the pleasant craftsman's bungalow on Bonita Street that Mai bought with Neil in 1972 for twenty-seven thousand dollars. It was worth about three hundred now, if you could sell it, but Mai swore she would die in that house.

"Are you sure you're not mad at me?" I asked Russ when we were standing outside the door.

"Why should I be mad, just because I tried to talk about myself and I tried to make love when and how I wanted to?"

"Then you are mad?"

"What difference does that make to you?"

"Russ, what do you mean?"

"I mean, you don't care about me."

Mai opened the door just then and we both smiled broadly and said, "Hi."

17

Rod was in the kitchen rolling enchiladas. MIT had not erased his accent or his identity. He still dressed like a young *vato* in buttoned-up Pendleton shirts and Levi's. "Hey," he said, and gave me a little hug. He shook Russ's hand, and pretty soon we were all clinking Bohemias in the bottle. Mai would never do anything as wasteful as pour beer into a glass. She set out some chips and homemade salsa on the butcher block table in the center of the kitchen.

"Mmmmm, Rod, this salsa is great," I said.

"Mai made it."

I worried for a minute that maybe it was an ethnic faux pas to assume that all the Mexican food was from Rod. Oh well, I guess he must be used to it by now.

Shoshona and three other girls, who all wore their hair like Shoshona and their eyeliner like Shoshona and their T-shirts like Shoshona and their jean cuffs like Shoshona, came in. They said "Hi" and took the bowl of salsa and the basket of chips out, and you could hear them trotting back up the stairs and giggling. Mai just put out another round of chips and salsa.

As soon as Rod heard that Russ was born in San Francisco, they started talking about whether the Giants were actually better than the A's.

"Their pitching is falling apart," said Rod.

"Clark sucks this year."

"I actually think Clark is the whole team. It's not good to depend on one guy."

"Well, there's only one Joe Montana . . ."

Mai and I went to the living room with our beers and some carrot sticks and more salsa. I sat down on the old divan, which was covered with a Peruvian blanket. Everything in Mai's living room was oak or woven or ethnic, with the exception of her books. Prominent on her shelves was the large collection of therapy books: *The Feminization of Dependency*, *In the Region of the Gonads*, *Marriage as Hysterectomy*, *The Stay-Together Orgasm Workbook*, *The Abuse of Abuse*, and my personal favorite, *Guilt-free Incest*.

"So, Mai, can I tell you a little about my problems? I don't know who else I can talk to."

"Everybody is suffering from compassion fatigue these days. It's getting harder and harder to get any unbilled sympathy, but go ahead. I mean, what can be bothering you with Dirk after you, and Bree on a spree with that horny screenwriter?"

"Mai, how is it you know all this? I mean, I hardly know what's happening myself."

"Neil called. He always seems to want to talk. We have a pretty open relationship, although I'd hardly call it a caring divorce. I certainly don't care what happens to him as long as he stays out of my life. He's like this mess I'll always have to rub my face in till the day I die. I was young. I made a mistake. Now why can't he just butt out?"

"Well, what do you think? About the idea of me flirting with Dirk and Neil flirting with Bree. Will it make them worry enough to get back together? Do you still think it'll work?"

"I always thought it was a good idea to do anything to get them back together. I'm a big believer in the old staying together for the kid. I know that's incredibly out of vogue, but I can see how my separation from Neil screwed Che up. Not that Che isn't great or smart, but he's pretty insecure."

"Will it work?"

"I think the real question is: Why is it so important to you?"

"Because I want that screenplay to happen even if it means working with Neil. I feel that's my only chance for greatness, to honor my father, to be in show business. And to make money. Real serious grown-up male-equivalent money. If I could ever make as much as Russ, I might feel like his equal."

"All I gotta say is: Beware of Neil Blender. Neil is not—"

Shoshona came to the top of the stairs. "Mom, can I wear your black velvet dress?"

"For what?" Mai asked.

"We're going over to Tojo's house and we decided to get dressed up."

"Shosh, can't you wear something of yours?"

"Oh come on, Mom. Besides, you're too fat for it. Even Dad said so."

"No! You can't wear it. And I want that mess cleaned up before you go out tonight. Do you understand?"

A slammed door seemed to say: Yes.

I found it interesting that Mai had such a negative line on Neil. She could be sarcastic, but generally she saw the good in people.

"Neil's a skunk," she said. "Don't trust him."

"You know he's gotten involved in the screenplay about Dirk and Bree. He says Cher's interested."

"Don't believe it until you see it."

"Actually, Mai, just between us, he told me he was going to set up a meeting with her down in LA next week."

"Who knows what he's capable of. So his interest in Bree is actually business. . . . That's good for our side. Does Dirk know about the screenplay?"

"I haven't talked about that with him in any detail. In fact, Mai, this is what I really wanted to talk to you about. I think Dirk is strung out on painkillers and I think Neil is supplying him. In fact, I know Neil is supplying them. That's going a little too far in manipulations. Even I have my limits." I described the scene over at Dirk's that afternoon.

Mai agreed to take on Dirk's case and get him into some dependency program as soon as she could. We agreed that he shouldn't go to Recovery, Inc., and besides, Mai thought it was a lousy program anyway—McRecovery.

I was to keep Bree guessing about me and Dirk, but Mai felt I didn't actually have to consummate the affair to be effective. "Just keep putting him off," she said. I don't think

she realized how hard that was for me. Not that I was a slut
or whatever you called it nowadays, but I think that if you
start something you should go all the way with it.

"You know, Mai, I saw this report tonight about some Native American healer who locks people up."

"Like a marriage intensive?"

I knew Mai felt better when she had the right label for
things, so I said, "Exactly." I also knew that if a Native American did it, that was it for Mai. I could see her wheels turning.

"You know, I've heard of this guy who does these relationship weekends in the wine country. We could try to get Dirk
and Bree there—without Neil."

"You really think Neil is a problem?"

"I told you, I don't trust the guy."

Rod called us to dinner. While eating the enchiladas, I
started to speculate on how much Rod and Mai were worth.
This was my new thing. If I could figure out other people,
maybe I could figure out myself. That has to be the hidden
agenda of any writer because the self is always the last to
know.

If I could estimate their worth, I could estimate my worth.
Given the fact that nobody gets what they deserve, this wasn't
so easy.

Rod and Russ were really hitting it off. They could talk
sports, they could talk politics, they could tell each other
dumb jokes. Rod was one of the few people who could actually
eat dinner and listen to Russ's famous discussion of Surgery
Bloops and Blunders.

What I really wanted to talk about was Dirk and Bree's
breakup. The main question was: Who initiated it?

I said I thought it was Bree because she was fed up with
Dirk's being distracted by his work, and his computer life,
and maybe she was even a little jealous of how much time he
spent with Rachel Whoopi. Russ said that if Bree had initiated
it, why did she blow up like that and hit him on television?

"Now, I didn't see the TV show and I've only met the
woman once," Russ said, and I knew from his voice that he

was feeling his beer. "I can tell you this: she thinks that her stools aren't odoriferous."

Rod laughed heartily at that one. Mai did not.

"Great enchiladas, Rod," I said. *"Muy bueno."*

Mai said that she didn't see the Warfield show either but from what she read about it, she felt, "Bree's anger was the outstanding emotional event on the TV show. I still find it hard to believe that a jerk like Dirk could ever turn away from a woman as beautiful, capable, and classy as Bree. Dirk was always a social climber. Bree represents his ticket to the club."

"Did you see what Herb Caen said?" Russ asked. "He called Bree 'one of those women who shove too much.' "

Rod sat there for a long time, slowly chewing his rice and getting every last drop of salsa verde on it. He got up and brought in some strong black coffee—decaf, it was getting late—and he set out a plate of cookies.

"I think Dirk started it," he said.

"Why?" Mai asked.

"I think maybe he felt since he had money, he didn't need her and her old man anymore. But I think it would be hard to live with a woman like that."

Mai broke in. "You find it hard to live with any woman."

"Well, I'll bet he did have a little chickie on the side—just to bolster his ego."

"You know him best, Laurie," Russ said, looking at me. "Has he been doing it with someone else?"

Was he thinking of me? I had no reason to believe Russ knew a thing about my flirtation with Dirk. I thought of blinking my eyes like Scarlett O'Hara and saying, "Wha, wh-ut evah can you mean, sah?"

Mai bailed me out. "They're both too busy working out and making dough for extramaritals."

"I don't know," said Rod. "These yuppies must carry those appointment organizers for something."

Russ liked that one.

While they were talking I was thinking: Rod must make at

least thirty-five a year from carpentry and Mai close to that
from therapy. They did have a teenager, but their mortgage
would be very low. Perhaps Mai even owned the house outright by now. Neil paid for Che's tuition. They had a little
rear cottage with an illegal rental unit, but I'm sure they
rented it really cheap. So they might pull in around seventy-
seven five. That's what Dirk and Bree were making seven
years ago.

Mai started to talk about what consummate consumers Dirk
and Bree are. I've always been impressed with how critical
people can be about their closest friends behind their backs.

"Bree once told me that even in wartime, she could never
sacrifice her whirlpool," she said with a snort.

We were interrupted by the sight of Shoshona coming down
the stairs in an antique black velvet dress.

"Mom, just take a look, OK?"

Instead of looking, Mai jumped up and started running up
the stairs after the girl. I followed her up. She chased Shoshona into the big porch turned family room at the back of
the house, where the girlfriends were waiting like body-
guards. Mai caught her and said, "Take that off."

"Oh, Mom, please." It was clear to me who would win.
Mai was smart but she was a pushover for her daughter. And
Shoshona looked too pretty.

I came up the stairs because I was nothing if not a snoop,
and while Mai and her daughter were arguing I went into the
girl's room. It seemed as if every piece of clothing she owned
must be on the floor, but there was still a packed closet. All
the drawers were thrown open and also full. Her mirror was
dwarfed by photos stuck in the wood frame. Shosh at twelve
in a baseball uniform. The school picture that Mai had shown
me. Shosh, Mai, Rod, and Che at Che's graduation with him
in cap and gown and Shosh a few years younger, smiling with
a mouth full of braces. A picture of Shosh and another girl
with a heart drawn around it and the words "Best Friends"
over the heart. A group of girls in soccer clothes, each with
legs more beautiful than Miss America's. A line of four photos

from a dime store booth of Shosh, another girl, and various
boys' heads popping in with various silly faces. On one wall
was a poster of a band called War and Peace. On another was
a framed baby picture and Shosh's birth announcement. Also
framed was a poem which appeared to be cut out from a school
paper.

My Mom

By Shoshona Rodriguez, Fifth Grade

I love my dad
He makes me glad.
But my mom's the one
Who when I'm a fretter
She makes it better.

I started to cry. I think it's because I was premenstrual. I
cry really easily around two days before. Then I get the urge
to clean. Then I'm myself again.

18

From midnight to five a.m., I could not stop thinking about
my father. When it was almost six, I dialed the Kai Kapu
Nursing Home. I thought it was two hours later there.

After the phone rang for about three minutes, a voice whispered, "Aloha, Kai Kapu."

I said that I was trying to find the nurse who had phoned
me about Harry Gurvitz. The person who answered said that
it was the middle of the night there and she didn't really know
what I was talking about and could I call back when the day
staff was in. I asked if I could speak to Harry Gurvitz, and

she insisted he was sleeping. I told her my number and asked her to have him call me the minute he woke up. "Please call back after nine a.m., *Mahalo*," she said, and hung up.

I just knew Harry wasn't asleep. Why were they telling me that? He was always up in the middle of the night. That's when we had our best talks. I'd come down the stairs of our little Georgian Colonial in Teaneck and find him sitting in the dark in the kitchen, smoking a Pall Mall in the breakfast nook and staring out the window toward the backyard. There was a night-light out there illuminating Harry as well as a ceramic yard gnome.

"A burglar, he won't know if it's a gnome or a tough midget," Harry used to say. That's exactly how I thought of Harry, a mighty little man on alert against the big bad world.

I remember the night I came down and, instead of smoking, he was weeping. "We're going to lose her, Laura Beth, we're going to lose her." I knew he was distracted because he hadn't used my middle name in seven years, since I was ten.

"No, Daddy, you can't give up hope. You've got to have heart, remember?"

"Sometimes, honey, you have to let go. You can't make things work."

"You can, Daddy, you can. Don't talk that way. I don't ever want to hear you talk that way."

And then I went upstairs. I didn't want to hear it. My mother lived another three weeks, and I told Harry once that she would have lived longer if he'd kept the faith.

I was trying to interpret the woman from the Kai Kapu's remarks—her exact tone of voice when she said, "He's sleeping now." Was the emphasis on "sleeping" or "now"? Was it a lazy lie because she didn't want to check, or was it a coma?

At eight-thirty, I tried calling again. I let it ring a full four minutes, and no one answered. I pressed redial twice and waited a minute each time. Still no answer. So I got dressed and left Russ an "I'm sorry" note and headed out.

Another day, another bridge. Russ and I were supposed to go on this long bike ride on the Silverado Trail, but I just had to talk to Bree in person. She'd sounded reasonably friendly on the phone, but Bree had such an official corporate demeanor, who could tell what was going on without the mitigating atmosphere of her clothes and her body language and that slightly crazed look on her face.

First of all, I had to understand what exactly had happened in court, because I wasn't sure what I was supposed to do. Do I hand the Honorable Bradford Corman my VISA bill or what?

I also had to figure out where Bree's head was at these days. What was going on between Dirk and Bree, Neil and Bree, and especially Bree and me. I wanted to convey an ambiguous message about my relationship with Dirk that left Bree at once concerned about him and confident about me. It wasn't clear that I could do both and still have a caring friendship with her.

"Shit!" I screamed out as loudly as possible, using my car, as I often did, as a moving primal therapy chamber.

Lately, it seemed a lot of my time was spent driving over bridges listening to oldies and talk shows. Today it was macro-eco-catastrophist Dr. Norton Erlanger on the Ron Walden show, talking about which way we were going to go. Would the toxics completely seep into the water table and the ocean, or would the ozone layer be Swiss cheese first? "We're talking about what's killing the earth. Go ahead, caller."

"Yeah, hi, Ron, this is Steve McCandless. I'm a carpet layer in San Mateo and I want to ask Dr. Erlanger what he thinks we should do for a living while he keeps putting us out of work. Ya know, I'm all for the earth but I still gotta feed my family."

"Good point, Steve. Well, Doc, how about it?"

"I think, Ron, it's important for us to realize that without a healthy planet there's nothing for us to work for."

"Excuse me, Ron. But would the doc like to get me one of those university jobs like his, because unless I get some work soon, there isn't going to be any tax money for his big salary."

I was driving by the Chevron refinery now, and the sight of that eerie industrial landscape so close to the blue bay made me turn off the talk show. Enough already. I didn't want to think about it. I had personal problems. Unless I could get my life back on course, I didn't care if environmentalists were putting people out of work and I didn't care if work was killing the environment. Well, of course I cared, but what could I do about it? I couldn't even prepare a financial statement or remember to water Russ's plants. I couldn't keep my own father alive.

When I finally arrived in Quail Glen, I had to stop again and check my map. I had found the circle, turned right at the house with the goddess, left at the one with the imitation Shinto temple gate, but I couldn't find the one with the blue spruce in the planter box. For me, an experience more terrifying than being left to fend in the wilderness would be to be left in the middle of some suburb—they're designed to confound you. Maybe it's a security measure. By the time a thief has been driving around for half an hour, he's ready to surrender the silver and the CD player. Anything, just to escape from Quail Glen or Deer Parc or Pointe Negras Blancas.

Bree was in her civvies—shorts and a T-shirt. Her suits were suits of armor that she only wore to do legal battle. Still, she had a composed and flawless air even in her own home, even in casual attire. I followed her into the kitchen and she poured us each a Calistoga with fresh lime in a frosted lime-green glass. She put the glasses on a lime-green tray with the Calistoga bottle and we went out to her redwood deck, just off the geese room. The deck smelled of roses and smoked almonds. There were a half dozen pots of tea roses around the periphery and an almond-shaped dish filled with smoked almonds on the table between our chairs. I thought this might be a time to drink booze, to let our hair down, to try to cross the bridges that divided us, but I didn't want to push. Besides, there's no telling who else is a three-ounces-of-Fumé-Blanc drunk.

"You know, Bree, I have never really talked to you about

this split. If you don't want to talk about it I'll understand. I'm sure there's a lot of pain that I don't know about, never having been through this. I mean, I've had my breakups but not from a marriage."

I stared into her Ray-Bans. I wondered if she was wearing them because she didn't trust me, or if she wanted the power to look but not be seen. Or if she had been crying a lot lately.

She continued to sit there for a minute quietly sipping her Calistoga, so I decided to fill in the void. "A therapist once asked me why I made my sex life the subtext of my writing. She said that it's not in the main events but in the subtexts that a person reveals her true nature. But I told her I thought—"

"I broke up with him to save my marriage."

"Then you initiated the breakup?"

"I wouldn't say that. I would only say that once Dirk started it, I decided to finish it. I can be very determined once I make up my mind. Only now I feel as if I may have pushed it too far. What really drives me crazy is his complete inability to see his part in all this. It's as if he thinks everything is my fault, when it's obvious the whole thing is his fault."

"Well, whose fault is it? How did it start?"

"Look, Laura, if we're going to try to talk, I think we should get a few things straight."

"Me too. Me too." I gulped down my Calistoga.

"One is that I want you to stop writing about us."

"Absolutely. I mean, I can't write about you until this is settled anyway."

A hummingbird was sucking nectar out of a hanging fuchsia just behind Bree.

"The other thing you have to understand, Laura, is that I know about the computer affair. What I have to know is did you ever consummate it, or was it just electronic? Or, what do you call it—virtual love? I really need to know if I can actually trust you. Trust is a very important thing to me right now. It was when I came to doubt Dirk—whether I could really trust him—that the whole marriage was in doubt."

She took the slice of lime out of her glass and sucked on

it. I wondered how I could reassure her yet still keep her guessing.

"What do you mean? About the computer thing?"

"I mean have you actually slept with him?" She sat forward, uncrossing her legs. "Physically? In real reality? I have to know this, Laura, because while I believe fantasy can be a good healthy thing for a marriage, adultery is not."

She was showing cause.

"I absolutely have not. Yet."

"At least he didn't lie about that. But you're still thinking about it?"

She was an expert at cross-examination. "Bree, I won't do anything to cross you. I don't sleep with other people's husbands. Only ex-husbands. That's the truth."

It was. I sucked on my lime.

"I appreciate your honesty with me, Laura. I guess I'll just have to trust you, although I don't know why I should. Time after time, I have. And time after time, you've betrayed me. I haven't talked about myself with that many people. You're one of the few."

I realized that was true. Bree wasn't a therapy consumer. She confides in journalists. She tries her case in the press.

"So, whose fault is it?" I repeated my question. An interview is a lot like cross-examination.

"OK, well, I'm not sure how much of this I should tell you because I really don't want you to hold this against Dirk, and I still hope we'll work things out between us, although I'm less hopeful as time goes on. When I first married Dirk, everyone said terrible things about him. You know, that he was intellectually or financially or socially my inferior. No one said more about this than my mother. Oddly enough, so did Mai Blender, who is as opposite Lydia Wellington as any human being can be. When I told Mai we were separating, she said, 'It's about time'—the same exact thing my mother said. But I felt Dirk had proved them wrong. He ended up being a big business success. He also proved to be a much better father than I ever dreamed he would be."

I began to see that Bree was caught between wanting to dump on Dirk and wanting to defend him, as a loyal wife must, against someone outside the marriage. By now, we had both sucked all the pulp off our lime wedges, down to the peel.

"He can also be a terrific lover. Perhaps you already know that."

"What do you mean, Bree? No. I don't. I said that we hadn't."

Bree looked behind her for a second as the hummingbird took off.

"OK. Good. Well, it was actually 'the computer thing' as you put it that caused the breakup. Not because of the sexual affair—the fantasy affair—but because of the fact that we were spending less time together after I started to stay home than before I left the firm. I noticed that Dirk was spending more and more time at the computer and each month the LoveNet bill was getting higher. This didn't seem right if he was as happily married as he claimed. He would tell me it was just something he did to pass the time, to unwind, to reduce stress. You know how Dirk is always monitoring his stress level, trying to stay between a five and a seven and panicking if he hits an eight? By June, he was spending three or four hours a day on the LoveNet. At thirty dollars an hour that starts to add up. By September, he had a five-thousand-dollar-a-month LoveNet habit. And Dirk is such a baby about money. He pays no attention to where it comes from. He thinks it will just always be there."

Bree reached for an almond.

I was right about Dirk. He and I were actually a lot alike. "So what did you do?" I asked her, and grabbed a handful of almonds.

"I finally figured out how to log on, just to see what he was doing that cost so much money. That's when I began to read about him and Hot Mama."

"Hot Mama? You mean Hot Mama and Big Boy?" Now Dirk's weird Demerol demons made a little sense.

"Yes, I stopped checking last week when you revealed your identity."

She took off her Ray-Bans and set them on the arm of the chair.

"*My* identity?" I wondered if she'd even believe me if I told her the truth, that I had no idea who was doing this.

"I'm not even mad at you. I understand it was all a game. What the real fight was about was the fact that Dirk was becoming a computer addict. I don't care what the particulars are; he was escaping into that screen like a mouse potato."

"Mouse potato. That's really good, Bree. Did you make that up?"

We were both gulping down the almonds now. Bree poured more Calistoga.

"I guess so. You can have it. Do you want some more lime?"

"No, I'm fine."

"Anyway, I had just read this book about codependency and realized that Dirk was a completely addictive personality and that I was aiding him. So I told him either he stops with the computer or he stops with me. And do you know what he did? He went to his room and packed. I couldn't believe it. I felt so hurt. Have you ever felt total emotional pain?"

"I suppose it's like when someone dies?"

"It's like when someone dies while you're in the middle of fighting with him. You feel all this anger and all of a sudden— he's gone. You want him back to kick around some more. I think that's why I just went crazy when I saw him on the TV show."

Then—I don't know why—I started to talk to Bree about my mother. I told her that what she was describing felt like what had happened to me when I was seventeen years old, only I didn't understand it at the time. Before long, both of us were crying and laughing. Craughing, Bree called it. We finished the almonds.

I wondered why we never talked this way before. Usually, when we met, I asked leading questions and Bree dutifully supplied quotable answers. We were never really trying to make contact—just shooting the breeze. By the time I left, I felt closer to Bree than I had to anyone in a long time. It's really different when you talk about these things with a friend. That's the trouble with therapy—it's like the land outside of time. What happens there is just talk. Like a talk show.

Bree said one other thing that I found extremely interesting. She mentioned that perhaps Dirk was too weak, too much the new sensitive type for a woman like her. "Neil thinks that I need someone I can't manipulate."

Yes, of course Neil would think that. Who will manipulate the manipulators? *Neil Blender—at your service.*

Why had I let him into the picture? I actually did want to be Bree's friend, hard as she was to like. Today's conversation was unique in our experience together. She usually didn't show any vulnerability. I tried not to either, but I used to wonder if Bree had any. When I first met her to do the story about her ad for friends, I think I was really hoping just to make a friend. It's like the writer who does a story about singles clubs and what she's really hoping for is the story "How I Met My Husband at the Singles Club While I Was Posing as a Writer Doing a Story About Singles Clubs."

19

Driving home, writing in my head.

I said to her: "Doc"—I called her Doc even though she was still working on her master's—"Doc, did it ever occur to you that it's all just talk about my sex life? It's just words. It's not real. It's only reality-based. You know what they say about girls who talk, don't you? They seldom do."

And then this therapist had the nerve to say, "Did it ever occur to you that all this talk in public about your sex life was a way to drive men away? What man could possibly trust

*a woman who was going to take the intimacies of the pillow
and turn them into newspaper articles?"*

So I just blew up at her and screamed, "Well, what the hell
am I supposed to talk about in my stories, my financial life?"

I was disappointed when I got home. Russ was gone. There
was no indication of where he went or how long he'd be.
Maybe he was still mad about last night. Maybe this was it
for us. I thought about where I'd go if I had to leave. I could
find a place in the Marina. I wasn't tied down here. If he was
still mad, I could just pack my stuff and get out.

Then I opened a new file on my computer called "My
Financial Life." I began writing.

Confessions of a Financial Illiterate

*My financial consciousness began in 1957, just before
kindergarten. We lived in a pretty poor part of Brooklyn
where both my parents had spent most of their lives. But
my family was starting to get rich. My father owned a
small Formica-manufacturing company, and when he
walked down the street, people would say, "Hey look.
It's Harry the Formica maven," or they'd call him "Harry
the Formica king." I guess that made me a princess.
Sometimes my father called me that. "Don't worry, Princess," he'd say, "you'll never have to want for anything.
Someday Gurvitz Counters will be Gurvitz and Daughter Counters." I was a FAP—a Formica-American Princess.*

*I hated having such old parents when I was growing
up. I was that surprise baby when they were in their
forties. Their only baby—the dream child they thought
they'd never have. I think they called me "precious baby
darling," until I was twelve and I made them stop. Their
house was like the Laura Gurvitz Museum. Every school
paper, every little award, every professional photograph, was carefully framed and hung on the walls of
the New Jersey Lauratorium. This was the one thing I
felt I shared with Bree. She was an only child too.*

But nobody had old parents in the fifties, the way they do now. Nobody had parents who were preparing them with something to do should vaudeville come back.

I heard the phone machine go off. "Laura, hi, it's Bree. I just wanted to say how very much I enjoyed our talk today." I reached over to pick it up, but she'd already hung up. I realized she didn't want to talk to *me*, would never have said what she said to me. Only to my machine.

I had everything I wanted. Nice clothes. Tap dancing lessons. Piano lessons. Harry bought me my own baby grand piano. My friends resented how much I had. Some of them would even call me "Moneybags." I remember feeling guilty because, as I saw it, we were very rich and everyone else was very poor. This was the first time I remember feeling guilty, but My Guilt Life could fill a book.

Around this time, my parents decided to move, to buy their own home. We looked in Scarsdale, but King Harry said he could never feel comfortable with those snobs, so he found a nice house in Teaneck, New Jersey, with a big backyard with a swing set and a ceramic yard gnome.

The next major event in my financial life came when I started working part-time at Lord & Taylor the summer before college. Ostensibly it was to help pay for college, although Harry said I didn't need to worry. I ended up spending almost all of my salary at Lord & Taylor's Ivy League shop. An odd choice, since I was going to Berkeley and would eventually put all my Ivy League clothes in the Free Box at People's Park from which I took my new wardrobe.

Phone machine again. It was another machine calling my machine, offering it a chance to purchase catastrophe insurance.

For the first twenty years of my life, money was something that I had and could give away to good causes. I also figured that if there was a God and he was watching, he would see how swell I was being with my cash and I'd have kind of an in with him. This was my "I'll scratch your back and you scratch mine, Oh Lord" attitude toward religion. I was behaving like a Trust Fund Liberal. Only problem was, I didn't have a trust fund.

In the late sixties, something major began to happen in my financial life. My father started to lose his money. He made some bad investments. He sold the house in Teaneck at the wrong time. But it was more than that. My mother died and he lost his will to succeed. That was part of it, but it was really the shifting winds of taste and style that nearly broke him. Formica was dead. Wood was back. This was when I first realized the importance of watching trends. I owe my financial success—insofar as I've had any—more to the impact of the death of Formica than to the impact of the death of my mother.

While I was mourning for my mother and trying to understand what happened to Formica I worked one more summer at Lord & Taylor. I worked in men's leather. That summer I was still seeing Larry and, as it turned out, he was into leather. He would come up to me while I was standing behind the counter and say, "Why don't you take off all your clothes and lie down on that pile of imported English briefcases?"

The sound of Russ's car pulling into the driveway alerted me to the fact that I had strayed from the subject—my financial life. All roads seemed to lead to my s-life.

If you want to know why I make my sex life the subtext of my writing, I think it's because it feels good. You know, as they used to say—whatever turns you on. So I think Bree was wrong when she said I was a voyeur. I'm really an exhibitionist. Maybe journalism requires more than one skill.

Russ was in shorts and a T-shirt, and his hair was all curled up from sweating. He even had a bandanna around his forehead like Bruce Springsteen.

"It's the Boss. Where've you been?"

"At a pickup basketball game down at that school near Milvia Street, with Rod. He mentioned that he does it every Saturday morning. He can be pretty aggressive. But fair, you know. Great guy. Maybe when his nose heals, we should get old Dirk out there."

"Russ, I've got to go to Hawaii right away. He's getting worse. I'm afraid he's really going to die."

"I've told you that these things are never neat and tidy. With drugs and proper life support, he could be maintained for another year or two."

"You're being too clinical about it. Look, you don't have to go with me. I don't need you, you know."

"Laurie, I want to go with you. If you want to go right away, it turns out that I can work it out this week. And by the way, you know, you *do* need me."

"For what?"

"You need me for sex. You use me for sex."

"Well, if that's how you feel, I can move out."

"Laurie, you're too uptight. I'm just kidding. You're worried about your dad. Please, go ahead, use me. It'll get your mind off things. Stupid, I want you to use me. Come on. Come over here and use me this minute."

I hugged him because I didn't know what else to do. I wasn't exactly in the mood, but I was thinking about what I had just written about Larry and the leather stuff. Also, Russ had a really good smell when he sweated. Like graham crackers.

We went to our bedroom, but there was no point in turning on the TV. It was Saturday afternoon and there was nothing on. I got a little aroused anyway just remembering Larry and his fetishes. I thought at the time it was disgusting, although it always seemed to work. I don't think the leather did anything for me. It was Larry's level of passion, and his willingness to talk dirty. Even when I was involved with various feminist groups, I always had a hard time with the fact that despite what I thought was right, dirty pictures still got me excited.

And that's the beauty of an imagination. You don't need a VCR. You can run your own tapes. For some reason, the tape I started running now was the one with Dirk and Bree watching us. I realized that I had done this before, used Dirk and Bree, even when Dan was on the television. In the tape, Bree starts commenting clinically to Dirk about what we're doing, as if I can't hear her.

"Look at the way his hand on her breast causes her labia to swell."

"Interesting. Interesting," Dirk was saying.

Russ could tell I was getting in the mood now. It was also a matter of the time of the month. When I'm ovulating and right before my period, I'm hot to trot. Get me another time and it's Miss November. I'll pose but that's about it.

We had our clothes off and were parallel-parking, lying side by side and reaching out and touching each other. Dirk and Bree were narrating the scene in my head.

"Women have so many, many more erogenous zones," Dirk said.

"But certain spots are really special," Bree added.

"Like where?" Dirk asked.

"Oh, inner thigh," she answered.

"Inner thigh is always good," he noted.

"I think she wants him to perform cunnilingus," said Bree. "Or is it fellatio when the man does it to the woman?"

"Oh, come see, get in closer," said Dirk. "He's really going now. He's at that point of no return."

"She wants him now. Right this minute, can't you tell? Yes, yes, oh yes," said Bree. "Oh, this is so much fun."

It was. Oh yes, it really was. It was more fun with Dirk and Bree.

20

The phone rang. I dashed for it when I heard Harry's feeble voice trying to talk to the answering machine he didn't know was a machine.

"Hello, Daddy. Daddy."

"Laura, is that you? You sound like Lenore. Is Lenore there?"

"Lenore is dead, Daddy. She's been gone twenty years now."

"Lenore dead?"

Oh God, where was his mind? Did he already have one foot in the world where Lenore was? I wanted to reach into the phone and grab him and hold him here. Don't give up, Daddy. Not yet.

"Daddy, how are you doing? Are the nurses treating you all right? Do you need anything? I'm coming to see you as soon as I can. I'll buy my ticket today. Wait for me, OK?"

"They treat me real good, Laura. A big nurse is standing right here now. She got you on the phone. She says you're in California. Are you in Hollywood, baby?"

No, not Hollywood, baby. Not Hollywood, babe. Not yet, babe. Oh, he sounded so far away.

"No, Daddy, I'm in Northern California."

"I always knew you'd make it in pictures, kid. Didn't I tell you that you were pretty as a movie star? You did that tap dance to "My Heart Belongs to Daddy." Do it for those producers out there, they'll love it. Wear that little sequined outfit with the top hat and the tails and the shorts. And Laura, hold the cane up like I showed you."

I couldn't believe it. He was describing something that happened when I was four years old. My TV debut on the

Cousin Dickie show out of Newark. I had completely forgotten it until he mentioned it. He couldn't seem to remember anything that happened yesterday, but 1957 was coming in loud and clear. I thought about how strong his hand was, backstage when I was waiting in the wings and he squeezed my sweaty little palm, and how protected I felt around my daddy.

"Daddy, I'm in San Francisco," I said.

"San Francisco? They make pictures there now?"

"No, Daddy. I live here. In Berkeley."

"Well, no matter. I want you to come home. I want you to come to Jersey and see me. Can you get here?"

"Daddy, you're not in New Jersey anymore. You're in Hawaii, in a convalescent home. A really nice one, the best. Remember what you always said: The very best is never too good for Harry Gurvitz. I'm coming in a day or two. What can I bring you?"

"So, you'll come. Good. Bring me my Pall Malls and a couple Havanas. I can't find my Havanas. Here—the nurse wants to talk to you."

"Hello, Miss Gurvitz, this is Nurse Grace. I hope you can come in the next week. He's fading a bit, you know. Oh, and nothing to smoke, please."

"Yes. Yes, I'll be there."

There had been so many false alarms in the past year since Harry went into the home, so many false deaths imagined, I couldn't help hoping that this one would not be real. Please, don't let it be real.

Russ and I went to a travel agent and got tickets to Hawaii. He really wanted to come with me. He had two days off and called a friend to cover for two more.

I warned him it could be grim with me depressed. I'd probably get my period and be extra mopey. And we'd have to spend a certain amount of time around sick people.

He told me that he was used to sick people, that they didn't bother him at all, and anyway, he could go surfing while I was visiting my dad. My period didn't bother him. My mood-

iness didn't bother him. My parking tickets didn't bother him.
My murky financial life didn't bother him. So what did?

"What I can't stand is a woman who seems uninterested in
sex."

As I said, he's a simple man. At least it was convenient to
think of him that way. There was no point in bringing up the
fight yesterday. He didn't hold grudges—let's hope not. He
probably didn't even remember. Why don't I marry him?
Maybe I'm afraid that if I did, I would stop fulfilling his one
and only requirement.

That afternoon I decided to bake Russ a chocolate cake. I
hadn't baked anyone a chocolate cake in about ten years. I
don't mean some French megachocolate thing. I mean an old-
fashioned cake, like in *The Fannie Farmer Cookbook*. I looked
through the house and found a bittersweet bar hidden on the
top shelf from when my friend Alison was visiting and we
went to Ghirardelli Square. It wasn't enough for a whole cake,
so I decided to make a marble cake in a Bundt pan.

Alison was my friend from New Jersey, and I hadn't seen
her for at least seven years when she showed up in Berkeley
last spring. She was my friend from when I made friends
instead of contacts. She had never been away from her kids
since the youngest one was born ten years ago. While she
was here, and I was talking to her, I began to see that even
though you ruin your life with kids, you don't know it's ruined
because you have a different life. One that would be ruined
without kids.

I soured the milk the way my mother had once shown
me, by putting a tablespoon of cider vinegar in the cup
and then adding the milk. I alternated the flour mixture
with sour milk and sour tears. Harry sounded so frail, so
far away. He had been really good to me. When I hear
people go on about their abusive fathers, I realize what a
peach Harry was.

Russ was watching the Niners. I put the cake in the oven
and got a beer and sat down on the couch next to him. I tried

to decipher the cryptic Madden diagram on the screen. The phone rang and it was Neil Blender. I grabbed it.

"The meeting's all set for Monday," he said.

"Will Cher be there?"

"Lots of people will be there. It's at Century's End with Tod Fuelle. Do you know how hard it is to get a meeting with Tod Fuelle? He's like red-hot now. CAA grovels at his feet."

"I'm sorry, but I just can't make it."

"Can't make it. Are you crazy?"

"Neil, my father is dying in Hawaii. I've got to see him." And even as I said it I wondered if I was just using my father to sabotage my career at this crucial moment.

"So, can't it wait until Tuesday? I mean, don't they have him on some kind of life support? What's another day or two? Do you have any idea what'll happen if you don't show? You may have to be out of the deal."

I hesitated, but some halfway decent part of my brain, probably even the same part that enjoyed sex with Dirk and Bree watching, seemed to remember that there were some things more important in life than a screenplay. "That's the chance I'll have to take. This is serious."

"It's your life, babe. I know Cher will be disappointed."

"She'll be there?" Was he tormenting me, or was it true?

"She told me she was looking forward to this. I'm telling you, she wants the Dirk and Bree property. She needs something radical. Her career's starting to cool down. She's actually a very smart woman."

"Neil, couldn't you set up another meeting. I mean, if you sell her on this, won't we have to meet again?"

"Look, I'll do my best. I'm busting my balls for you, baby. Well, hang in there. Ah, hang ten."

When I hung up, I realized with a renewed sense of urgency how much I needed Dirk and Bree. The fantasy would never work with Bree and Neil.

21

There was Hawaiian Musak on the plane. A faint ukulele played a hula. I looked at Russ's profile, his curly black hair, his strong dimpled chin, and the train scene in *Some Like It Hot* came into my mind. Give him a blazer and a captain's hat and he could be Tony Curtis. But I was no Marilyn Monroe. I was more of a Jack Lemmon.

The plane was a Noah's ark of people in their thirties. It looked like a Club Med special. Boys and girls together. Or groups of girlfriends—all in brand-new resort wear. Everyone was on vacation. I was the only one on the plane wearing black. You're not supposed to be going to Hawaii to face facts. You're supposed to be going to get away from it all, not to get more deeply into it.

I had picked up the new edition of *Lifestyle* at the airport, and when Russ got up to use the bathroom, I opened it. I saw my piece, "An Open Letter to Dirk and Bree." I remembered my promise to Bree not to write about them anymore. She was going to be pissed when she read it. I looked at the closing line: "And so, I'm outta here." I was, sort of.

I had left Dirk and Bree behind me; they were figments of my computer, stored on my disk in California. I had left the world of relationships and careers that fills up your life between adolescence and middle age. I was flying into the kinds of problems older people think about every day.

I pictured myself squeezed in between my parents in the front seat of our '57 Bel Air station wagon, riding down the highway to the Jersey Shore, Harry at the wheel singing, Lenore riding shotgun and shouting, "Slow down, Harry! Slow down before we go off the road." How was I to know then that that was as good as it gets?

"How did someone like you ever get stuck with a loser like me?" I asked Russ when he sat back down.

"Laura, what are you talking about? You're a successful writer."

"Yeah, but everything seems to be falling apart. It's been one disaster after another."

"I take exception to your use of the word 'disaster.' I think a real problem for you, for people in general these days, is separating the trivial from the serious. That's what surgery teaches you. That's what triage is all about: what's really serious."

"But what about losing my movie deal?"

"Trivial," he said.

"Fifty traffic tickets and the threat of going to jail?"

"Trivial."

"Betraying Bree?"

"Trivial."

"You and I having a fight and breaking up?"

"I hate to say it, but in the big-picture sense—trivial."

"My dad getting worse?"

"OK, here it is. Here is what I know is serious. Loss of airway. Loss of pulse. Uncontrolled bleeding. Loss of brain function. In that order. That's it. And what I've been taught, what experience has proven, is that next to these things, everything else is—relatively—trivial."

I stared out the window, at the clouds, and he went back to his magazine. There was truth in what he said. When you lived in the world of people between twenty-five and forty-five, a sense of what is really serious was hard to come by.

It was incredibly hot when we arrived at the Kona airport. My black turtleneck felt like a wool blanket. We hurried past the tour greeters placing fresh flower leis around the necks of those who had paid $999 for car, condo, cocktails, and complimentary lei packets. I had the pamphlet from the funeral society in my hand.

We got our rental car and I dropped off Russ and the bags at the Hilton and headed through Kona to the Kai Kapu. Over the last few years, I had watched Kona grow as Harry Gurvitz went downhill. I noticed the Burger King after he had his first stroke. And the Taco Bell was finished around the time he had a bad episode of congestive heart failure. The ATMs went in when his emphysema got worse and he could no longer be cared for in his retirement complex.

It was dark when I got to the Kai Kapu, and the nurse told me he had been sleeping more and more. It was his congestive heart disease, she said; he was exhausted. Russ said that meant his chest was full of fluid.

His heart was full. I sat by his side for about an hour and a half, meditating on the tiny remains of what had once been my dad—my big, strong, cigar-smoking, schnapps-drinking, quick-quipping dad. He had to be tough to have survived this long, after a lifetime of breaking every health rule now held sacred. But who knew, as Harry might say; who knew from fitness back then?

He opened his eyes only once that night. I held his hand and squeezed it. I tried to give him strength, the kind of strength he gave me when I needed it, when I was little. He was the little one now. He looked at me and I said, "Daddy, it's me, Laura."

He said, "Hi, doll," and went back to sleep, breathing in and out with a plastic Y in his nostrils.

I sat there for another hour just staring at his face. Little black lines like auras danced around him. I couldn't tell if it was the fluorescent light overhead or my fatigue or if I was really seeing something otherworldly teasing him. I kept blinking my eyes to ward it—whatever it was—off. I was afraid if I left, it would take over.

I jerked up, awake, as a nurse came by, and she told me to go home and sleep for a while. I kissed his forehead and tried to convey with the kiss my thoughts: This kiss will protect you and keep you until I come back tomorrow.

The next morning, Russ wanted me to go for a swim and I told him there was no way in the world I could do anything like that. I felt so weighted down I was sure I would drown.

I hadn't even packed a bathing suit. He asked me to walk into town and have breakfast with him before I went to see Harry. I watched him eat a big breakfast while I drank coffee and nibbled on a little pineapple. Kona was the only place I have ever been that had better coffee than Berkeley. Russ insisted that I let him buy me a bathing suit even if I didn't use it. Sometimes I hated being mothered by men, probably because I knew how badly I really wanted that. Even before my mother died, Harry was such a great mother, so tender and giving. The idea that Russ wanted to take me shopping for something to wear was hard to resist.

At eight o'clock, the tourist shops were open. We went into one of the five hundred stores in Kona that sell bathing suits and sunglasses and hula dolls and off-key plastic ukuleles and macadamia nuts and suntan lotion that smells like coconut and coconuts with painted faces and sunglasses.

I let Russ pick out a bunch of suits and I tried them on for him—one more outrageous than the next. I was floating around on automatic and Russ was controlling me. I knew I could count on him to keep the ship afloat until the Kai Kapu opened to visitors at nine. He bought me a black one-piece with electric-green palm fronds and a huge diamond shape cut out of the back. I never even looked in the mirror. I'm sure if I had, I wouldn't have bought it, but Russ loved it. I gave it to him in the bag when we got back to the hotel. Then I took off to see my dad. Russ offered to come along, but I said that it was something I preferred to do alone. Maybe I just couldn't risk being any more indebted to him.

Harry drifted in and out several times during the day. I spent the hours mostly looking at him. I combed his hair and helped groom him and wondered if he had ever changed my diaper when I was a baby. He was a traditional sort of man, but he must have developed that strong maternal streak long ago. I know how much it helped me when my mom died, even though I lived at the house only a few months after that. I suppose if I had thought about Harry, I would have stayed and gone to school back east. He never told me I couldn't go.

Now I considered the years we could have had, the years I could have had of his mothering—and that maybe I could have given a little more back than I had managing his affairs from California the past five years. I should have learned early on that people don't live forever, but I had closed my heart to that little detail.

At one point, when I was fixing his hair, he looked up and said, "Take a couple inches off the top."

He was a shrunken Harry Gurvitz. He still had a mustache and I suppose, if he could, he would still smoke a cigar or at least a cigarette, even with the oxygen tube. When I was growing up, I seldom saw him without a wreath of smoke around his face. He now weighed about 130 pounds. He'd been almost 180 in his fifties and sixties, with a big potbelly on his five feet six inches, and tough, muscular little arms and legs.

We had our longest conversation in the late afternoon. He sat up in bed and I fed him his dinner.

"Laura, you remember the time I took you into Manhattan to see *Damn Yankees* when you were five years old? Just the two of us."

"I don't really remember it, Daddy. But you've told me about it so many times. You wanted to see the real Yankees."

"You said you'd only see the musical. Remember that song? We used to sing it—me and you and Lenore. We'd go for a drive when it got too hot and we'd sing . . ."

"*You gotta have heart* . . ." I remembered the song from before I had a memory, the way I remembered that pink and gray Chevy wagon and my mother saying, "Slow down, Harry, slow down. You'll get us all killed."

And in a very slight breathless voice, he joined me:

> "*Miles and miles and miles of heart.*
> *Oh it's great to be a genius of course*
> *But keep that old horse before the cart*
> *First you gotta have heart.*"

And then he went to sleep. He looked so peaceful now. No black shadows circled him. I kissed him and said, "I love you, Daddy. You are always so good to me."

When I got back to the hotel, Russ made me put on the bathing suit and come down to the pool. "Just do it. Just do it. Just listen to me," he said. Even though it was against all my feminist instincts, I did love being ordered around in my confusion. A sign by the pool said, "Beach Party Night!" and the hotel had a band and a stand with hot dogs and hamburgers and a volleyball net set up nearby.

I felt drunk even before I sipped whatever was in the pineapple with a straw in it. Russ took my hand and we walked over to the band and did the stroll and the jerk and the frug and the bugaloo and the mashed potato and a lot of other dances I didn't know I could do. I usually drank to escape but now, on an empty stomach and with a big hollow growing in my heart, I was really flying. I could have been on speed. Russ and I just kept moving in a frenzy and he kept laughing, and I kept laughing, and I don't think we exchanged a single word. I really don't think being a doctor helped him deal with a grieving person at all. Once he told me, "As soon as I tell the family the bad news, I say that I'm sorry and then I am out of there."

But he was a master at escape. I sat back and watched him win the limbo contest. His prize was a pound of Car-Macs, macadamia nut turtles, and a free mai tai, which he gave me to hold. I downed it like it was mother's milk. Later, when we had a chance to request a song, I asked for "I Could Have Danced All Night."

They played it in that lounge cha-cha-cha style, using a computerized rhythm section. The bandleader insisted I come up and sing it. I got up there in my bathing suit in front of all these people, holding an electronic hand mike and looking at Russ, as if I had just been crowned Miss Kona Coast. I was so out of it I didn't care. I said into the microphone, "Harry Gurvitz, this one's for you."

First I sang "I Could Have Danced All Night" as a cha-cha.
Then I segued into *"You gotta have heart . . ."* Cha. Cha.
Cha.

"Miles and miles of heart. . ." Cha. Cha. Cha.

"Oh it's great to be a genius of course. . ." Cha. Cha. Cha.

"But . . . first you gotta have . . ." Big pause. Everyone
applauded wildly.

"Heart."

The crowd roared. The bandleader took off his lei and put
it around my neck. Russ lifted me off the stage. All the men
and women and groups of gals looking for love just stared at
us as if we had the perfect love they were all longing for.

We didn't make love that night. Russ didn't even suggest
it. He knew we had just been flying on nervous energy, and
when we got to bed he tucked me in. I let him baby me. I
wanted that now. He had been on the beach all day and was
already tan. He was just beautiful, and I had to wonder what
I had done to deserve Russ Nelman.

We got the call during the night. Harry died. I felt a door
slam in my face. I was glad that I had come, that I had been
in touch with something that told me this was really it, but I
also wondered why I hadn't spent more time with him in the
past twenty years than a week or a weekend here and there.
He had so many stories to tell and I'd never even written
them down.

In the morning, we arranged his funeral. Even though it
was against Jewish tradition, Harry left clear instructions that
he be cremated and his ashes scattered over the ocean. He
told me a long time ago that he was going to do his part to
save the whales.

We hired a boat, and Russ and I and an old hippie in an
aloha shirt rode out to where there were no tourists or glass-
bottomed boats or marlin hunters and scattered him there.
The hippie was what passed for clergy in the town of Kona.
The Aloha Society covered the cost of the boat and his fees.
I threw out the lei from my singing debut after Harry's ashes.
He would have liked that, a souvenir of my show business

career. I thought for a moment of jumping in. Would I find
my parents down in the deep? And if I did, what would I say?
Would I address my mother as I had when I was seventeen?
Would it be any different now that I was thirty-seven and a
half?

We got a flight home that night. Someone played the "Hawaiian Wedding Song" on a plastic ukulele; the plane smelled
of coconut and frangipani. Russ ate the Car-Macs on the plane.
I told him how Harry always wanted me to be in show business. I described the time, when I was about five, that he
had me with him in a TV commercial for Gurvitz Counters.
He was wearing a crown, and my line was, "My dad is a magic
king. He can make your whole kitchen modern overnight."

Then Harry said, "It's not magic, Princess. It's Formica."

Russ said all his father cared about was whether he made
the swimming team at Stanford, and when he didn't his father
never really cared much what he did after that, until he became a surgeon. That was good, although his father was a
banker and viewed even doctoring as servile.

"You know, my dad once said to me, 'Really, Russell, you're
just a high-priced barber.' "

I realized again how few children felt what I felt from my
parents: wanted, unconditionally wanted. But what false training for the world. And I felt ashamed for the bitterness I still
harbored toward Harry and Lenore for not being able to give
me a world that welcomed me the way they did.

I asked Russ if he had a kid what he would want him to
be, and Russ just said, "A girl."

When we got home, I had these strange emotions. I felt
as if I'd been on a long, peculiar vacation, and yet what had
really happened was that I had been orphaned. I also realized
with some astonishment that only death had kept me from
thinking about Dirk and Bree, because they were the first
thing I thought of when I walked in the door.

22

A dream. Russ and I are driving down California Highway 1, right on the coast, on a winding portion of cliff with a steep drop into the ocean. I'm driving, and as we head downhill I realize the brakes are out. I barely turn in time to stop us from falling off the cliff. We start going faster and faster and the curves become less and less negotiable, and finally it happens. We go off the cliff. Time seems to slow dramatically as we realize we only have a few seconds before we plunge into the rocky, churning water. We cling to each other and I tell Russ I love him. But I'm thinking: Who will look after Harry now? Who will see that he gets what he deserves? Who will make sure he has the best?

I woke up in terror just before we hit the water. The empty feeling I had came from the fact that not only did I not have a father or a mother, I really had nothing—no one—to worry about.

My father's death was completely different from my mother's, but no less unreal. By going off to Hawaii to die, it seemed as if he'd been in some kind of tropical purgatory, waiting for the final boarding call. Now I was back home and Harry was in heaven or Hawaii. If it was heaven, there would be no more phone calls.

I let Russ sleep, and got up and tried to decide which machine to turn to. I went to my phone machine and thought, hoped for a second, that I might hear, "Hi, honey. Daddy's home. Daddy's home to stay." I once read a story in the newspaper about people getting phone calls from the dead, but that was only on the New York phone system.

Instead, I got Bree. "Laura, you are just scum. Once again, you sat there in front of me, looked me right in the eyes,

acted as if you were my dear friend, and swore you weren't
going to write about us anymore. I pick up the paper and
there we are—"An Open Letter to Dirk and Bree." That's
my child you're joking about. This may be a lot of laughs for
you, but it happens to be painful for me. Not that you care.
Get a life."

I was actually relieved to hear the next message, even if it
was from the grotesque Mr. B. "Hi, Laura, Neil Blender here.
The project was an incredible hit. Cher is crazy nuts to do
this. We need to talk. Call me."

Another click. This one was for Russ, and I knew it couldn't
be the hospital because they usually use the beeper or his
business phone. "Hello, Russell, this is your father. Mother
and I would like to see you. It's been a while. Why don't you
bring that woman and meet us for dinner?"

That woman. Harry Gurvitz would never refer to my boyfriends that way. He would say, "Bring the schmendrick
along." Harry would have liked Russ—"Solid, very solid. A
mensch. Don't let this one get away." I think he would have
even liked Neil Blender. "I admire his chutzpah," he would
say. But Dirk and Bree—"A couple of cold fish." I'm sure he
would say that.

Now we'll never know. He'll say no more. I guess in the
back of my mind I kept hoping for some miracle. In the last
few months, a plan began to take hold. I began to imagine
what it would be like to bring Harry to Northern California
to live with me, and take him around to meet my friends.
Maybe it was never realistic; he was too far gone. I even
picked out a place for him to stay, The Bay Royale, A Fully
Automated Retirement Community. I imagined him in his
yellow V-neck and plaid pants playing golf in Tilden Park.
He'd have been so much fun, so different from everyone here.
Think of Harry at a party with my friends—where they're all
tsk-tsking about censorship in the arts—saying, "What that
Madonna needs is a good spanking."

From another time and place, he was an original. There'll
never be anyone like that again.

Now I was back and without him, back to going through the motions of pressing buttons and running tapes and turning on the power. One of the strangest things about the past decade was the *way* the machines had taken over our lives. We always knew they would, but the fantasy, back in the fifties when we had fantasies about a rosy future, was of a life of ease, where the machines did the work. And in the sixties when we had fantasies of a dark future, we imagined the machines enslaving us. Now I turned to machines not to save labor or surrender to a robot but merely to be engaged, to pass time, to interact with the world. To live was to push buttons.

I pressed play again: Chuck Chernoff, producer of the Del Warfield show—"Are you going to make the show?", Berkeley traffic court—"Confirming the time to review your materials," Mai Blender—"I've got a plan for Dirk." And finally, an upbeat Sean Garrison.

"Laura, hi, Sean here. I hope you can make it Saturday night. You know it's our Halloween party and we're asking our writers to come as their copy. Also, I haven't gotten anything from you for this week and I'm wondering if you're going to make it?"

I was just wondering that myself.

I pressed stop and went to get some coffee and look at that antique distraction, the newspaper. Instead of turning to the gossip columns first, as I always do, I looked at the obituaries. Nothing about Gurvitz, Harry L. It would help to read it in the paper, but as the last descendant of the House of Gurvitz, only I could have placed such a notice. There was one other way to look at it. Maybe it wasn't true.

I turned to Liz Smith and read: "Cher was in Milan today to confer with noted designer Antoni O, who is creating a new line of Cher-inspired leather fashions. Cher herself was sporting a black leather minidress and her frequent pal German teen rocker Babar."

I speed-dialed Neil Blender. "Oh, those columns are always a week or two late. Yeah, Cher just got back from Italy and

she's already working with a makeup man for the Dirk look.
She'll use a red wig for Bree. I'm really sorry you couldn't be
there. Tod Fuelle will produce, and he wants to get Norm
Desmond to direct. But look, we've got to sit down and work
out our deal. Maybe next week we can fly down and iron
things out with Slow-go. You wanna stay at my place?"

I thought of telling him that my father had just died, although I still hoped it wasn't true, but I got off quickly. I
couldn't talk. One didn't want to deal with Neil Blender from
a position of weakness. He could probably smell uncontrolled
bleeding over the phone.

I went back to the computer and "My Financial Life."

> *According to my checkbook, I have fifteen hundred in
> cash right now, but that doesn't really mean anything
> until I get my VISA bill. I have a habit of using my ATM
> card without writing it in the book. I frequently end the
> month by going to my money market account, which now
> has almost twelve thousand dollars, and taking a thou-
> sand out to cover the plastic confusion.*
>
> *My father died. He's gone. The fortune he once made
> in Formica was down to around fifteen thousand dollars,
> which would have covered just three more months at the
> Kai Kapu, so he seemed to have let his life run out just
> as his money did. I don't know what to do with the fifteen,
> but I'm thinking of buying my boyfriend a new car—
> maybe a Mazda Miata. I owe him rent and food for the
> last nine months, and I think it would be a good idea to
> even the score. Maybe even make him feel a little in-
> debted. Then all that would bind us together would be
> sex—great sex. Not money. Not rent. Not marriage. We
> don't even have anything to say to each other. Just a
> pure, no-strings-attached physical attraction.*

There I go again. My sex life, my self.

I noticed a Post-it note I had attached to my phone machine
reminding me to call the LoveNet. I scrolled to "Pen Pal"

and there was Hot Mama. Hot Mama and Big Boy had been carrying on a correspondence since April. There were over three hundred entries. The most recent was:

To: Hot Mama
From: Big Boy

I have been a bad boy
But help is on the way.
Hot Mama, come and validate me.
At least come over to play.

Then:

To: Big Boy
From: Hot Mama

I can validate you.
You can park in my spot.
Tell Bree you want to see me
Or Laura will cry a lot.

Then Dirk/BB responded.

L is for the virtual love she gave me.
A is for her ass so firm and white.
U is for the undercover playmate.
R is for the romance of the night.
A is for the arms I want to hold me.
   Put them all together, they spell Hot Mama. See me tonight?

I turned off the computer and felt slightly nauseous. Who could be posing as me on the LoveNet? I just couldn't see Neil Blender, aging hacker. Besides, he'd have written a better poem.

23

There was no point in calling Bree. What could I say? I found it very hard to tell anyone my father had died, especially over the phone. All reality seemed artificial, once removed, electronic, over the phone, a jet ride away. Maybe Harry Gurvitz wasn't really dead in California. Maybe he was just dead over the phone, in Hawaii. Which way did the time delay work? Perhaps it worked in Harry's favor, and he still had a couple hours left in other parts of the country.

But I felt it was important to square things with Bree, so I decided once again to ride over to Quail Glen. On the Richmond Bridge, the talk show was on whether older men/younger women romances always represent some kind of father complex. The guest was Fran Cefisco, author of *The Gepetto Syndrome.*

I considered what it was I liked about Russ. He was close to my age, and I realized that I loved him when he was being both paternal and maternal, the way he was in Hawaii. He could be authoritative and gentle, the surgeon who carefully explains what he will do to you, and then once you're asleep, sticks the knife right into your heart—for your own good of course. Why don't I marry him and let him take care of me? I could be the warm parents he never had, and he could be the Harry and Lenore I still needed. I'll never forget him buying me that bathing suit, even though I won't wear it again.

"Hi, Ron, my name is Ralph Stevens and I'm an attorney in the city. I'm fifty-six and I frequently date women in their twenties and thirties, and all they want is a daddy. I don't care how independent or liberated they seem. They basically want their behinds kissed—"

I turned it off. I couldn't stand to return to the stupid world just yet. I was thinking about ashes in the sea. Russ had stood next to me as they were scattered and held my hand, as if he knew I needed something to keep me from going down with them, some anchor. I decided I would get him the Miata today.

My car started lurching suddenly, as if the transmission went out. I almost skidded into the car next to me. I seemed to have set off some kind of chain reaction. All the other cars were swerving and veering—trying to get away from me. I must have blown a tire. Or maybe four of them.

I tried to pull over to the side, but a car behind me started honking and the driver was waving his hands around like a madman. As he passed me on the right he yelled, "Keep going! Keep going! Get off the bridge!"

My car seemed all right, so I kept going and stopped just near San Quentin. A siren was sounding somewhere; then I heard several sirens, and I thought maybe there was a prison break.

I imagined Charles Manson, with that little swastika cut in his forehead, running from the bushes and commandeering my car. "Take me to LA and don't stop. We've got a meeting with Universal. I've got a deal in development with Tod Fuelle. We've got De Niro lined up to play me. Isn't that just too perfect?"

Why I would mix up Manson with Neil Blender was obvious to me, especially when I considered Blender's confidence that he could lure women into his cult. Bree was his Squeaky Fromme. I was his Susan Atkins. Women who love creeps too much.

I got out and checked the bushes for Manson and the car for problems. No damage was apparent to the tires, nor was any maniac hiding in the foliage wearing a creepy-crawly suit and brandishing a prison shop shiv.

As I continued north toward Quail Glen I kept passing fire trucks and hearing sirens. Maybe there was a forest fire— things were still pretty dry.

I turned on the radio and Ron Walden was gone. It had to be the end of the world, and maybe it was.

". . . we don't know the extent of the damage yet," said

the voice that had eclipsed Ron Walden, "but we have a report of damage to the Bay Bridge. A plume of smoke is rising in Oakland and another can be seen in the direction of the Golden Gate. Again, there has been an earthquake and preliminary reports indicate that it has affected a wide area. We still don't know the magnitude or where the quake was centered, but I can tell you that we here in the KBAY newsroom have never felt anything like this before."

OhmyGod! was all I could think, because God is a very useful concept in a disaster. Now I had conclusive evidence that I really was the Queen of Denial. I never even felt it.

I decided to go on to Quail Glen. I was close enough and would try to call Russ when I got there. On the way over, the reports kept changing. First it was a 6.3, then it was a 7.5. First it was centered near Santa Rosa, then it moved to Morgan Hill. First the plume of smoke was in Oakland, then the University of California was on fire in Berkeley. First there was very little damage, then there was a report of people buried alive in a bookstore.

It took me a while, but somehow I found my way to Bree's street without a map. Lots of people were standing in front of their houses talking to their neighbors, holding their babies. They were out of their yards, out of their tasteful wooden fences. I think this is when I began to feel that something extraordinary had happened.

A new Alfa Romeo Spider was parked in front of the Miller-Wellington Spanish hacienda, with the license plate: RECOVER. Maria came to the door holding Rachel Whoopi.

"That was really scary," the little girl said. "I'm glad my mommy was here. And my daddy came home. He hurt his nose but we're all fine. I don't like earthquakes."

Maria pointed toward the deck, and when I got out there, Dirk and Bree were standing there stark naked except for the large fresh bandage taped over Dirk's nose. Bree stood beneath a showerhead that was hooked up next to the hot tub. Neither seemed surprised to see me.

"Look," Dirk said, "If I'm going down the hill I'm going in the tub."

I swear, he said that. This happened. I couldn't make this up.

24

The surreality of it all didn't hit me for several hours, but the earth shook something in my soul.

How else can I explain the fact that I, too, threw off my clothes and jumped into the tub with Dirk and Bree? See, I'm actually a pretty modest person—about my body, I mean. I always pull the curtain or go into the toilet stall in women's dressing rooms. Don't judge me by my debut as a lounge singer in a bathing suit doing the "I Could Have Danced All Night" cha-cha-cha. That was just a dance of death. So too was the scene I found myself in—sitting in a redwood vat, on a redwood deck, in a suburb carved out of what had once been a redwood forest. I was in the Dirk and Bree soup now.

"Please don't splash—I have to keep my bandage dry," said Dirk as I got in the tub.

"I'm so glad I was home with Rachel," Bree said. "But I'm amazed at how fast both of you got here."

"I was actually on my way here to explain about the piece in *Lifestyle*," I said. "I was just coming off the Richmond Bridge and I didn't even realize there had been an earthquake. I thought it was my tires or a prison break."

"I thought it was withdrawal," Dirk explained. "I had just come out of a meeting trying to come to grips with my addiction to painkillers. At first I felt shaky and thought; Oh no! Higher Power, don't fail me now. Then I felt the Alfa jump up in the air, and I knew it was an earthquake. I raced here as fast as I could. All the way I was thinking—Just let Bree and Rachel be OK. Nothing else matters. There's nothing like an earthquake to put things in perspective. Should I turn on the jets?"

"Please, no bubbles," said Bree. "I want things as still as possible. This house really shook. For a minute I contemplated the end of the world."

"Well, we all seem to be OK," I said. Little did I realize that I would be having this where-were-you-when conversation nonstop for the next few months. And what could I say when people said, "I was in the liquor store and the bottles started flying off the shelves," or, "I was on a ladder and the house started swaying." What could I say? "Oh, I was in denial."

I would hear tales of people who experienced mini tidal waves not only in hot tubs and swimming pools but also in bathtubs and on the toilet; of others who saw the shock waves coming, who felt soccer fields turn into billowing blankets. I would speak to one man whose acupuncture treatment during the quake turned him into a bleeding Saint Sebastian.

Little did I suspect, as I once again swore to Bree that I was through writing about her, that I would be calling in a few days and asking for just one more. I wrote my "Earthquake Survival, California Style" piece about our postquake moments in the tub. People assumed that I made it up. Sean Garrison said, "Terrific, Laura, one of your best," as he spilled his caffè latte on it. The Media Union gave me its Golden Tacky Award for the very worst piece of quake journalism. The wife of a man who died in the quake wrote to me and said, "Do you have any idea how your cavalier treatment of this tragedy affected me?" She included a photo of her late husband with their three children.

But this was all to come. I naively thought the earthquake was something in the past tense as we sat there in the tub, and Dirk and Bree talked about how the earthquake was a spiritual experience, a way to get them back in touch with their real feelings. "Now we can proceed with our caring divorce," said Bree.

"You know, Bree, I was hoping I could move back in and we could work on our marriage with a therapist."

"I think it would be better if you stayed in your place and we worked on our marriage with a lawyer."

"Could I move back in after the divorce?" he said.

"My father died," I said.

Either Dirk and Bree did not hear me or they chose not to. "When do we do the Del Warfield follow-up?" Bree said to Dirk.

Maria came running in. "Ber-ree!" she cried, and I realized it was the first time I heard her talk. "Ra-chel is asleep but the radio say the bridge is collapse and San Francisco is burning."

We scrambled out of the tub and wrapped towels around ourselves. Those were the last seconds before we knew that the earthquake was actually going to affect us, inconvenience us, shake us up.

We stood there dripping in front of Bree's TV as the live coverage of the burning Marina came on. "Holy shit!" screamed Dirk. "My computer's in there."

"Your computer!" yelled Bree. "How can you think about that? People are in there."

"People are in my computer too!" Dirk shot back. "My friends, my network—oh no! My hard disk!"

I dressed quickly. I tried the phone and couldn't get a dial tone. In a dreamlike state, I headed back toward the Richmond Bridge, never considering the possibility that it wouldn't be there.

I was driving right over the bay when I heard that the Bay Bridge really had collapsed. I could have been on it! Of course, I didn't picture one piece falling in. When they said "collapsed," I pictured the whole thing crumbling like in a Godzilla movie. Not a modified limited hangout.

I could have been on it. And that was another theme that was to dominate our conversations in the weeks to come. I could have been there—there, where people actually died.

Reality was beginning to feel like looking through the wrong end of a telescope. The earthquake was diminishing the death of my father, which had diminished my court problems, which had diminished my screenplay deal. Only one thing was important now. Where was Russ?

On the radio coming home I got new updates. Confirmed dead. Expected dead. Epicenters here. Epicenters there. Looters. No, not looters—rescuers. Please, stay home. Turn your gas off. Do not, we repeat, do not turn off your gas. Read the front pages of your phone book. Now we go to Wendy Chavez live from the KBAY Telecopter.

All of the stations were the same. Either no signal or your correspondent here at the devastation on the Oakland front. What I wouldn't have given at that very moment for the comforting voice of Geraldo saying, "Marilyn Monroe—Was She Really a Lesbian?"

I drove up to Grizzly Peak. Night had fallen, but without power. You could look out across the bay and see that Marin was on, but most of the city lay in an eerie darkness except for a huge blaze near the Golden Gate. I was behind a bus that seemed like a shining beacon, although there were no passengers. It screeched to a halt as a buck deer with antlers ran crazily across the busy street.

That was the first of those little Shakespearean "the times are out of joint" moments I had that week. Later that night, I would see a lumpy harvest moon, huge and red as a forest fire, rise over Inspiration Point. I would see an owl fly at dawn the next morning. I would hear stories about earthworms all coming out at once and hundreds of oak moths hatching on the spot and caterpillars leaving their cocoons and pregnant women going into premature labor.

Our power was dead and Russ was not home. I groped around looking for a flashlight. I also found a candle, but I just sat down on the floor and started to curse the darkness. The phone machine was out. The computer was useless. I couldn't even use the TV. I was powerless. Then I saw the outline of a man coming in my doorway holding a flashlight. "Hello," he said. "I heard you come home. Are you OK?"

It was the jogger, the man next door. I just knew him as the jogger because every morning at six a.m., he would wake up and go jogging. I knew his routine. Sometimes I watched him turn on his Mr. Coffee and heard him singing in the shower, and then I would see him put on his UC Bears T-shirt and his blue shorts and run off into the sunrise. He would come home at eight, shower again, and go off to work in his business suit.

"Are you OK?" he asked again. I shone my flashlight at him. Today he was wearing an A's shirt and red shorts. Another sign that the times were out of joint.

I went over to him and instinctively hugged him. I was happy to see anyone I knew, even though he was my neighbor and I knew his routine but not him.

"I'm Rabbi Birnbaum," he said.

A rabbi! Somehow I always thought of him as a stockbroker or perhaps an architect. So he actually drove off every morning to slave over a hot soul.

"Would you like to come next door and stay with us awhile?"

It was so incredibly kind. I followed him in a daze. His place was well prepared. He had several large battery-operated lanterns and dozens of bottles of Evian on the table. His wife, Myra, offered me some gazpacho—she had been making vegetable soup before the power went off. But I wasn't hungry. I told them how worried I was about Russ, and they said he must have had to stay on call if he was a doctor. They had two little kids—Noah and Molly—who kept fighting, and were arguing about who would sleep with Mommy that night. Noah had a toy remote-controlled car which he kept sending off to run over his sister's foot.

"Would you like to sleep here with us tonight?" Myra asked me. I thought about it, and it was really sweet, but it also put me in contention with the children. "That's OK. I guess I'd better go check my place," I said.

The jogger, now The Rabbi, came with me. He checked my gas lines for leaks and my chimney for masonry damage.

Russ Nelman's house hadn't been damaged at all. Now, if I just knew about Russ. Losing him was beyond imagining. But with all that had happened recently, I was imagining it.

The rabbi gave me several batteries from his box labeled, "Preparedness." I thanked him for everything and told him that he was very kind. "I just praise God we're all OK," he said, and told me if I got scared to come back anytime during the night.

I put on my Walkman and got out a bottle of Cakebread Chardonnay. Why not go for the good stuff?

I fell asleep as the body count went up. I woke up several times during the night. Each time, I made sure that the lights hadn't come on, that the red moon wasn't the end of the world, that the fire in San Francisco hadn't gotten any bigger, and that Russ still was not there. Russ, oh, dear, sweet Russ, where are you? I love you.

I knew what I had to do. Maybe it was the electromagnetic field that told me. Later, all sorts of people would claim that they had predicted the earthquake, that they saw a rise in electromagnetism and knew. The rise in electromagnetism told me: Marry the guy.

I listened intermittently to the sounds of KBAY, now "Your Earthquake Information Station," and my own internal monologue: Yo, God, if you're there and this is all as arbitrary as it seems, then could you please see fit to bring him back to me.

At what I think was about four a.m., Russ came in. He said he'd had to stay on at the hospital in case any victims were brought in. He was glad I was OK. He was really tired and had to go back in a couple hours. He fell asleep in my arms and I lay there awake, unable to do anything but rejoice in the sound of his snoring.

The next morning was hot and sunny and extraordinarily lovely—in part because I was alive, in part because the same forces of nature that shook us also give this place its rugged beauty. Russ and I ate some ice cream, which was still semi-solid in the nonfunctioning freezer, and he went back to the hospital. I realized our relationship was holding up amazingly well. We hadn't just survived a week with a death and an earthquake. We had survived five days without intercourse. I made a mental note that as an offering of thanks to God I would not reveal this incredible fact to the readers of *Lifestyle*.

I was surprised to hear the phone ring. The power was still down, so I had no choice but to answer it. It was Neil Blender.

"You OK, babe?"

"How on earth did you get through?"

"Hey, a real man knows how to do these things."

"You're too much," I laughed. I felt the most bizarre post-earthquake emotion—I was happy to hear the sound of Neil Blender's phony voice.

He was calling from his car phone and wanted to know if I'd mind if he came over. "I'd be delighted," I said, and you know, I meant it.

I guess the worst thing you can say about a natural catastrophe is that even the greatest cynics on earth start gushing with love for their fellow man.

A minute later, there was a knock on the door. It was Neil.

"I was right outside," he said, laughing.

He gave me a hug, but I got my mouth away before he could unroll that red carpet of tongue into it. "No, no, no," I said, shaking a finger at him.

"So, you want to hear where I was?" he began, and without waiting for an answer he continued. "I was at the Kamikaze Kafe with Mai. My experience of the earthquake was completely narcissistic."

"How is that different from any other experience you have? Sorry, I couldn't resist, Neil. Go ahead."

"Hey, I don't mind. Good line. Anyway, no one can piss me off like my ex-wife. We were talking about Che. You know my son, don't you?"

"Che Guevara Blender—an unforgettable character like his dad."

"Yeah, well, believe me, that name was Mai's idea. I wanted to call him Clark. Anyway, we were talking about Che—some

problems of his that we had to talk about—and she starts
attacking me, doing one of her monumental bitch head trips.
All of a sudden, I feel like everything is shaking. I just assumed
it was all an *internal* event, my anger toward Mai bubbling
to the surface. Then, when I see everyone else diving under
the tables, I start thinking: Hmmm. They can really sense my
anger. Finally Mai, who has already dived under in her usual
save-her-own-ass way, tugs at my pants cuff and shouts,
'Earthquake, schmuck!' It reminded me of our wedding night.
So you, Laurie Glory, what were you up to?"

Even Neil Blender using my derisive nickname could not
make me have an internal event on the day when I and the
man I loved were survivors.

"Actually, I was on my way to Bree's when it happened,
and just a few minutes afterward I was sitting in the hot tub
with Dirk and Bree."

"Are you kidding?" said Neil. "That's fantastic. Can we put
it in the treatment?"

"What treatment?" I asked.

"Well, I'm about to send a little five-pager to Tod Fuelle
so he can show it to Cher. That's why I stopped by. We can
do another meeting next week and cement this thing. I hope
you can make it, because I had a hard time convincing Cher
to go with an unknown screenwriter. She wants a heavy hitter
for this. Oh, I also need you to sign this letter of agreement
from Slow-go saying we share the ownership of the Dirk and
Bree concept. Just a formality to get the deal rolling along for
our meeting next week."

"But I can't fly away at a time like this. I heard the airports
were down anyway." I was in no mood to leave Russ now. I
was not thinking of my career at all as I signed the paper Neil
handed me on Rosenbloom & Associates stationery. I was
thinking of my bride-and-groom Barbie and Ken.

"Well, I'm going to go fax this stuff to Slow-go and let him
take it to Tod."

"Using what for power?"

He gathered his papers. "Babe, this is why God invented
car fax."

I watched him walk out to a beat-up old Mercedes. He waved and drove off. I noted the license plate: SINEMA. I saw the bumper sticker: "No Caution—Single Man on Board."

The phone rang again. It was Alison, my best friend from high school, calling from New Jersey.

"Thank God, you're alive," she said. She had been trying to call all night, but kept getting a recorded message about the earthquake. She told me some reports on the East Coast suggested that Northern California was leveled and that roving drug gangs from LA were looting all the bodies.

I told her about my dad, and she said her parents would be sorry to hear it. I realized I hadn't told anybody. Not my aunt Lo or any of my parents' friends or relatives who were still alive.

During the next few days, though, they all began to call to find out if I survived the quake, and I gave them the good news about me and the bad news about Harry. Telling it to people made it a little more real, although many of them were people I had hardly seen in the last twenty years, so they seemed somewhat imaginary themselves.

I guess everyone was getting these calls from out of town. When I called Mai I got her machine, and the message said: "Yes, yes, we're OK. If you're calling from back east, California is still standing. Sorry."

No cracks in her sarcasm, but I knew what she meant. The other coast seemed obsessed with California disasters. We hadn't had a major flood or mudslide in years, and they were getting restless.

As the day went on I was starting to go crazy, realizing that even though I could get calls, I couldn't call screen, and I couldn't access the LoveNet. At one point, a man called and said he was from Nordstrom and they were doing a survey on pantyhose and would I mind answering a few questions.

"In the middle of a disaster?" I said.

"Well, you know, the hose must go on."

I didn't laugh.

"I was wondering what size pantyhose you wear?" he asked.

"I don't know—B, I guess."

"Firm support or control top?"

"Just regular," I said, and then added, "Wait a minute—
I'll go look."

I ran to my drawer and found a pair still in the package.

"OK, they are size B, nothing about control top, and the
color is coffee bean."

"Cotton crotch?"

"Yeah. Sure. Cotton crotch."

"And do you put them on right over your pussy, or do you
wear panties with them?"

"What?" I said. "How can you ask me that?"

"Well, even in an earthquake, I'd like to lick your pussy."

I slammed down the phone, but after a while I started
laughing. I heard a bird outside. The sun was shining bright.
The perverts were calling again. Life goes on.

All the lights in the house came on at once, and the radio
and the TV and the refrigerator and the computer and the
VCR and every other appliance I had tried to turn on last
night. I turned everything off but the TV. I had power.

Every station had live earthquake coverage. I began watching, transfixed. In between, I answered phone calls from
everyone I'd ever known from out of town. Later, I would
make a list of the people who didn't call and decide I'd hate
them forever.

I finally went out to buy some food. As I drove around
Berkeley, and listened to reports on the radio of all the sudden
heroism, I noticed that Berkeley responded in its usual way.
Everyone was eating. Every cafe and restaurant had set up
extra tables outside on this balmy day, so that people could
comfort themselves with pasta and frittata and focaccia and
goat cheese calzone and calamari and blueberry muffins and
seeded baguettes and pumpkin pie and flan. I stopped at a
grocery store and bought a quart of mint chip ice cream and
Mint Milanos and butter pretzels.

"Ah, earthquake food," said the lady at the cash register.
"Everyone's buying it. Comfort food."

"I noticed you were almost out of ice cream. I guess all the
freeway closings affected your deliveries."

"Oh no," she said. "We got our regular deliveries, but people were here early this morning buying everything we've got, especially ice cream."

I got home and opened the mint chip. I didn't bother with a dish. Just a spoon.

On the TV, KBAY correspondent Maria Chow was outside a collapsed freeway in Oakland. "And with me is one of the many heroes of this event, Dr. Russ Nelman. Dr. Nelman, aren't you risking your life by going back in there?"

"Look, Maria, there's a job to do and they need doctors to do it."

I turned off the TV and got in the car. If Russ was going into that dangerous place, I was going with him. If we were going over the cliff, we were going over together. Nothing else was important. Nothing else really mattered. I knew what was serious now.

I parked as close to the collapsed structure as I could. It was as big and horrifying as they said, but an even greater horror was the surrounding neighborhood. It was cut off, destroyed, and scarred long ago by the now ruined freeway. The neighborhood was referred to as "Crack Town," and there probably hadn't been this many white people around since the construction crews sealed the community's fate in concrete thirty years ago.

The police were keeping people back. I anticipated this and put on the white coat and the stethoscope I had taken from Russ's doctor-costume trunk. Nobody stopped me as I floated by disguised as a healer.

The closer you got to the freeway, the more unbelievable it seemed. Crushed, twisted concrete as far as the eye could see. It was not America. It was like the set for *The Last Days of Pompeii*.

I saw a mob gathered in front of one of the worst-looking sections. I thought maybe they had dragged a body out. I pictured Russ as moribund as Harry was when I last saw him. Things had been moving so furiously lately, as if life were on fast forward, that even the worst downturns were now imaginable. My deal falling through, my father dying, the earth quaking, the economy collapsing, my lover caught in a death-trap. I became aware of my breath coming in audible pants and my heart beating heavily.

I moved through the crowd the way a ghost moves through walls in horror movies. When I got to the center of the circle, I saw him. Him.

It was really him. Ten feet in front of me, surrounded by people.

Dan Rather. He was standing there in a combat jacket, and the cameras were rolling.

"Death. Destruction. Devastation," my Dan was saying. "We can actually smell death here in Oakland, California."

Smirk. Smirk.

How dare he smirk at a time like this?

25

Dan, to me you were always The News. Now I know you're nothing but melodrama. After twenty years, we're through, Dan. Your mother should have told you long ago that if you persisted in smirking like that, your face would freeze. It's one smirk over the line, baby. It's over. MacNeil-Lehrer may not be sexy. They may in fact be boring. But while you were out there smirking in a combat jacket in Oakland, in front of a collapsed freeway, MacNeil—or was it Lehrer?—was sitting at a desk having a half-hour discussion with an earthquake safety engineer.

I read this over, closed the Celebrity Sex Fantasies conference in disgust, and then logged off the LoveNet. I started to realize that the TV shrinks were right: the earthquake was driving everybody crazy.

"It's not just the aftershocks. It's the emotional aftershocks," one said in an exclusive interview with Tom Brokaw. And now I was starting to feel this strange letdown. It wasn't just my breakup with Dan. It was the urge to merge. I wanted to be married to Russ right now, this minute. I think as soon as I realized that I was using Dan Rather as a way of avoiding real relationships, it hit me—now was the time.

I called the hospital and asked to speak to Russ. The nurse said that he couldn't come to the phone. A man had been pulled from the rubble that evening and Russ was part of the surgery team trying to repair his injured leg. They were calling him "the miracle man" for surviving the ordeal. His name was Jesus Firm.

I swear to God.

I was going to write an article about the earthquake, but when I heard that, I thought: People will think I made the whole thing up. They'll never believe it.

Behind Russ's house, there was an old apple tree, a remnant from the time when there had been a farm up here. It had the most wonderful apples—red Delicious. Not like those red Delicious apples you buy in the store that look perfect but taste bland. Having just ripened, these tasted even better than they looked. I picked the most perfect ones and put them in a big straw basket. I found some red ribbon and tied a bow on the basket and wrote a note saying, "In times of trouble, one remembers kindness most of all." I put them on the jogging rabbi's doorstep.

The phone. This time it was a producer from *Night Time*, the network late newscast. I picked it up. They wanted to send a film crew over to interview me for their Earthquake Experience special. "Chuck Chernoff gave me your number," she said.

I decided to skip all mention of Dirk and Bree and the hot tub, realizing that in the immediate aftermath, with the focus in the media still "the smell of death," such comments might seem frivolous. I would use that in my piece for *Lifestyle*, which would be out in a few weeks, when frivolous would be back in demand. I hoped.

I talked on *Night Time* about my neighbors who helped me

pull through when I was frightened and alone. It was true.
One truth. The appropriate truth, and I could just see the
reporter lighting up as I fed her lovely copy, tender sound-
bites, perfect apples of experience.

I was watching myself on TV that night when Russ came
home. I was taping it, so I turned my attention to him.

"I've decided something fairly major," I said.

"Me too," he said. He was standing by the bed. I was lying
there holding the remote. He began to undress. He had all
his clothes off and I could see the tan above his navel. I told
him that I admired his tan. He turned around to show me his
white rear end.

He got under the covers and cuddled up to me. "I want to
get married," I said.

"That's your major decision?" he asked.

"Yes."

"Here's mine: I want the volume turned down. You can
leave the TV on, but I want the volume off." He looked at
the screen and said, "Hey, that's you."

I was on the TV saying, "A rabbi, a man of God, a neighbor
I hardly knew, took my hand and gave me batteries. That's
when I realized we would all pull through this somehow, those
of us lucky enough to be among the living—"

I clicked the mute button on the remote, and we watched
me moving my lips and walking in front of the house as I
showed the reporter a downed chimney up the block.

"How's Jesus Firm?" I asked Russ.

"Holding steady."

And then he fell asleep on me. I couldn't believe it. I've
never known Russ to be too tired or too distracted or too
anything for sex. He was like the Rock of Gibraltar that way,
a pillar of strength. This was all the proof I needed that the
earthquake had permanently altered life as I knew it.

And let me tell you another thing: there is nothing on earth
as sexy as a man who doesn't want it. It is the ultimate challenge to every trick a woman has ever learned. At first I tried
the simple things—rousing him, kissing him, a light pass or

two on his dormant penis. Then I got out the big guns. I threw
off my nightclothes and hunkered up to him. I recalled the
shirt the guy at *Lifestyle* had been wearing. Grab your board
and go butthole surfin' with me.

When Russ finally woke up for a second and said, "Not
tonight, honey," I felt incredibly guilty. People had died,
structures had collapsed, and all I cared about was getting
laid.

The next morning I woke up to a restored pillar of strength.
I was so excited I almost forgot to turn on the TV and put in
my diaphragm. Then I remembered: I didn't need the TV. I
didn't need Dan Rather. I had Dirk and Bree. This time they
were like John Madden and Pat Summerall, watching and
calling the play-by-play.

"OK, now first, he tries to get through from behind the
line of scrimmage. A lot of these women, they like it that
way," Dirk Madden was saying.

"But no, she seems to want it her way. She's down on her
back and he's scrambling around her," said Bree Summerall.

"He's at the goal line," said Dirk.

"Touchdown!" yelled Bree.

I could see the Madden diagram of the whole thing on the
screen in my head.

Russ kept thrusting and the aftershocks kept on coming. It
was something memorable. Something I would keep in my
trunk of earthquake memories beside the morning Extra! Extra! and the chunk of chimney brick I found down my block.

About ten minutes after the last aftershock, I remembered
that I still hadn't gotten my period. I was a week late. I said,
"I want to get married. Today."

"Not today, honey." His beeper went off and he went to
the phone.

Not today, honey. Not tonight, honey. What was happening
here?

He got dressed and told me he might be late that night.
There was still a lot of postquake stuff to deal with at the
hospital.

"Like what?" I asked. "Did you have many patients or surgeries related to the quake? An emergency hemorrhoidectomy?" When you actually thought about it, so few people were injured for an event that hit such a big area.

"No, not really. Just Jesus Firm, and a few minor emergencies. But our regular schedule had to be shifted. So just go about your business. Don't wait up for me."

"Now, wait a minute. We have this great sex and you're just going to leave me. Don't you care about me? I know you care about your patients, but what about me?"

"Gee, Laura, now you're sounding like my ex-wife."

This of course was the biggest weapon he'd ever used on me, and I thought it was a hell of a time to do it. "Russ, I just asked you to marry me and now you're going to walk out like it's nothing."

"Laurie, calm down. I think the earthquake has really gotten to you."

"Now, what's that supposed to mean? What are you—unfazed by it?"

"No. I'm fazed. I'm tired. I've been working hard and there's still a lot that needs to be done. I think these natural events affect women more. Are you premenstrual?"

"I can't believe I'm hearing this. One: I'm no Earth Mother with a direct line to the forces of nature. Two: I'm a week after my period," I lied. "And three: Whatever happened to 'I'll marry you anytime you want'?"

"Laurie, let's not say anything radical. I'm not ready to bury this relationship in the rubble. I've got to go."

He headed toward the door. I grabbed one of his dirty shirts and went out after him. He was down the steps and opening the garage door. "Russell!" I screamed, and I realized I had never called him that. His parents called him that. Now I had turned into his ex-wife and his cold parents. He looked up at me impatiently.

"I'll call you later," he said. "I'm outta here."

My line. Your Honor, he took my heart, my soul, and my line. I watched him drive away in his beat-up VW Rabbit. His

ex-wife got the Porsche and the big house. It suddenly occurred to me that Russ Nelman was not the all-perfect godlike
man I had always fancied him. He was just another Porsche-
driving bastard in a Porsche-driven world.

I looked out from our front steps at San Francisco and the
bay. It had to be the most beautiful day I'd ever seen. When
it was this clear, the city looked like a mirage on the horizon,
close enough to touch, fragile enough to shatter. I thought of
all the people who'd called me in the last two days saying,
"Are you still going to live there?" What was I supposed to
do, move back to New Jersey and die of boredom?

All along, I had been much more worried that modern
civilization would kill San Francisco—traffic, crime, drugs,
pollution—but the ancient forces were still the strongest.
That's why, I think, we live here. It may look like any other
city, the way Manhattan looks from New Jersey, but it is still
a place where nature has power.

I would go to the city today. I would meet the challenge
of the downed bridge. I could see the crane out on the bay
moving the little erector set pieces of bridge around. In the
great spirit of sacrifice, I would take public transportation.
Besides, the common terror of the shaking earth had erased
all distinctions, had made us all one—victims. And victims
was exactly what we all felt we were anyway.

The rabbi disrupted my ruminations. "You all right?" he
called up to me. He was stretching his hamstrings, pushing
his hands forward and his legs back, as if he were attempting
to move his house. He was returning to his normal jog routine—as sure a sign of life returning as the sea gulls flying
overhead, the traffic whizzing by, and the pervert phoning
me. I realized that I was standing there in nothing but Russ's
shirt and staring at the rabbi, who was staring up at me. I
was also aware that I was in the mood for an ego boost, but
I have a religious belief in not flirting with a man of God.

"Thanks for the apples," he shouted.

"You're welcome, Rabbi Birnbaum."

"Shelly."

"Huh?"

"My name's Sheldon. Call me Shelly."

"Sure," I said, and heard the phone ring.

I ran in the house to get it. It wasn't a pervert, it was Dirk, and what a story he had to tell. He and Bree had a terrible fight after I left. He drove back to the Marina and discovered the house he had been staying in was condemned. Dirk was homeless.

He'd been spending most of his time in the emergency shelter, where volunteer masseuses had been giving him acupressure. He was getting sick of all the elaborate food that restaurants had been sending to the victims. I told him I was going to BART into the city, and that I would meet him at his favorite Burmese place. With the fight with Russ still fresh in my mind, I decided I needed to shore up any outside action I could muster. And Dirk was the closest thing to a backup flirtation I had.

After I hung up, I looked at my calendar—something I hadn't done for days. I saw that this afternoon was my appointment with Judge Corman. Then I counted the weeks from my last period and realized that I was actually six days late.

I went to the bathroom and collected my first morning urine. I remembered from my last pregnancy test that this was what you used.

OK, I'd BART into the city, take the urine to a clinic there, where Russ and I were not known. Then after lunch with Dirk, I'd go directly to court. Russ would be calling and wondering where I was. Let him wonder. And if he came home and saw my car there and me gone, so much the better.

I grabbed my checkbook and my VISA bill and the Dean Witter statement about my IRA. I couldn't find the passbook from my money market account, but they could always call, couldn't they? I would kind of like to know exactly how much is there anyway.

After a shower, I put on my sexiest T-shirt and tight black jeans—which were even tighter because I'd been eating nothing but ice cream and pretzels since the earthquake and my breakup with Dan Rather. I took the jar of pee and put it in a bag with my financial papers.

The Berkeley BART station was more crowded than the few other times I'd been in it, but it was certainly no uptown IRT. Perhaps there were a couple more people in the station than would normally be there at ten a.m. I walked down to the very farthest edge of the platform, hoping to get a seat on the last car. At least this was the Bay Area and not New York— modern trains, clean stations, no graffiti, and no beggars.

I enjoyed a kind of giddy liberation from my car. Nothing made me feel stronger than the knowledge that I could survive without a private vehicle. A shabby-looking young man walking my way made me slightly uneasy, but my unease was more guilt than fear; guilt about how I lived in an isolated, middle-class, protected world—largely because of Russ Nelman's free housing program. I never intended to live that way, so apart from poor people. I never intended to become a chronicler of the petty taste snobbery and shopping passions of a generation of aging boomer babies. It all just kind of happened. Now with the earthquake, I felt at one with the great mass of humanity.

"Hi," I smiled at the young man coming toward me. I almost said, "Hello, brother."

He didn't say a word, but kept moving faster, and when he got up close, he tried to grab my purse. I held on to it and started screaming. He snatched the paper bag out of my hand and ran away.

It all happened so fast I couldn't believe it—and just when everyone had been talking about how there had been less crime because of the earthquake. Now another sign of things returning to normal: I get mugged. The San Francisco train roared into the station. I thought about whether I should report the incident, but then I got on the train. As we pulled out I started laughing. People on the train probably thought I was nuts. I laughed harder. Somewhere, there's some sad putz holding my urine and my IRA.

26

Most of the time, we try not to think about what we're really doing, because if we did, we would all be paralyzed with fear. I mean, just think about flying in a plane or driving in a car or buying processed food and heating it up in a microwave. What are we doing risking our lives like that?

Since we live in the modern world and all the kids on the block are doing it, we go along for the ride. And we resent, even hate, those madmen who insist on rubbing our noses in it.

So it was that when the BART train got to the transbay tube, a generic little white man who had been sitting there cleaning his nondescript black-framed glasses, suddenly stood up and screamed, "Repent! Repent! San Francisco will pay for fornication, homosexual fornication, abortion, subversion, and perversion. We will die in this tube. The earth will shake like it did before and shatter us. Repent. Repent. Repenteth now or we're all going to die."

Perhaps the greatest monument to the great city by the Bay is that no one in the crowded car, racing through a tunnel many leagues down under the sea, touched the man. No one even spoke to him. Instead, we continued on—experts in the art of eye aversion. We had all walked those urban gauntlets of grief we were powerless to relieve. We had learned to deny the spare-changers and rationalize that the thin mother begging for food would only spend it on drugs anyway. So we shook off the prophet of the transbay tube, and went back to reading about how IBM was doing or whether Montana would start or if paisley and velvet would be back this year or if Delta Burke was fatter than Liz Taylor.

Really, once someone has ripped off your precious bodily

fluids, what else can they do to you? Force you to face your
terror of modern civilization? The madman of the BART train
only tightened our defenses. We fly. We drive on erector set
bridges. We live on fault lines. We shoot through tubes under
the sea.

I got off at the Embarcadero and walked toward the Burma
Road, where I was supposed to meet Dirk.

The sunny Indian summer day was offset by the ghostliness
of the city. This was Friday, a business day, but the besuited
troops had mostly stayed home, waiting for some official sign
that life was to resume. Things were emptier. This cleared
the way for more homeless—homeless before the earthquake,
homeless after—to sleep in doorways or carry on one-way
conversations on uncrowded benches. Most of the shops were
closed. The Bay Bridge, of course, was closed. The cracked
freeway, which obstructed the view, was closed and the tourists were gone.

I found Dirk at the Burmese place, but it was Closed Due
To Earthquake/Sorry No Power. He looked his old self again.
A neat pair of beige slacks, a clean, pressed white shirt with
blue stripes, and a blue lamb's wool sweater vest. His hair
was tidy. His look was confident and his eyes were clear as
he stared toward the water. Only a small bandage on his nose
and a small amount of discoloration under his eyes told of his
televised debut as a battered husband eleven days ago.

As we walked along the still waterfront I felt as if Dirk and
I were actors in one of those only-survivors-of-the-A-bomb
movies I saw around the time we were being taught to assume
the air raid position in kindergarten. Dirk was the last man
on earth and I was the last woman. Our petty little differ-
ences—the fact that he drove an Alfa and I drove a Toyota,
that he liked bran muffins and I liked scones, that he liked
postmodern art while I liked Murphy Brown, that he used
psychobabble and I swore, that he held stocks and I might
believe in God—mattered not a bit. We had the survival of
the race on our hands.

We came upon a street vendor selling hot dogs, bought a

couple with the works, and walked over to one of the piers
to eat. It was the first time I had ever seen him eat meat.
After he described in painstaking detail what happened on
the Warfield show, Dirk asked me what I was thinking.

"Oh, I was just wondering how anyplace could look this
beautiful in the middle of a disaster."

Dirk seemed almost beatifically calm. He was proud of
getting off his painkillers despite the chaos of the last few
days.

"I don't know. Maybe I'm addicted to recovery," he said.
"But I never seem to feel as good as when I'm working on
my addiction. That's why All-Anon is the perfect twelve-step
program for me. Some people have one problem, but I have
multiple addictions. When I get up and say, 'Hi, my name is
Dirk, and I'm addicted to anything,' I feel this tremendous
burden is off my shoulders and the truth is going to set me
free. I know it must seem corny to you, Laura, but my life is
lived in two stages: hooked and recovering."

"No, Dirk, I think it makes sense and I'm glad you've found
yourself."

"Well, I suppose it's a plus that I'm not so insecure that I
can't show my vulnerability."

"Absolutely. I couldn't have put it better myself."

"Although I seem to be more vulnerable to addictions than
other people. I'm afraid recovery has peaked as a business
proposition. I'm talking to a friend about a new start-up. We're
going to market California lifestyle products to the Japanese.
You know, they've got money, the Pacific Ocean, and they're
totally miserable. I think we've found a niche there."

"What are California lifestyle products?"

"Oh, you know, T-shirts with nature scenes, sunglasses,
beachware. We're working on the California Dreamin' motif.
I've even registered the name."

"But don't the Japanese already have these things?"

"Yeah, but they don't say California Dreamin'. That's what
makes it. . . . Laura, there's something I really want to say
to you."

"Go ahead."

"I want to apologize for the computer stuff. The misunderstanding. I thought you were seriously flirting with me. I guess I have to learn to be less trusting of people. Especially people named Neil Blender. But I'll die before he gets Bree, believe me."

I wondered then if I should tell him that it wasn't his wife Neil was after but his wife's story, but I didn't want to undercut Dirk's determination to get her back. Besides, what had I been doing with Bree—social work?

"What will it take to get you two back together?" I asked him.

"Oh, I think time, and the right kind of program. I haven't quite figured out how to get Bree to work on the marriage. She's very resistant to therapy. And you know, she isn't blameless in this. I think once Rachel Whoopi was born, she took me for granted. She expected me to win the New Fathering Award, do everything. I once actually heard her bragging to someone that I insisted on becoming a househusband. I mean, I hate to use a Freudian word like castrating, but that's how it felt. That's why I joined the LoveNet, for empowerment. I started to feel that she only wanted me for convenience, for social purposes, and baby-sitting. I don't know if she told you this, but we hadn't made love for a month before I moved out. She just wasn't interested."

Suddenly, I saw Dirk for what he was—a very needy guy, a man who had turned on the power for empowerment. At that moment, I felt moved. I hugged him and he gave me an incredibly sweet kiss.

"I don't want your pity, Laura," he said.

"It's not pity, Dirk. I see you as a man struggling to change, a work in progress." And to tell the truth, if he were really sensitive, he could have figured out that anyone who just lost her father and had a fight with her once perfect lover was feeling pretty needy herself. I hadn't actually told him these things—I wasn't feeling confident enough. What I felt, mixed in with my needs, was a little bit of real desire.

He stood up as if he was uncomfortable. "I'm going to look for a new room now. I'll call you when I get settled."

"Why don't you move in with us?" I said, leaping up. "Russ has plenty of room. It might be a good base for you to try to rebuild with Bree." And of course, I'd be there for every move. Taking notes. Making Madden diagrams.

"I don't think it would be such a good idea, Laurie," he said, and touched my cheek very sweetly. "I'll call you." He walked toward the silent freeway.

Amazing, I thought. Amazing how little it takes for a man to go from a jerk to a mensch. I stood there for a while aching for another of Dirk Miller's sober, recovered kisses.

I couldn't face the traffic court now or the clinic. I didn't have my urine or my IRA. All I had was my checkbook and my VISA bill, and I didn't feel like peeing at all.

I walked along the docks where makeshift signs pointed the way to the Oakland ferry. It was funny to remember that these were still working docks, that there were still long-shoremen and fishermen. The whole place had not been torn down and turned into Waterfront Place or Pointe San Francisco or Parc Pier Village, but it was a shadow of its former port. It coulda been a contender instead of what it was—a bunch of pretty, old industrial buildings of historic interest to architecture junkies.

I walked the length of one of the old piers to board the eastbound ferry. There were maybe fifty other people who came on. The boat was a three-decked affair with a TV blasting the latest disaster news on the lower deck. You could buy coffee and beer and doughnuts and red licorice for your basic postquake meal on the middle deck. Someday when things calm down, I thought, the dentists are really going to come out ahead on this earthquake.

I went up to the open top deck and looked at the unreal city. It was like a blowup of the tiny skyline I saw from Russ's living room. What was I going to do about Russ? I needed him now. Maybe I was being selfish, thinking of my wants while he was busy caring for the sick. I was useless during a

"This is not a problem. I suppose when I say I'm a rabbi, it conjures up some pretty conventional images. But I'm a rather unorthodox rabbi. Let me give you an idea."

He walked over to his car and picked up a flier. "Here's a seminar I'm giving. It's for couples in crisis, so I'm sure you won't need it. But it'll let you know where I'm coming from."

"Thanks, Shelly. I think I've heard about this from a friend of mine who's a therapist. You know Mai Blender."

"Oh, yes, Mai—from acid-head to acid tongue."

Shelly Birnbaum seemed to be a natural at making you feel good. I got a sort of contact high holiday off him, although I wasn't quite prepared for his act. The flier said:

Rabbi Sheldon Birnbaum of the Temple Without Walls presents:

Wine, Men, Women, and Song: a special weekend for couples who are in trouble, in conflict, or interested in relationship renewal.

Rabbi Birnbaum is the leading practitioner of Zen Judaism, a school of thought that combines the ancient wisdom of the East, the ancient wisdom of the Middle East, and the land of plenty called California to improve our sense of inner and outer peace.

We will meet in the classic Queen Anne environment of the Leafy Creek Inn, located near the town of Sonoma in the wine country. There, through drink, through song, and through individual and group sessions led by Rabbi Birnbaum, couples may revisualize love. The fee includes a room furnished in authentic antiques, meals from Fri through Sunday, and evening port or sherry. Massage available upon request from Myra Birnbaum, licensed Esalen practitioner. Come play The Love Game!

Weekend Rates: $250 for a vineyard view room.
$300 with prv. bath.
One suite available for $350.
All persuasions, all sexual orientations, all denominations welcome. Om Shalom.

disaster—nobody cared then about what's hot and what's

A loud whistle blast announced our departure. It really
a boat! It was really real. A voice came on the loudspea
and said, "Oakland, ho. All not bound for Oakland—ya bet
abandon ship."

We sailed under the huge harp of the suspension bridg
and I saw things I had never seen before. An old Victor
lighthouse clung to the side of Treasure Island, its gingerbre
trim announcing that it was a survivor of all the Big Ones

Me too, I thought, me too. Laurie Gurvitz, girl wimp a
earthquake survivor. As we sailed around Treasure Island a
into the Oakland estuary we could see the place where t
piece of bridge had fallen. People rushed to the decks wi
Nikons and camcorders and Instamatics to record for posteri
what previous generations had needlepointed: A chain is ;
strong as its weakest link.

27

Russ Nelman was my only link. I had to seal it. I walked
off the boat and took a taxi straight to the nearest Mazda
dealer and bought him a candy-apple-red Miata convertible
with the last of Harry Gurvitz's Formica fortune.

I got home and parked the car out front. Then I found a
piece of posterboard and some markers and wrote JUST AL-
MOST MARRIED on it and put it on the trunk. The Birnbaum
kids came out and helped me decorate the car with balloons
and some old beer cans. Shelly joined us and said, "Listen,
if you do decide to tie the knot, I'd be happy to perform the
ceremony."

"Oh, my boyfriend's not Jewish," I said. "And I'm not really
very religious. I hate to say it to you, but my parents were
so reformed they worshiped at Temple Emanuel Kant."

I couldn't wait until Russ came home. Not only did I have his new car to spring on him but this classic piece of Californication. He would love it.

I waited and I waited and I waited. At seven, Dan Rather came on from New York in a suit and tie. I guess that meant that more was over than my relationship with him. It meant our disaster was over as far as TV was concerned. I upchanneled to Peter Jennings.

After the news, I started an enchilada casserole modeled after Rod's special, except I used canned tomatillo sauce. I took the casserole out at eight-thirty. It was starting to dry out even though I had it on 300. I was not in the mood to risk my life on the microwave.

I hated to call him—it seemed like being a harpy. But finally, at nine o'clock, I couldn't stand it anymore. I got someone to page him, but they said he wasn't answering and they would try his beeper.

He called back in about fifteen minutes.

"Laurie, what's up?"

"Where are you?"

"Oh, I'm sorry—this damned thing has really thrown my sense of timing off. I think I'm going to be on all night. I was going to call you, but things got jumpin'."

"Really."

"You bet. We're getting all sorts of weird cases."

"Like what?"

"Oh, you know, phlebitis, stomatitis, cherry angiomas—stuff like that. Listen, go to sleep and before you know it, I'll be there."

I called out his name but he wasn't there.

Russ had a study in the little alcove off our bedroom, the room that looked into Shelly Birnbaum's yard. I found his medical dictionary and looked up all those words. None of it made sense. A cherry or senile angioma was something that old people got. Why would a surgeon bother with it?

I kept getting diverted, as I often do when I look something up in a medical book. It was like reading mythology. One weird thing led to another, and I fell asleep reading about "port-wine stains: the big blotches that appear on the faces of infants, sometimes called 'mother's mark'; and 'witch's milk': the phenomenon of lactation seen in a newborn." Reading about the science of medicine was as engrossing as reading the *National Enquirer*.

I woke up at six and Russ was still not home. I called the hospital again, and this time a nurse said he had not been there all night. That was it.

I got out the bag of "fun-sized" Milky Way bars I had bought to give out for trick or treat. I was feeling tricked. I needed a fun-size treat. I ate ten of them.

Russ finally walked in at seven o'clock looking dazed. He was as surprised to see me up as I was to feel like the detective who had caught him red-handed.

"Laurie! Did you see that car out there?"

"I bought it for you," I said.

"Very funny."

"It's true."

"No. No. You've got to be kidding."

"Here," I said. "The pink slip is in your name." I went over to the buffet where we piled up our mail and our receipts.

"But why?"

"I wanted to pay you back for the rent, the food, and most of all, for all the love you've shown me recently."

He sat down at the table near the living room window, the one looking out at the tiny unreal city. "I feel terrible," he said to me.

"Why don't you tell me what's going on?"

"Let me change." He went into the bedroom, and I could hear him taking a shower. Bryant Gumbel was broadcasting "live from the devastated Marina," interviewing the mayor, who was talking about how we were survivors and were just going to pick right up and rebuild.

"The entire city is in recovery, Bryant."

If Bryant Gumbel was here, the danger was over.

Russ came out looking spiffy and heroically handsome.

"I've gotten involved with somebody else," he said.

"Why didn't you tell me?" I said stupidly. My voice seemed to be coming from far away. I did not want to be having this conversation. This was worse than the earthquake, worse than death. It felt like I was being forced out the window. But when I thought about it, I *knew* something was up, something was wrong. I saw it coming.

"It just happened this week. And I don't even know what *it* means. It could be nothing. It could be something. I haven't had time to sort it out. And I'm afraid I really do have to go back to work now. When I come back tonight, we can sort it all out."

"Who is she?"

"Laurie, you don't want to know."

"Don't tell me what I want. Who is she?"

"She's a nurse. A nurse. We were working together on the disaster relief."

"What's her name?"

"Her name is Cherry."

I started laughing. "Cherry Angioma?"

He smirked. A smirk is what a man does when he's embarrassed about how heartless he is. "No. Cherry Saunders."

"Come on, you're making this part up. Cherry Saunders, R.N. Didn't I read those books in fifth grade?"

"Laurie, I'm sorry," he said, and hugged me.

I froze. "Take the car," I said, and handed him the key.

"I couldn't. I just couldn't. Not until we talk."

"Take the car. Take the car, you asshole." I shoved the keys in his pocket. "If you don't take the car, I'll get on the porch and start screaming."

"I haven't got time for this now."

I watched him walk out. I watched him grimace as he pulled off the JUST ALMOST MARRIED sign and the cans and the balloons and put them in the garbage. Then he got in. He put down the top. He turned up the radio and smiled. And he drove off.

OK. All righty. No problem. I would kill Cherry Saunders, R.N.

The shower stall still smelled of his Selsun dandruff shampoo. I cried in the shower, I screamed in the shower. I swore a curse on the perfect ass of Cherry Saunders, R.N.

I lay down in bed to dry off and pictured Cherry Saunders. She looked remarkably like Cherry Ames on the cover of *Cherry Ames and the Halloween Surprise.*

She was petite and adorable as a cheerleader. Her snug white uniform poured like satin over her pinched-in waist. Her little nurse's cap with the tiny red cross sat perfectly on her crown despite her high blond ponytail. Her blue cape flowed from her delicate shoulders. The coloring was different, but Cherry Saunders, R.N. bore a striking resemblance to Bree Wellington, J.D.

I pictured Russ following the blue-caped crusader into the hospital utility room and throwing a stack of sterile blankets on the floor. I saw him knock her hat off, and in one deft motion pull the band off her ponytail so that her blond hair fell like silk down her white satin back. Her unblinking blue eyes stared up at his cartoon-perfect male profile. The hair bristled at the top of the V of his surgery suit.

He kissed the tip of her upturned nose. And sensed—yes! sensed—the prominence of her upturned nipples.

I could go no further with this fantasy, tossed as I was between despair and desire. Was this sick? Or do other jilted women torment themselves by picturing their lover getting it on with the she-bitch man stealer?

And not just torment themselves. Do they get aroused picturing their man doing it to his other woman? I had nothing left to do but slip my hand under my robe and satisfy my lonely urging. As I tried to be my own best friend the phone rang and I heard Neil Blender say into the machine, "Hey, baby. Come on, put down your vibrator and answer the phone. Have I got a deal for you."

The man must have eyes in the back of his dick. I didn't answer the phone, but he certainly spoiled it for me. I would go off now and kill Cherry Saunders—angry, crazed, and horny.

Driving to the hospital, I continued to form images of Nurse

Cherry in my mind. Now she was wearing a striped apron, like a candy striper, and she seemed to be more a molded Barbie doll than a living person. All my life I have feared this perfect blue-eyed monster, this American icon who can be all I could never be: the dream woman the Laurie Gurvitzes and the Laura Glorianas and the Laura Khomeinis can never compete with—we with our dark eyes and dark hair and our hints of mustache above our Mediterranean, Aegean, Caspian lips.

Was Cherry married, or a kid just out of nursing school? Some little angel from some Southern California beach town with her favorite things listed next to her centerfold photo?

Favorite books: Everything I Know I Learned In Kindergarten *and* A Snoopy Thanksgiving.
Favorite movies: Teenage Mutant Ninja Turtles, Gremlins 2.
Favorite food: Meatball sandwich.
Turn-ons: Having my ponytail band ripped out in the heat of passion.

As I approached Oakland, traffic was diverted off the freeway and I realized that they were still trying to find some bodies in the wrecked section up ahead. What kind of person was I—going off to commit murder in the middle of a disaster?

Who knew if Cherry would even be there or be on duty. Maybe she was out at the disaster scene giving aid and succor or whatever it is she gives.

And once I found her, what was the plan? I had no gun, no ice pick, no bottle of acid, no poisoned apple.

I guess I just wanted to see her, to face my worst nightmare—the little princess who would do her ballet-lesson steps on my life.

I parked at a meter across from the hospital and realized I had no change. Fuck it. What's another one to me? I might not even need to drive home. I might be carried off in handcuffs, for real this time.

I went to the information desk and asked, "Can you tell me where I can find Miss Cherry Saunders?"

"Yes," said the old lady in the blue smock labeled *Volunteer*. "Miss Saunders is the charge nurse in postop on the fifth floor, section D." She spoke in that eager-to-assist-you voice. Did she by any chance have a gun in the smock?

On the way up in the elevator, I decided maybe I wouldn't kill her right now. I could always hire some guy in a leather jacket to do that later. Maybe he'd take VISA until I could return the Miata. Hey, I was starting to take an active role in My Financial Life.

No. Don't let her die right now. Maybe she's Catholic. Cherry sounded like a Catholic name. Sister Cherry Teresa. So, let her feel a little anguish. Let her suffer. No state of grace. Now I was Prince Hamlet.

Fifth floor. I thought I saw the little princess behind the desk. But no, I was at section B. D was down the hall just past A. There is a logic to hospitals that defies the sane.

As I rounded the section with the big *A* on the floor I decided I would just humiliate her. I would yell at her, "How could you ruin my life? You've always had everything."

I wandered around for about five minutes, my anger building, my fuse burning. Finally, I asked for directions to section D.

There was nobody at the D desk. I went up to a nurse and started to ask how to find my little Cherry, but I saw the tag "Saunders" on the pocket of her white polyester pantsuit. She was tall, black, and bony with a short natural. She wore no makeup and her skin was light enough to show freckles.

"You are Cherry Saunders?" I asked.

"Yes. Who are you?" she said.

"A racist pig," I said, and walked away.

I went down the elevator and got in the car. This was the worst thing I could have imagined. My rival was a black nurse. I didn't have a self-righteous leg to stand on.

28

To make matters worse—and believe me, I was becoming an expert at that—I realized when I got home where I had seen Cherry Saunders before. Her picture was in the newspaper that morning. She was posed with a large group of people labeled "Heroes of the Quake."

For the rest of the day, when I pictured my rival, it was not in some wanton, clandestine closet groping with my man. Instead, I kept picturing her pulling people out of the wreckage, securing them to stretchers, giving them mouth-to-mouth. I no longer imagined the idyllic adolescence of Cherry Saunders, white beach baby, but the years of struggle and poverty of Cherry Saunders, African-American supernurse.

I turned on the TV to get the latest quake news. Wendy Chavez was reporting from the studio again. "Another hate crime in the East Bay tonight. It happened at Kaiser Hospital in Oakland, where Cherry Saunders, a nurse who had been active in relief efforts, was on duty. A mysterious woman came up to her, muttered a racist message, and then left. Saunders, who is black, described the woman only as young, white, and apparently deranged. . . . Coming up next on sports: The Quake and How It Can Affect the Forty-niners."

My only diversion was going to the computer to see what was happening in the Pen Pals Conference between Hot Mama and Big Boy. Wasn't Big Boy or Fat Boy what they called the atom bomb? I mention this only because what I found in this computer conference hit me like a ton of TNT. I include the entire printout here.

To: LoveNet Users
From: Hot Mama's Mama
My name is Mai Blender and I am a therapist in Berkeley,
California. I detest dishonesty in any form, even in computer sex. That is why I have decided to inform all those
involved here that the communications from Hot Mama
are not what they appear to be. In one entry Hot Mama
identifies herself as Laura, and those involved may have
been able to figure out from this that Laura refers to the
journalist Laura Gloriana, best known for her pop an-
thropological explorations of Dirk Miller and Bree Wellington, the first North American yuppies. Some of you
may have also figured out that Dirk is Big Boy. What
needs to be made clear here, since so much has already
been exposed, is that Hot Mama is not Laura Gloriana.
Hot Mama is my son, Che, a computer science major at
MIT. Che was encouraged in this computer cross-dressing by his father, my ex-husband, Neil Blender, for his
own manipulative and nefarious purposes. I have spoken
to my son about this, and I regret any injury or confusion
he may have caused.

To: LoveNet Users
From: LoveNet Management
We all regret any situation which forces LoveNet users
to expose themselves, but we applaud the actions taken
by Hot Mama's Mama. LoveNet relies on the concept of
honesty and mutual respect. We try not to make any
rules, feeling that LoveNet performs a useful, safe sex
function in these troubled times, but if individuals are
going to abuse the system by outright deception rather
than the playful fantasies which are the bedrock of
LoveNet, then action must be taken. What if straights
were to enter the gay conferences and egg innocent people on for their own amusement? We have an obligation
to protect our fantasies from liars. As a result we are
taking the unprecedented step of banishing Hot Mama

from this service. Much as we hate to inject an author-itarian head, we feel Big Boy must be protected from Hot Mama's and Hot Mama's dad's scams.

To: LoveNet Users
From: Stiff Arrow
As a longtime LoveNet user, I applaud management's decision to eject the electronic transvestite. There are times and places for such behavior and I for one don't want to have to feel paranoid here.

To: LoveNet Users
From: Anything Goes
I'm sorry, but I think someone done Hot Mama wrong. One man's fantasy is another man's lie. If you can't stand the heat, stay out of the virtual kitchen.

To: Hot Mama
From: Big Boy
I am disgusted and saddened that I have been misled and involved in a man's fantasy. Even if you yourself are not gay, how do you think it feels to have had this image of a woman in mind, only to have the screen pulled out from under me. I feel like throwing up.

To: Big Boy
From: Queen Mary
I find your reaction offensive, homophobic, and maybe even a sign of closet hysteria. Bring back Hot Mama and tell him to e-mail me any day. Methinks Big Boy doth protest too much.

To: Everyone
From: Erotic Modem
I find this whole thing sad. I give everyone permission for everything.

To: Friends, Romans, Lovers
From: Hot Mama's Papa
My son and I were only out to have some fun, not to
hurt anybody. In fact I think it is my ex-wife who has
hurt people by exposing us all to this public scrutiny. I
think the earthquake is driving everyone crazy and that
Mai Blender should go take a cold shower instead of
forcing everyone else to.

Now I understood Dirk's remarks about being too trusting.
He must have read this whole thing and sobered up when he
realized the extent to which Neil Blender was manipulating
him. But what about me? Was I another pawn in his game?
I didn't really see how he could be using me any more than
I was using him.

This must have been the trouble Che was having that Neil
and Mai were discussing when the earthquake happened.
What a sicko Neil was to encourage his own son to lie. Now
Mai will have to remember what he was doing to their son
every time someone asks her where she was when the quake
happened. This reminded me that I had better get my quake
story in so I could earn a little money. Especially if I was
going to be forced out of the house soon. Of course Russ
would choose Cherry Saunders—I respected him for that. I
clicked on my story.

Earthquake, California Style
Rub-a-dub dub, three survivors in a tub. There was Dirk
and Bree and me, spending our flextime and quality time
relaxing. When the Almost Big One hit, a wave nearly
wiped out Bree.

I decided to claim that the three of us were in the tub
at the time of the quake, rather than afterward. It was one of
those little compromises I made for the sake of a better story
that I chose to think of as creative journalism. Of course, how
different was that from creative judiciary? Speaking of that,

I remembered that I had to reschedule my urine and financial screening, and called the offices of Judge Corman.

"I have bad news for you, Ms. Gurvitz," His Honor said.

"No, Judge, you can't have bad news. I've had my fill today."

"Well, in addition to missing your court-mandated appointment yesterday, I'm afraid a man was picked up attempting to make a drug purchase in Oakland and the only identification they found on him was a copy of your IRA. He then agreed to testify against you in exchange for dropping the charges against him."

"You've got to be kidding. That guy was a bum who mugged me and stole my bag in the BART station yesterday."

"Did you report that assault to authorities?"

"Well, no, because all he stole was the IRA statement and my urine."

"Your what?"

"My urine. I was taking it to a laboratory for testing. And that's why I didn't show up yesterday. I was robbed."

"And you didn't report it?"

"No, I was too embarrassed to say I'd lost a bag of urine."

"Was it for a drug test?"

"No, actually, pregnancy. I'm late this month and I can't tell if—"

"Look, Ms. Gloriana—uh, which do you prefer, your real name or your alias?"

"The pen name is fine. You know, I don't think anyone ever referred to 'George Eliot' as Mary Ann Evans's alias. You've been hanging around with the wrong crowd too long."

"Perhaps, yes. Well, look, Ms. Gloriana, I think the simple solution here would be for us to just come to some kind of agreement. Why don't you agree to interview me about my book and I'll agree to forget your tickets. Providing you pay the amount of the original warrants, which is a thousand dollars."

"But, Your Honor, isn't that a kind of bribery? It would require me to compromise my journalistic integrity which,

insofar as I have any, consists of the fact that nobody tells me
what to write about. I mean, surely you would be horrified
if I had proposed that you drop the charges in exchange for
some favor."

"Of course. But this is not bribery, this is creative judiciary
in the best sense of the word. I'm trying to move the system
away from Justice Burger—an obvious cretin—toward Justice
Solomon, the original creative judge. Look, do we have to
haul your ass back in here, or can we work this out in a
mutually and socially benevolent way?"

"Your chamber or mine?"

29

Dirk looked down, the opposite of the confident and renewed person I had seen yesterday morning. He said
he'd been trying to find a place to stay, but to no avail. Bree
would absolutely not let him come back home. Neil Blender
was there when he tried to speak to her, and Neil sat around
grinning while they fought. At one point, he saw Neil take
out a notebook and start jotting things down. This, while he
and Bree were watching their life together go down the drain.
What kind of person would take notes at a time like that?

"But despite all this, I am still drug-free," he said. "Look,
I'm feeling pretty fragile and I'm wondering if I could stay
with you after all. There are other old friends I could stay
with, but some of them might put me back into behavior
patterns that would be risky right now. I won't be any trouble,
and all I've got is this one suitcase and a laptop."

I couldn't say no, but I hated the idea of telling anyone
that Russ was dumping me for a better woman. Besides, I
still had this omniscient relationship with Dirk and Bree. They
were supposed to be the characters, and I was supposed to

be their chronicler. I mean, what would happen if Boswell started coming up with the one-liners? Maybe it would be best to have Dirk close at hand where I could maintain some control over him. But then, I didn't want to have my scene with Russ in front of him—not in front of the subjects, please.

"Why don't you stay here tonight and I'll stay with Mai? I think that would be best."

"Oh, Laura, I don't want to trouble you. I just need a place to crash for the weekend."

I called Mai and asked if I could spend the night there. She started to go into the whole Che thing and how much she hated Neil, but I said we could talk later. She wondered if I was going to the *Lifestyle* Halloween party that night. Mai was a friend of Anita Tass, the sex advice columnist; she and Rod were going with Anita and would be dressed as an egg cell and a sperm cell.

"Mai, I want to talk to you about something. I think Russ and I just broke up. But I can't talk now. Dirk is here."

"What? You broke up with Russ?"

"He got involved with someone else this week."

"So? Does that mean you have to roll over and play dead?"

"Mai, you don't understand. She's black."

"And what are you—chopped liver?"

"Yeah, well, kind of."

"Look, why don't you come to the party with Dirk and we'll talk later when you come to spend the night. Hey, spend the whole weekend. Shosh always has friends sleep over."

"I can't go to the party with Dirk. You're supposed to come as your copy. What should I do?"

"Simple. Come as Dirk and Bree. He already has his costume. All you need is the wig and the tennis racket."

Dirk loved the idea. I wore my beige shorts and found a T-shirt that said *Claremont Pool and Tennis Club*. I wore those coffee bean pantyhose to give my legs a Bree-like tan.

We stopped at the drugstore and bought a red Halloween wig. "You know she dyes it, don't you?" Dirk told me.

He helped me put the hair up in a Bree-esque ponytail. I

guess in my mind, Bree was a kind of spiritual sister of the imaginary Cherry Saunders. I was a wicked stepsister of the real Cherry Cinderella Saunders.

The party was in the old *Lifestyle* headquarters on the Oakland docks, which was now used as a mannequin warehouse. Sean Garrison had chartered a ferry to take the San Francisco crowd across the bay. There was a terrific old rhythm-and-blues group, the Jesters, who could have been the Temptations or the Impressions, but they were not so lucky. Now they were all school bus drivers and picked up a little change doing their act on weekends at fraternity gigs and white liberal soirees.

The mannequins were arranged in arty little groupings with nothing but colored lights on their hairless, anatomically incorrect bodies. In the dim light, one could imagine that half the party was naked.

I ran into Cinnamon Hardwig, the rock critic. She was dressed as John Lennon's ghost, and her boyfriend, a Japanese drummer, was Yoko Ono. He looked pretty good since he had hair down to his waist and even his mustache seemed to be part of the statement.

Kevin Rose, the film critic, was wearing nothing but gauze. "What are you?" I asked him.

"I'm Jack Nicholson's nose in *Chinatown*," he said. He pointed to Dirk's nose, which still had a small bandage, and said, "You and I should go together. I could say I'm a blow-up of your nose. Say, who are you supposed to be, Laurie?"

"Can't you tell? We're Dirk and Bree."

"That's great. I loved your last piece about them. That Dirk is such an asshole."

"Ah . . . Kev, this is actually Dirk," I said. "Kevin Rose, Dirk Miller."

"Good to meet you. I admire your work," he said, and walked off toward Sean Garrison, who was standing with Elena Cholent-Cimmino, the dance writer. We watched Kevin go up to Elena and kiss her and say, "Good to meet you. I admire your work."

Mark Garvey, the political writer who does the "Left Out" column, was there with his girlfriend Dana Chun. He was wearing a red devil costume and she had glued real dollar bills all over herself.

"Hi, we're Dirk and Bree," I said. "Who are you?"

"We're the CIA," he said.

"I love the costume, Laura. Is this your boyfriend Russ— the one who has to get laid every night between six and eight?"

"No, actually this is Dirk."

"The real Dirk?" said Dana. "I have someone who's dying to meet you."

She ran across the room and grabbed a woman who wasn't in any costume and brought her over. "Betsey, this is Dirk. The real Dirk. Dirk, this is my friend Betsey, who makes documentaries for public television."

Dirk said, "Hi."

I decided to leave him with the two women. "Dirk, can I get you a drink?"

"No, absolutely nothing for me, thanks."

I walked away as Betsey was saying, "So, Dirk, I'm making a film on the nineties called *Whither the Yuppies?* and I've been dying to get a hold of you and see if I could interview you . . ."

I found Sean Garrison standing between two naked, bald mannequins and a woman dressed as a snow leopard. "Laura," he said, and extended his arms for a big hug. I handed him the copy for the earthquake-in-the-tub story. He started to read it and spill red wine on it, but I told him to read it later.

"Sean, I wonder how you would feel about an exclusive interview with Judge Corman. He's the judge who's written the book *The Creative Judiciary*."

"Oh, yes. That guy. He's so publicity-crazy. He keeps calling me. I think I'll pass on this."

"Umm, Sean, I really am hot to do this."

"Well, what's your spin?"

"How about the sex life of a jurist? He's no David Souter, you know."

"OK, OK. That might work. Let me see it."

The woman in the faux-snow-leopard suit started pawing Sean. He introduced us. The faux was Sarie Bauer, the nature writer. "Glad to meet you," she said. "I admire your work."

I hardly knew what to say. I hated everything I'd read of hers, especially her holier-than-thou friend-of-the-earth tone. "I was wondering," I said, "since you write so infrequently, what you do the rest of the time."

"Oh, my dad is retired from Chevron—thank God. He bought a cattle ranch in Montana and I go there in between gigs to find peace and ride my horse, Solar. I'm working on a piece now that's kind of abstract. It's a view of New York City as seen by the last bald eagle on earth. I haven't found a publisher yet. I think I'll try *The New Yorker*—what do you think?"

"Well, they usually go for those darn big names."

"I know, but I've gotten a couple of beautiful rejection letters from Bob Gottlieb in the past. I mean, really thoughtful."

"Sarie!" It was Don Dahl, the guy who did the twenty-thousand word feature called 'Sittin' on the Shlock of the Bay,' about how landfill and pollution were killing the bay. They embraced and began to talk about a recent dead bird find near Santa Barbara.

I walked over to Dirk to see if he was OK. Steven Sachs, the crime feature writer who just covered the Fed Ex rapist, came up to him and said, "Hi, I'm Steve Sachs. I'm working on a nonfiction book about rape and alienation. What are you working on?"

"Hi, I'm Dirk, and I'm a recovering Demerolic. I'm working on my problem."

I took the opportunity to walk over to the food table. All the usual subjects had been rounded up—smoked Gouda, creamy Havarti, Boursin. I grabbed a couple Wheat Thins—they always sounded like diet food. Whoever thought of getting the word "Thin" in the name was a genius—eat these oily Wheat Thins and you will stay healthy and thin. I poured myself a big glass of the '86 Bordeaux and started dipping the Wheat Thins into a very soft, creamy wedge of Brie that was slowly collapsing.

"Who says we're Brie and wine liberals?" someone said. It was Jeremy Crawford, an assistant editor at *Lifestyle* and my lover for most of '83 and part of '86.

I laughed and held up my wineglass. "To '86, a very good year."

"And who are you, Lucille Tennis Ball?" he said, yanking my fake red ponytail like the naughty schoolboy he was.

"No, I'm Bree, the one I write about."

"Oh, Bree on Brie," he said.

Jeremy was oh so clever, someone who thought that because he could spell he was superior to his writers. I found him tiresome. I already knew he was a pedant, a premature ejaculator, and a Sanskrit scholar. I realized he was flirting with me.

"You know what I always admired about you, Laurie? You didn't have the usual agenda. Most women are trying to trap you into marriage whatever they say. But you were different. You just wanted free editorial services. I could live with that."

I would have actually preferred a simple, insincere "I admire your work."

As more people came and the band got louder and the Brie got runnier and the talk turned to who could do what for whom, I had the strange feeling I was in the bar scene in *Star Wars*. Seeing Mai in her big egg suit and Rod in his paisley sperm suit with the long tail did not decrease that impression.

"Laura, this is Anita. Ask her to solve your sex problems," Mai said, and presented her friend, who was dressed as Mr. Condom. Anita was older and chubbier than I would have imagined from the racy answers she supplied in her columns. But I guess sex therapists can't seem conventionally sexy. No one would dare admit their inadequacies to some babe or hunk.

"Zo, vat zeems to be za problem, Boobie?" she said.

Well, I was pretty drunk so I just spilled my guts. "I divide the world into the women who are more conventional and stupider than me and the women who are less conventional and morally superior. Right now my boyfriend is involved with one of the latter and I feel lost."

She seemed surprised that I actually said what was on my mind. "Why don't you seek professional help?" she said, and walked over to flirt with Sean Garrison. Sean's power over publication seemed to be the strongest aphrodisiac at the party. He was surrounded by several young women who had shaved their heads and pierced their noses and who all wanted to be writers when they grew up. Sean Garrison loved it. I was probably one of the only people there to whom he had confided the awful truth. He could only come if he was bound, gagged, blindfolded, and had his dick tickled with a special feather quill he kept on his desk.

It made Dan Rather seem like a minor sex toy.

30

Now and then, Mai was capable of dropping the therapist thing and just talking. We were sitting in her living room. She made up the couch bed and brought me a cup of Sleepy Time tea.

"Look," she said, "no one is more sensitive to race issues than I am. But in a way, to assume a black woman is better than you is a kind of racism too. I think you should respond to Cherry Saunders the same way you were going to before you knew the color of her skin."

"Mai, I was going to kill her."

"OK. Well. Forget that."

"Look, I feel like the only support I've had has just been taken from me, like the Big Guy in the sky just pulled out

the chair and let me fall on my ass. Maybe I should talk to
Rabbi Birnbaum about this."

"Do you know Shelly?"

"Yes, he's my next-door neighbor."

"Have you ever taken one of his seminars? He's great. You
should do it. In fact, hadn't we talked about trying to get Dirk
and Bree to come? Actually, Rod and I are going to one in
the wine country next weekend. You should come. Take Russ
and work the whole thing out with him right there. If anyone
can help you solve your problems, it's Shelly Birnbaum."

"But why are you and Rod going? You two seem to have
the perfect relationship."

"Oh, come on, Laura, that's your problem."

"What is?"

"This 'perfect relationship' bullshit. Nobody has it. The
very concept is a burden. I think that's why Dirk and Bree
broke up. You hung that albatross around their necks."

"So you're saying it's my fault they broke up?"

"No, I actually think you were being sincere. You were proj-
ecting your own fantasy onto them. Dirk and Bree were a comedy to you. Other people are always comedies. We're tragedies."

Her husband called from upstairs, "Mai? Are you coming
to bed?"

"Just a minute."

"Well, what is the problem with you and Rod?"

"It's not a problem as much as it is a need for renewal. Too
much of our life together is bogged down in the politics of
the past. Shelly is into renewal rituals."

"But I can't help thinking you and Rod have it made. You've
been together for fifteen years. That's got to be some kind of
record."

"Laura, how long were your parents married?"

"When she died? Let's see . . ." I started thinking. They
were married twenty years when they had me, and she died
when I was seventeen.

"Thirty-seven years. They were married thirty-seven years.
That's as long as I've been alive!"

"And did they have a—to use your phrase—a perfect relationship?"

I pictured them old and funny-looking, having the same fights over and over again—Lenore always yelling at Harry that the cigars were going to kill him, that he got too aggravated about everything, that they would find him "keeled over on a slab of Formica." . . . Funny, huh? And he outlived her by twenty years.

"No, it wasn't perfect, but something kept them going. It wasn't bad. I mean, I do believe they loved each other and I don't think they needed any therapy or renewal rituals."

"Well, maybe they had their own. Maybe your being born so late in the relationship brought it new life—literally."

I had never thought of myself in that way, as Harry and Lenore's little renewal ritual, but it was true—in a way.

The phone rang and Mai went to get it. I could hear her talking in the kitchen. I figured from her tone, and the fact that it was past midnight, that it was one of her clients having some kind of emergency. Perhaps some inner child from some long-gone dysfunctional family had just had a breakthrough.

"Oy caramba," Mai said as she came back in the room.

"What's wrong?"

"That was Bree. It seems she had a big fight with Neil Blender and somehow you were involved. She began to feel that Neil was trying to get some kind of screenwriting deal similar to the one you had for a movie about Dirk and Bree. She's not so dumb, is she? In true Neil Blender fashion, he claimed it was all your doing, that you had involved him and were trying to get him to manipulate Bree into a reconciliation with Dirk for your own selfish reasons. After she threw him out, she tried to call you, and when Dirk answered the phone at your house, she went bonkers. Now she's sure you are after her husband and her screen rights. I told her you were here but she didn't believe me. She accused me of being in cahoots with you and said she will never trust anybody again."

"Mai, come to bed," Rod yelled from upstairs.

"Go ahead," I said. "I'll be OK." I knew that at one a.m.

there was a talk show—*In the Middle of the Night* with Jon Darlington.

"Sex with animals. Is it a human rights or an animal rights issue? Tonight we will be speaking with Dr. Kit Stieglitz of the Veterinary Therapy Center in San Diego; Ruth Wolf a dog trainer in New York; and from Brookfield Zoo in Chicago, Paco the Parrot. We'll be back in a moment to talk about sex with animals . . . *In The Middle of the Night*."

31

Dirk called at the crack of dawn to describe the bizarre night he'd had at my place. Alone with my things and Russ's drugs, after his fight with Bree, he started to feel that old devil anxiety playing tricks on him.

"Dirk, it said to me, you are in a doctor's house. And that means that somewhere in this house is a doctor's medicine kit. Maybe I should have a drink, I thought. Alcohol was never really my drug. Alcohol would take the edge off my anxiety and keep me from looking in the medicine chest.

"But as soon as I visualized that medicine chest, I thought: Well, maybe just a peek. So I went into your bathroom. Laura, I couldn't help noticing your silk bikini panties and lacy bra lying in a pile outside the shower. I considered picking them up. People do things like that. Better a pervert than a junkie."

"You didn't, Dirk, you didn't?" And now I thought of another good reason to try to stop being such a careless slob. You simply never know when one of your friends will come over and start fondling your underwear.

"No. I *should* have gone straight to the bra and panties, but I found myself looking in the medicine cabinet instead."

"Kid at a candy store" would not describe his tone as he told me what it was like to look at Russ's collection.

"Laura, I couldn't believe it. There were sample bottles of every imaginable thing on earth. In fact, that was part of the problem. You couldn't tell from the names, like Vibracycline or Combuteral or Monicide, what the hell they were used for. I was looking for downers, perhaps a muscle relaxant, but an upper would do. Yes, I thought, an upper would do very nicely, especially with that bottle of Chateaux Margaux I saw in the dining room."

Oh no, not the Margaux. We were saving that for some special occasion. I had imagined breaking it out to toast our engagement after the Miata-giving ceremony.

"Of course, I considered that the cabinet might contain some horrible experimental drug, something you would only take if you had an incurable disease and didn't mind side effects like loss of hair and loss of sense of touch. So I slammed the door shut and ran to the bedroom and climbed on Russ's rowing machine. I sang out a few choruses of 'Row, Row, Row Your Boat' as I rowed, and imagined heading for some shore that never came. I thought maybe I would go out to an all-night drugstore and buy something I knew—something over the counter. Advil. A couple Advils and maybe a little NyQuil. I'd done those before, a Quilvil cocktail.

"I remembered that I had the phone numbers of some twelve-step buddies in my wallet. I was struggling, Laura, really struggling. I went to the phone and dialed one. First I got: 'Hi, you have reached the home of Nick, Jodie, Ethan, Dylan, and Cassie. We can't come to the phone now, but please leave a message.' I went down the list to: 'Hi, this is Megan. If you have a message for me or Isis or Osiris, we'll get right back to you . . .'

"Finally, I tried my assigned buddy. His message was: 'Hi, my name is Jordon and I'm a recovering paregoric freak. If you are calling from All-Anon, I'm really sorry I'm not in. Don't hang up. Hang in there. Wish I could hold your hand, but please leave a message. I'll call you soon. Talk as long as you like. Even if I don't hear your words, a Higher Power will.'

"Well, fuck this! Fuck this, I thought. I decided I would just go back and try something. Instead, by some incredible act of will, I got back on the rowing machine and started singing like a man possessed, 'Life is but a dream tra-la-la-la-la.' "

"Singing can help at these times," I said.

"Then I hear a knock at the door and see a man in a football jersey standing there. 'Hi,' he says. 'I live next door and we couldn't help but hear that singing.' "

That would be Rabbi Birnbaum, I assumed.

"I felt like a real jerk. 'I'm really sorry,' I said. 'Did I wake you?'

" 'Well, yeah,' he says. 'Are you a friend of Laura's?'

"I said, 'Sort of. Look, I'm really sorry I woke you.'

" 'Are you drunk?' he asks me.

"I explain that that's the problem—I'm sober. And I told him that I'm having a hard time. 'I'm Dirk and I'm a recovering multiple substance abuser,' I said.

"So he shakes my hand and says, 'Hi, I'm Shelly, I'm a rabbi. An MSA, huh? Well, I'm here for you if you need me. Did something precipitate this episode?' he asks me.

"So I tell him that I've been separated from my wife and we had just had a terrible fight on the phone, that she thinks I'm here with Laura, but Laura had a fight with Russ, so she let me stay here and she went someplace else.

"Shelly says, 'Wait a minute,' and then he disappears for a few minutes. I row a little more; then he comes back and hands me this paper.

" 'This will explain who I am and what I do,' he says, and the paper is an advertisement for a weekend for couples who are in trouble. Exactly the sort of thing Bree and I need. It was almost an act of God, a sign pointing the way. Then he asks if I want him to stay for a while and talk to me. I tell him how considerate that is, but that I think I can make it now. I apologize for waking him. Then he gives me some advice. He says, 'If you're dealing with the twin demons of relationship problems and drug addiction, you need to break the circuit. Do something completely different to get out of your usual patterns.' He told me to remember that the earthquake had lifted everyone's stress level a notch or two. That seemed so perceptive to me. I'd been an eight point five all night. I couldn't believe he was a rabbi. He told me that he really was a rabbi and had a Ph.D. in therapy. We talked a little bit about everything from therapy to religion to psychology education. I told him I had my degree in that also. He said that in addition he did triathlons. He suggested that I try that as a way to stay high without using anything.

"After he left, I felt incredibly strong. Empowered. I marched back to the bathroom. I looked at the medicine chest and shook my finger at it and shouted, 'You won't get me! Not tonight. I can do it. Shelly was the messenger. Thank you, God.'

"Then I threw off my clothes and jumped in the shower, alternating hot and cold for about five minutes. I came out and grabbed a towel and that's when I saw your bra and panties again. 'Break the circuit'—that was the phrase that kept going through my head. So I picked up your underwear and went into the bedroom. I had heard of men who did things like this, and really, I'm not one of them. I've never done anything even remotely like this. But just for the hell of it, just to give the old circuit a real jolt, I put on the pants and bra. The pants barely made it over my knees and the bra was, as they say, a stretch. I turned out the lights and lay there under the covers with your underwear on, trying to understand what this trip is, what it does for a man and his maleness.

"But when I touched the lacy cups on my chest, all I could think about was Bree, Bree's beautiful body, Bree's little lacy white bra. Once, it was there for the asking, and now the feel of the lace made me profoundly sad and lonely. I wept, I actually wept, Laura, and then I feel asleep.

"The next thing I knew, I woke up some time later to find a man throwing himself on me saying, 'Laura, Laura, I'm so sorry.'

"I bolted up out of the bed, forgetting all about wearing

your bra and panties. It was Russ. 'Shit!' he screamed. 'What the fuck is this?'

" 'It's not what it looks like,' I said.

"Russ had his pants off and he was screaming, 'OK. Here's what it looks like. Some crazy guy is sitting here in my bed, in my girlfriend's underwear, laughing'—I am laughing by now. He continues raving. 'Great, that's what it's not. Great. Now suppose you tell me what it is, because I'm delighted that it's not what it looks like.'

"I tried to explain it to him. I said that it was kind of a game, an attempt to break the circuit. I told him that I had a problem with drugs, that I was trying to find some way to cope. You know, do something different.

"Then he started to get irrational. He asked, 'What have you done to Laura?' And Laura, he actually started looking through the closets and under the bed. I got dressed and told him you were gone.

"And then Russ kind of blew it. He was screaming things like: 'Where is she? What have you done with her? It was bad enough hearing nothing but Dirk and Bree, Dirk and Bree, night after night, month after month. And now I find you in my bed with her clothes on. What is going on?'

"He was extremely agitated. I realized that we were cross-communicating. I was fully clothed now, and handed him the bra and panties and said, 'I think we need to talk about this, man to man.' "

32

Call me a bad girl, but I can't help it. I loved it. When Dirk told me about this, I just lost it. Hysterical. Loved it. LOVED IT! I kept picturing the look on Russ's face when he saw Dirk in the bed. You know, in his own way Russ is the most conventional guy's guy kind of guy. And later, when Dirk tried to talk to him man to man, with all that male-bonding jargon, I could just see Russ cringing. Anyway, what happened is that Dirk and Russ talked for several hours. Then Dirk spent the night on the couch, and in the morning, when Russ left to join the volunteers at the freeway disaster, Dirk told him he would come that night and help. The volunteers were spending one more night trying to make sure no one was left in the collapsed freeway. He told Russ he would arrange for me to show up and talk to him. This was great. Now Dirk was trying to get Russ and me back together.

In return, I persuaded Mai to call Bree and tell her that as a healing experience we would make some food for the rescue crews and bring it down to the disaster scene that night. Mai convinced Bree to come over to her house. Bree accepted my explanation that I had spent the night there, especially when she saw my stuff on Mai's couch and heard the whole story about Cherry Saunders.

"At least Dirk wasn't cheating with a real person," she said.

"Oh, this is even worse," I said. "She's black."

Mai jumped in. "In her weird way, Laura assumes that means Cherry is automatically both a better human being and a better piece of ass than herself."

"Ridiculous," said Bree. "I saw a Del Warfield on Sexual Dysfunction in Black Women just last week. Del even admitted that she was anorgasmic with black men."

"You're kidding," I said. "Then she's seeing a white man?"

"No, an East German woman. They met when Del did her show on anticommunism in the refugee community."

"You mean Del is gay?"

"Well, this is strictly gossip from a therapist who was on *A Current Affair.*"

We sat around Mai's for the rest of the afternoon. I suggested Bree stay that night and we have a PJ party, but she said she had to get back to Rachel Whoopi. We went off to Price Mart to get some food for the rescuers.

Price Mart is one of these discount places where you join

and pay wholesale, but only if you buy in quantity. Bree had
joined when she and Dirk had Rachel Whoopi. Why a family
of three would need to buy a five-pound bag of tortilla chips
or a six-pack of tabasco sauce or a thirty-count package of
fresh-baked cinnamon rolls is beyond me.

We bought a three-pack of bread loaves and a huge res-
taurant-size vat of peanut butter and another of imported
raspberry jam, a hundred-count box of orange juice cartons,
a three-pack of oatmeal, and three hundred chocolate kisses.
All the huge containers gave one a comfortable feeling of
smallness. Not the way a cathedral tower humbles you but
the way an enormously fat person makes you feel like you're
just right. I wondered if Mai and Bree were reading reassur-
ance in sixty-four-ounce pickle jars or the crates of five
hundred individually wrapped maxipads.

We went back to Mai's and spent the evening making peanut butter sandwiches. Shosh and her girlfriends made oatmeal cookies, and we put each sandwich in a bag with a cookie
and a carton of juice and a chocolate kiss. The kitchen was a
cross between Santa's workshop and a sorority house before
women went in for anorexia. We made sandwiches and ate
kisses and scooped up fingerfuls of cookie batter. It was almost
nine o'clock before we headed for the rescue scene.

I was a little nervous to be going off in Bree's BMW to that
neighborhood at night. Who knows what we'd find there. It
was totally dark as we got near the area, because power was
still off to all the houses that bordered the collapsed freeway.
We saw the flashing red lights of a police car blocking off the
street. We approached and the cop cast the beam of a flashlight
into our car.

"I'm sorry, ladies, this area is closed for the rescue efforts."

"Hi," I said. "We're from the Emergency Support Network. We have some food for the rescuers." And I pointed
to the cartons in the seat next to me.

"Oh, food," he said, and he issued us a pass that said "Emergency Vehicle" and posted it on the windshield. He waved
us on through.

As we came to the disaster scene we saw huge floodlights shining on the streets, enough power to turn night into day. At first, I thought it was because someone was taping for a TV news show, but as we got up closer I saw it was weirder than that. Dozens of tables were set up with food for the rescuers. Restaurant Poulet had set up five barbecue tables with rotisseries where dozens of chickens were being spit-roasted on the spot. Chez Panache had set up a table where cold poached swordfish was sitting in a creamy rosemary vinaigrette. The Monterey Market had donated enough baby lettuce to feed a baby army. Jeremiah Puck had made his special Southwest caramel soufflé. Everywhere there were men in hard hats and white coats and orange vests trading comments on the best food. A handmade sign read: "Carnival Against Carnage."

I found Russ standing near the table with fresh-baked baguette and Maurice Edell's duck pâté. "You've got to try the curried lamb. It's excellent," he said.

We talked for a while. I could see that Bree had come upon Dirk and they were tapping a keg donated by the Pacific Brewing Company—Bree no doubt getting back to her brewery roots. I moved around so I could give Russ my undivided attention and still watch what Dirk and Bree were doing over his shoulder.

Russ told me he was sorry for what happened. The Cherry thing, as he called it, was not serious, he said. He could understand how I felt. When he first saw Dirk in the bed, he assumed the worst, until he saw he was wearing a bra.

"Cherry is over there near the burritos if you'd like to meet her. It's not what you think. She's really a great person. I know you would like her."

"No thanks." I said, and realized I had better get out of there before Cherry saw me and recognized me as the perpetrator of the hate crime. What could I say to her? It's a love/hate crime thing—you wouldn't understand.

"Laura, you can come home." Russ was giving me his understanding-surgeon look, the look of someone so clearly in the superior position that he could afford to be generous.

"Not until we straighten some things out." Holdout power was all I had left.

"OK. Look, I found the thing about the weekend with that weird rabbi next door, and I want you to know, I'm willing to go."

"You are?" I was shocked. Russ was the kind of man who avoided therapy like the plague.

"Yes, and Dirk is going to ask Bree to come. We'll all be working on relationships, as Dirk would say."

I could see Bree looking at Dirk now. She was shaking her head no. I wondered if she was refusing to go for the Birnbaum cure. Maybe Mai and I would have to kidnap her and take her. I had to get to her before she blew it with Dirk. I told Russ that I was going now and would meet him Friday night at the Leafy Creek Inn in Sonoma, that I'd ride up with Mai and Rod who were also coming.

"I wish you'd come home tonight, Laura."

The only advice on dealing with boys Harry Gurvitz ever gave me was: "Make 'em beg." As soon as I thought of him, I again prayed that I would find a way to do justice to his memory.

"I'll see you in a few days in Sonoma," I told Russ, and did not kiss him goodbye.

Cherry Saunders was coming my way. I grabbed Mai and said I had to get out of there, that my rival was near by. When I pointed her out to Mai, it turned out Mai knew her from a Friends of El Salvador group.

"Guess what," Mai said. "She actually is a saint. She has a son, you know. Adopted. An abandoned crack baby."

Great. Why wasn't Mai a liar?

Cherry was getting closer. "Please, I've got to beat it," I said.

We decided that we couldn't leave our crummy peanut butter sandwiches around all this incredible food, so we drove over to where the people displaced by the rescue efforts were being housed. Extra food from the rescue scene was sent there and they really didn't need ours either.

We drove back to Berkeley to the homeless shelter there

and saw that they, too, were enjoying the disaster abundance. By this time, we were so tired we just put our cartons of mundane sandwiches on a table next to day-old brioche from La Boulangerie, and Bree left us at Mai's.

Before we went to bed, Mai told me that Neil Blender had already arranged to take Bree to the wine country anyway, and would be dropping her off at the Leafy Creek Inn. Just to keep Dirk nervous, Bree told him to be there but said she couldn't commit to anything yet.

Always keep 'em begging, because once they've got you, they've got you. I fell asleep easily that night on Mai's couch, imagining Dirk getting into my bed wearing my old red flannel nightgown with the matching granny cap.

33

Have you ever seen a dog try to find his way home across a road that's been washed out? I think that's what we were all like during those days after the earthquake. We kept trying to go down roads, cross bridges, get on freeways that no longer existed.

No one was more disoriented than me. I had lost my father—the road back to my childhood. And now I seemed to have managed to misplace my lover—the road to my ego. I had lost Dirk and Bree somewhere along the way on the road to success. And to complicate matters, I woke up that morning in a strange house.

Sunlight poured through the French doors at the back of the Blender-Rodriguez house. Streaks of it landed on the Turkish rugs and the Mexican chairs and the foot of my sofa bed. I realized where I was as soon as I saw Mai's collection of demon-faced masks hanging on the wall across from me. A big red and silver devil was sticking out his tongue at me.

"Hi, Neil," I said.

I found some of yesterday's coffee still in the Melitta on the stove and heated it up. I wanted to get out of the house early and not be any trouble to Mai. I was sure Rod would get annoyed—he seemed like a very private person. And to tell the truth, whenever I was around black or Chicano or gay or handicapped people these days, I was always tense, certain I was going to say something insensitive, wrong, revealing of my incorrectness.

Last night Mai had told me a little more about Cherry Saunders, and it was all bad. Cherry lived with her four-year-old son, Akin, in Oakland. She was actually from a middle-class family—her father was a math professor at Cal State and her mother a quilt artist. She was well known in political circles, on an "Alice" and "Ron" basis with Alice Walker and Congressman Ron Dellums. Despite this, she was also known for her sense of humor and her *joie de vivre*. Give me a break. Couldn't she just be another self-righteous bitch for peace?

I drank three cups of coffee, then vowed that I would start a new life this very day. I would find a place to live so that I didn't have to live with Russ, even if things worked out. The Miata more than evened the financial score. That kind of payback had to continue. After I found a place of my own, I would stop eating all the junk food I'd been eating lately. I would go on a whole-foods diet. I would stop writing fluff and start doing investigative reporting. I would never get another parking ticket. Trouble was, I didn't think I could even get dressed.

I had shorts and a sweatshirt in my bag and managed to get those things on. I decided I would go jogging. It was the one thing I could still do—so little concentration needed, so much stubbornness available.

Mai's place was not too far from the BART path and I headed there. Running under the train reminded me of something when I was little, something in Brooklyn where I lived at the dawn of time. There was a train to Manhattan on a track above a store called Ma's. Ma's had paper dolls and comic books, pink Spalding bouncing balls and red wax lips, Double Bubble gum and Clark bars. All the good things in life in a tiny luncheonette with a counter with four stools and an old gray-haired lady everyone called Ma. I can hear Harry just as if it were yesterday, saying, "Hey Ma, gimme a stogie. And throw in a licorice whip for Shirley Temple here."

Harry was gone. It was really true. Every day I woke up and remembered it made it truer. Gone, but not forgotten, never forgotten. And maybe I would find a way to give him a proper memorial. The grim rituals of funerals and tomb-stones and dedications and even prayers made sense to me now. It's so easy to discount these things until you need them. When my parents were growing up, no one questioned the rituals, they just did them.

But the nineties were not the thirties, at least not yet. And the BART track was not the old Brooklyn train. The BART track was sleeker than anything in Brooklyn, of concrete strong enough to withstand a 7.5, and under it was an organized exercise path and par course. Arrows pointed to where the joggers should go and the bikers should go and the walkers belonged.

Plum trees that turned pink in February were kept trim below the tracks, and now graffiti blossomed here and there: *El Cerrito Rules; Jolene + Spider; Fuck the Police; White Punks on Dope; Metallica—metal up your ass.*

I thought of adding, *Actually, didn't Edward II die that way?* But it wasn't the kind of thing you wrote on a wall.

It was eight when I got back to Mai's, and they still weren't up. I took a shower, made up the bed, and left Mai a note saying I'd be home late and not to let my presence interfere with her family's life. I had a plan. In an attempt to make peace with Bree—funny how when you lose your boyfriend you start being nice to your friends, huh?—I had offered her something. I said I would like to take Rachel Whoopi out for the day so that she and Dirk could spend some time together and work on their relationship. I almost wanted to see those two get back together aside from the popularity of romantic

comedies in the movie houses. *When Harry Met Sally* . . .
Ghost . . . *Perfect Love, The Story of Dirk and Bree* . . . Oh
well, even if it was not to be a major motion picture, at least
let it be an example of relationship salvage. Especially since
my own relationship was something that looked hopeless. I
didn't buy Russ's "it's over with Cherry" line for one minute.
The best woman would win. And guess who that was?

I drove by Russ's house, which I guess was still sort of my
house. My files were in there. My old half-used makeup and
deodorant and olive oil were in there. My computer was in
there, so I couldn't work even if I wanted to. Even Dirk was
in there. His car was out in front. But was Russ there? The
Miata and the Volkswagen could be in the garage. Or the red
Miata could be parked in front of Cherry Saunders's house.

I found a phone booth down on Shattuck, the main street
in this strange town. Thornton Wilder once lived here. Is our
weird town Grover's Corners? I found an intact, unwatched
phone booth without any gang graffiti. Nobody had cut out
the phone book. I suppose that in Our Town in Our Times,
that is some sort of miracle.

I looked through the S's. Past Saefong, Saeng Tsing and
St. Joseph The Workman Church and Samsel, G. until I came
to Saunders, C. Unlike most single women, she had the cour-
age to list her address—a house in the Rockridge section of
Oakland. Hmmm. Maybe she would rent me a room.

When I was ten, I watched a soap opera about two women
who loved the same man. I think it was called *The Hands of
Time*. When woman number one found out, she went to the
cosmetics counter where woman number two worked and
poured acid on her face. The guy left them both. They ended
up living together, and the one who did the pouring went to
work to pay for the other's plastic surgery. I thought it was
such a beautiful tale of friendship.

Of course, I would never throw acid on Cherry Saunders's
face, but I did stare with envy at her wood-shingled house
with the stone chimney. Desiring this woman's hair and that
woman's house, I comforted myself with the thought that

maybe she just rented instead of owned. I did not see either
of Russ's cars parked in front or anywhere in the five-block
area I combed like a hawk. I could have missed him, though,
and just to make sure, I drove back across Oakland and up
to Grizzly Peak. No cars in front. I parked down the block
like a cop doing surveillance. I realized that somewhere, right
now, someone is watching someone.

I saw Shelly Birnbaum pack his wife and kids in the car
and then load up four bikes on the bike rack. I slid down in
the seat when I realized he was going to drive past me. To
my horror, he stopped.

He parked across the street and got out.

"Laura, I just wanted you to know that Russ made a res-
ervation for the two of you to come to the workshop this
weekend, and I think if you just hang in there, everything
will work out for the best."

I sat up from my disaster-drill head-in-my-lap position.
"Shelly, in your professional opinion, can this relationship be
saved?"

"I think it will work out for the best, whether that means
saving or abandoning. Remember, there are things people
want that are no good for them, and desire is not an accurate
measuring spoon."

Thanks, Shelly. A pearl of wisdom is not a life. And see, I
actually needed to get a life. Quick.

"Shelly, will you tell me one thing?"

"If it is within my power to know."

"Was he—was Russ—home last night? I mean, did you
notice his car coming home?"

"I heard that new Mazda pull in at around eleven o'clock.
Your friend Dirk was playing the adult rock station, singing,
'You've Really Got a Hold on Me.' I noticed because it's one
of my favorites and he really can't sing. So I looked out the
window until it was over. That was exactly eleven—just before
Russ got home."

"Thank you."

There really wasn't any time for Russ and Cherry to get it

on between the rescue work and his arrival—unless they did
it in the car, and that would mean even more bad news. Either
Cherry Saunders was one of those women who could come
anywhere on a dime, or worse yet, she was one of those women
who just cared about pleasing a man.

While torturing myself with fantasies of the moral, sexual,
political, and ethnological superiority of Cherry Saunders, I
saw Dirk come out of my house and get into his car to go
meet Bree and me at the Neon Cat diner. I quickly turned
the car around so I wouldn't be caught spying.

Outside the diner, Dirk and Bree thanked me profusely as
they passed Rachel Whoopi into my care. Dirk whispered to
me, "He came straight home last night."

They kissed Rachel Whoopi many times, and Bree kept
telling me important things like, if she starts to suck her thumb
that means she's tired. She gave me her backpack, a blanket,
and a teddy bear to put in the trunk of my car just in case. I
was happy to see it was the bear I gave her. Dirk gave me
their camcorder and told me to "get everything on tape."

I was afraid Rachel Whoopi would start crying when her
mom left, but she was a pretty poised little girl and I guess
I had sucker written all over me. I told her she could indeed
order a sundae for Sunday brunch instead of the veggie ome-
lets that most of the couples at the Neon Cat were ordering.
They didn't make them, so she settled for a doughnut, a cocoa
with whipped cream, and a fruit plate. I stood up on the seat
in the booth to get an establishing shot of the table.

The cocoa was unfortunately the genuine Mexican kind,
and Rachel just ate the whipped cream and said the rest was
"yuk." I got some footage of her toying with the fruit plate,
most of which she left. I read her the things that were written
on the walls of the Neon Cat about how the place was a
reconstruction of a historic diner in Ho-Ho-Kus, New Jersey,
but she just laughed and said, "Ho. Ho. Kiss. Kiss."

I had barely eaten my scone and was nursing my latte when
Rachel Whoopi was finished. "Can we go yet?" she kept asking. I gave her a couple quarters to go play the jukebox. Since

she couldn't read, she just pressed buttons, and that's how
we happened to get "Those Lazy-Hazy-Crazy Days of Summer" twice. But fate led her to Elvis's "That's When Your
Heartache Begins," and I swear he was singing just for me.

> *"When you find your sweetheart*
> *In the arms of your friend,*
> *That's when your heartache begins . . ."*

Maybe Cherry Saunders was not my friend, but she could
have been. I would choose her over me. Maybe Mai was right.
Maybe my breakup with Russ was a self-fulfilling prophecy.

I asked Rachel if she'd like to go for a hike and she said
sure. "My mom and dad are dating," she told me.

I drove up to Tilden Park, which just happened to take me
past the Nelman aerie one more time. Again, no indication
of what evils lurked. On the hiking trail, I discovered something about Rachel. She would run but she wouldn't walk.
She'd take off with me chasing her, then stop and say, "I'm
bored. This is boring."

Kids show you no mercy, do they? When some jogger
passed us, she'd start running again, and I'd start the camcorder and run after her.

I carried her on my back the last quarter mile. I let her
grab a stick and hit my butt and yell, "Giddyup horsy." She
told me her dad let her do that.

And forgive me, I pictured how Dirk and Bree might be
working on their relationship at that very minute. Bree naked
on naked Dirk, hitting his behind and yelling, "Giddyup
horsy." You see, Your Honor, I have this one-track imagination. Always have, always will. Nobody loves a dirty lady—
except a guy with an erection and the readers of *Lifestyle, A
Magazine.*

I just didn't want Rachel Whoopi to cry. I would have done
anything to prevent that. I wanted to think that if she were
my little girl, I could make her happy. I guess, for that one

day, she was my little self, and I was determined not to see my little self cry.

The trail ended at the City Farm, and Rachel Whoopi seemed excited about the prospect of getting to pet some animals. Everyone was taping their kids. At first, Rachel held her nose and kept saying, "P-U. It stinks here." But pretty soon, she was making contact with a baby goat. Then I couldn't pull her away. I got some great footage.

We drove to the merry-go-round. It was hand-painted with pastoral American scenes; there was even a panel showing an Indian capturing a buffalo. It was a stunning carousel, with more than just horses. You could ride a carved cat or a giraffe or even a deer with antlers. I bought Rach—she was Rach by now—a book of tickets and she took a turn on each animal.

I read the history of the merry-go-round in a little display set up next to it. It had been built in North Tonawanda, New York, in 1911 and had done time in San Bernardino and Ocean Beach and Griffith Park before coming to Berkeley after the Second World War.

Another beautiful feature was its music. The carousel had a calliope-type music box, and a series of waltzes and fox trots cheered on the scared babies and excited schoolkids and happy lovers who rode around and around before my eyes. I put the camcorder down.

There were gargoyles across the top which seemed to make faces at me as the thing whirled by. It was studded with mirrors and light bulbs, and I let my eyes go out of focus as I stared at it like some time-lapse photoplay of American life, my life. I went into focus as Rach came by. She smiled and waved at me, as I had smiled and waved at Harry and Lenore at Coney Island when I was four years old. The music was a beautiful old song, "Bye Bye Blackbird." I imagined my mother smiling and waving at her mother on some sunny day when she was a little girl and that same music was playing that same way. It was so nostalgic I sobbed out loud.

Then I saw Harry go by, and he was waving too, waving

and calling, "Bye-bye. Bye-bye." I was sitting on the bench next to an old man of around eighty, and whatever his memory yielded, his impassive face gave no clue.

34

Neil Blender was renting a house in Marin to be close enough to manage what he called Operation Breedom. It was a sixties-style ranch on a hilltop overlooking the bay, a nondescript suburban house, decorated inside in late Hefner. The living room was mostly white and gold, with a huge black leather wraparound sofa, wrapped around a large gold-trimmed glass coffee table. An enormous blown-glass figurine of Rodin's "The Kiss" stood on the center of the table. Surrounding all this were bookshelves filled with videos and CDs. Neil said the place belonged to a friend of Cher's, and he had called this urgent meeting because "Cher wants the treatment for our screenplay faxed to her yesterday."

He greeted me in a white silk shirt, baggy black slacks, black cloth slip-on shoes, and a black kimono-style jacket with a golden dragon on the back.

"Anybody ever tell you you look like Bruce Lee?" I asked him as he signaled that I should sink into the giant sofa.

"I think the concept here is Oriental potentate in his off hours."

I thought: Occidental pimp. "Do you mind if I run this tape recorder as we talk?" I'd decided to protect myself should Neil and I ever have reason to dispute who said what, wrote what, and who owned what.

"Not at all, although you do know it's not admissible." Cheshire grin, then: "Coffee? Calistoga? Wine?"

I saw that he had a wineglass on the glass table with the

glass "Kiss," so I said, "Sure. I always drink when I'm on duty. I'll have some wine."

"Red or white?" he asked, going to some cut-glass decanters on a black lacquer cabinet. Before I could answer, he poured me the white and himself the red. He put on an opera CD— *Madame Butterfly*, I believe—loud in the background, loud enough to make any tape recording inaudible.

He sank into the couch next to me, handed me my glass, and then put his chilly hand on my knee. I picked it up and took it off. He laughed raucously.

"Don't worry, baby. This is strictly business. So, Cher likes the basic idea: Boy meets Bree, Boy gets Bree, and they become cultural stereotypes. Then, as the stereotype stops dominating the culture, as money gets tighter, as Boy and Bree get older, they fight over the pie and start acting weird. They go off together into their own strange sunset as the *fin de siècle* fever starts heating up. I figure if all goes well—and in this business it never does—we open on seven hundred screens in the fall of '95."

I was staring out the window. The fog was moving in, obscuring the thousands of lights below us.

"By '95, who knows if there will be any theaters left or what?" I said. "Think of our demographics—the first baby boomers will be approaching fifty. I'm just wondering how romantic comedy will play to that age group."

"Babe," he said, punctuating the air with his finger like Phil Collins hitting a high note, "you're thinking good. You have to read the future to make a movie, because what plays today will seem dated in a couple years."

"Right. Like Formica tabletops in the sixties."

I put my glass down on the glass-topped table. He got up and brought over the decanter and filled it again.

"Odd example, but yeah. See, that's where the weirdness comes in. When the baby boomers start to get seriously old, things are going to get very strange. You hear everyone crying about turning forty now. Imagine what kind of psychotic breaks turning fifty will bring out. This is what Cher wants—

something to show her at fifty, but in all her Cherness. So, what do you think of Cher playing both Dirk and Bree?"

"Well, it would make it really interesting if she played Bree in Bree makeup, and how about if Dirk ends up a cross-dresser and his female drag is vintage Cher—you know, big wig of Cher hair, Cher black lace lingerie, Bob Mackie navel-alert dress."

"I love this," he said, writing furiously. I was feeling the effect of the wine and realized there was another reason why I thought of this, besides the Dirk Does Laura episode. The whole craziness on the LoveNet with Che. I asked Neil about that.

"Laura, don't lose this creative surge you've got going here. Forget about that. Che and I were just funning. Cross-dressing is a growing trend. Now dig this scene: Bree's parents come for the tenth-birthday party of Rachel Whoopi and Dirk is in drag and Bree now collects exotic pets . . ."

"You know who I see as the parents? For some reason, I see Tony Curtis and Janet Leigh."

"Oh, I can't believe it. Inspired. Inspired David Lynchian casting. Forget Norm Desmond. Can you imagine what Lynch could do if he directed Aging Yuppies Get Weird? Or John Waters . . ."

We were swimming away from *Perfect Love*, down some bizarre channel that I even feared might be appropriate. We had come full circle, metaphorically approaching the real Dirk and Bree, the weird couple I met at the coke and popcorn party back in 1983 when we watched the Bree soft-core demographics videotape.

"How about if we start the film with a scene of Dirk, Bree, and Maria, their au pair, sitting on a couch watching family videos of Dirk and Bree?"

"Wrong. That should come later. I say we start with the Warfield Fiasco. It's a scene everyone in America has seen— if not on the show, then on the news where it was replayed a million times. That's the actual publicity chip we're going to cash in here: Whatever happened to Dirk and Bree after that? Everyone wants to know."

He was right. He was very sharp. But I started getting sleepy and felt I'd better get out of there before I fell asleep in Neil Blender's rented bachelor pad/command post. I asked to be excused, and he said we had more than enough; he'd fax it in the morning. He showed me to the door and said, "I'll see you in Hell A on Thursday. Drive carefully—you can't miss this meeting."

When I got outside, I realized a thick fog covered the hilltop. I could hardly see my car, let alone the road out of there. I rang the bell again, and he came to the door with his shirt already off. He threw on his kimono and offered to get in his car and let me follow him down the hillside to where I could see the freeway sign.

That was kind. You know, Neil Blender did have a good side; he was fun to work with, responsive and direct and animated. As I said, everyone changes when you get to know them. That's why you don't want to get to know some people too well. You don't really want to know, for example, that Hitler is a fun guy to play board games with.

The thing is, I was beginning to understand Neil's appeal— to Mai, to Bree, and now, even to me. He was exciting. He was bright. And most of all, he was decisive. Unlike Dirk, who was always concerned with expressing his feelings and listening to your feelings—at least that was his official position—and unlike Russ, who never let on what he thought, or Rod, who thought only the politically correct thing, Neil was a loose cannon. He might say or do anything. Anything. There was energy in that. A man like Neil might sweep you in his arms and carry you off into, if not the sunset, at least the backyard.

Was I having a rape fantasy about Neil Blender? I couldn't have sunk that low. Although wasn't any fantasy about Neil Blender a rape fantasy?

As we came out of the thickest fog I could make out more than the red taillights of Neil's car. I could see the license plate: SINEMA. We seemed to have reached flat ground and were speeding up.

I popped the tape of our discussion into the deck. In between the screaming soprano and the bleating tenor of *Madame Butterfly*, I could make out Neil saying, "You know, it won't kill you to work with me. Cher had her doubts about me too, but a driven man is not the worst thing to have in the driver's seat." Then he said something I couldn't make out and I leaned forward to press rewind.

A sharp jolt and things came to an abrupt halt. Wherever my mind was, the front end of my car was now firmly inserted in the rear end of Neil's old Mercedes. He had stopped for a light. I hadn't.

I got out of the car to survey the damages. It was clearly my fault. I should not have been driving under the influence of even one glass of wine, listening to a tape, imagining the unimaginable, and trying to rewind at the same time. I don't know where my mind goes when it takes these little vacations at the wheel, but one look at our enmeshed vehicles and I knew that this little vacation was going to cost me plenty.

"Oh, no! No!" I screamed when Neil got out and said we'd better file an accident report. That would mean cops, that would mean a ticket. "Neil, please. Don't you understand?"

"What? You don't have insurance?"

"It's worse than that. Don't worry. I'll pay for it, I promise. I have some money saved. Take your car in and I'll just pay for the repairs—whatever it costs. But please, Neil, I beg you, don't file an accident report."

I was crying now, and maybe a little hysterical, replaying the moment of impact, chiding myself for being so stupid and inattentive. Neil got in his car and after some manuevering was able to disengage it and drive over to the curb.

I could see that we were in downtown San Rafael, but it was late and the street was deserted. There were no witnesses.

"OK, relax, Laura. See if you can drive your car."

It started and it moved, but it was not a pretty sight. I pulled it over in front of his. I begged him again not to call a cop. I took out my money market passbook to show him that I had twelve thousand dollars.

"Neil, remember my fifty tickets?"

"Yeah, but I thought that was all taken care of, that Bree had arranged everything."

"Well, I still have to interview him."

"Interview who?"

"Judge Corman. That was our deal, that I interview him and publicize his book."

"Laurie, I've known Brad Corman for twenty years, and publicity will not be enough."

"What do you mean? You're not going to tell him about this, are you? I promise I'll pay for your damages. Neil, please don't."

"Don't worry. I know you're good for it. I'm not worried about that. And as far as Corman goes, it's a done deal. One blow job and he'll have your record expunged. He'll say you performed your community service."

35

The next day, it was trick-or-treat time. I called traffic court first thing and agreed to pay a thousand dollars for the tickets and another thousand in fines. I left a message for the Honorable Bradford Corman canceling the interview. The last thing I needed was to get involved in another writer's fantasy—I already had one in a kimono; I certainly didn't need one who dressed in robes.

Now I could get ready for Halloween. What I love about Halloween is the total indulgence. You can be what you want to be and eat what you want to eat. And if there's one thing I know about life, it's that you have to spend a lot of time being things you're really not and eating a lot of what you don't want to eat.

Not that I've ever been one of those grown-ups who dress up on Halloween. In San Francisco, it's kind of the gay Yom

Kippur, but I just like the anything-goes aspect. And I like the memories. Memories are beginning to occupy more of my life than experience.

Memories of my father kept flowing back now—the oddest little details, like the kinds of things he remembered near the end. In particular, I remembered the Halloween when I was dressed like an Indian squaw and Harry took me to meet some real Indian who worked at a restaurant with a cowboy motif in Brooklyn. This Indian spoke Yiddish and my father said it was proof that the Indians were really Jews. The Indian, Chief Swift Running, gave me a little orange wax harmonica and a black velvet cat mask. My father told me he was the man who posed for the nickel. As we left the Wagon Wheel Harry took out a nickel and pointed to the Indian in profile and said, "See? Look at that schnoz on him. What did I tell you?"

That was the first year I noticed how beautiful the colors orange and black were together, and that nothing more cheerful occurs in nature than a pumpkin. We stopped and bought our pumpkin on the way home from a big pile out in front of Louie's, The Vegetable Man, and Harry helped me carve a face on it like an Indian chief. We used a cigar for the nose.

What meant the most to me, this year especially, was the whole happy view of death you get on Halloween. I like to be reminded that the spirits are always with us. After my mother's death, I never doubted for a moment that she was around. And now I knew Harry was out there too. I felt he was waiting for some communication from me, some act that would remove the empty feeling I had when I thought of him, and replace it with a sense that I was honoring him. What is sad is that you can't actually talk to the dead when you know they're right out there, a touch and a universe away.

So the sight of skeletons and ghosts everywhere makes me feel much better. And as if all this weren't enough, add to the night of the dead the spirit of giving. An unbeatable marriage of concepts. The idea that any stranger who comes to your door deserves a little treat. Not like Christmas, where you have to go to stores and make choices and spend money

and be clever and wrap things. Just a little treat—a Tootsie
Roll, a sucker, a bag of M&Ms. Seeing little kids come and
go. It's the nicest night of the year.

I had a hard time persuading Bree to let me take Rachel
trick-or-treating. I figured that with Neil in LA, it was the
best way to give Dirk and Bree a chance to get together. I
was horrified when I heard that trick-or-treating was forbidden
at Quail Glen. Instead, the parents pay twenty dollars for a
child to attend a party at the Quail Glen Pool and Sports
Center. There, a professional clown dressed in a pumpkin suit
gives each child a bag containing a milk chocolate witch from
Au Cocolat, a small pumpkin pie from the Country Bake Shop
at Quail Glen, a certificate for a small toy from FAO Schwarz,
and a book, *An Illustrated Meaning and History of All Hal-
low's Eve*. Each child gets to carve a pumpkin with a special
safe instrument. A prize is given for the best costume, and
according to Bree, some mothers pay over a hundred dollars
for a seamstress to make a costume. The parents camcord the
entire evening. If they can't come, they ask a friend for a copy
of the tape.

As if kids today haven't been robbed of enough, many mothers won't let their kids out to play on the streets, even in front
of their own homes in the best neighborhoods. Bree was one
of these. She pointed to a kidnapping last year not too far
from Quail Glen. So, in addition to spending their childhoods
under house arrest, many children will grow up without ex-
periencing the miracle of Halloween. To me, that's a crime.

I promised Bree that if she let me take Rachel for just the
evening, I would walk up to every house with her. I would
throw away the unwrapped stuff, and I would stop at the
hospital for the free X ray of her candy. I said we'd even CAT-
scan it if she wanted me to. Dirk was on my side because it
meant that he and Bree would have another opportunity to
be alone together. And, I promised, I'd get the whole thing
on tape.

Again, I was doing it for myself. It gave me a chance to go
up to all these houses and see the hard faces of adults soften

as they lit up for the innocents on their doorstep. It also gave me a chance to look into the houses and see what the furniture was like, who was eating dinner by candlelight, who was alone, who was drinking what. There were certain houses of particular interest to me.

Rachel was Little Red Riding Hood and used her basket for her trick-or-treat goodies. I wore a rubber Barbara Bush mask and my red flannel nightgown and went as Granny. Most people assumed I was a kid too and gave me candy. At first Rach was a little shy, but when she saw all the candy, she started running from house to house. We did Mai's block; then we got in the car and drove up to the hills.

Fortunately, Russ Nelman did not recognize me, and I don't think he'd ever seen Rachel. He handed me one of the "fun-sized" Milky Way bars I'd bought and left on his kitchen counter. All he said was, "Grandma, what big pearls you have." I didn't dare say a word. I had the camcorder ready to record anything shocking, but when I peeked in, I saw that he was alone, eating something out of a Styrofoam container, drinking his third beer, and watching Dan Rather. I took all this as a hopeful sign.

Then, just to be sure, before taking Rachel to get her stuff X-rayed, I stopped at one house in Oakland. Cherry Saunders was there with Akin and a bunch of his friends who were having a party. Of course she was one of those moms who would give her kid a Halloween party. She probably even made him trick-or-treat for UNICEF.

She held out two baskets. One had raisins and one had chocolate bars. "Does your mom let you eat candy?" she said.

"This isn't my mom. This is my friend," Rachel answered.

I stood there terrified that she was going to say my name.

"Candy," I muttered quickly, and grabbed a couple bars and threw them in Rachel's goody basket. I took her hand and started to leave, but Cherry yelled out, "Just a minute."

She reached for another basket and held out a tiny kit with a portable toothbrush and a little tube of toothpaste. "Candy is all right," she said, "but what do you do afterward?"

"Brush my teeth!" yelled Rachel, and took the kit.

"Happy Halloween," called kind, considerate, healthy Cherry Saunders.

On the way home, Rachel and I sang "The Eensy Beensy Spider" three times, once in pig Latin. When I dropped her off, she ran to the house, stopped, turned around, and said, "My favorite lady was the toothpaste fairy."

<h2 style="text-align:center">36</h2>

All the way down to LA, I kept trying to imagine what it would be like to be in the same room with Cher, how hard it would be to look her in the face and keep from smiling and saying dopey things like, "Wow, you're Cher." I wondered if she'd actually be nice. What if we hit it off, became friends? Me and Cher, my old pal Cher. I realized that I spent almost as much time imagining having friends as I did imagining having sex.

Neil had already flown down, and he picked me up at the Burbank airport in a rented jet-black Jaguar. He kissed me but I held my jaws tight. "You look great, babe. Relax. My car's being fixed. I got an estimate of maybe two grand. You can cover that. So relax."

"Of course. I said I would cover it. I feel nervous about this meeting." I spoke candidly because I felt closer to Neil since the marriage of our cars.

"Don't worry, this project is a goer. Cher told me again last night that she was more excited about this than any part she's done since *Mask*."

The Santa Anas were blowing, and had I only been a symbolist, I'd have read some meaning in all that hot air. It left enough visibility to see the mountains, but not enough to see what Neil was up to. On the way to our meeting, the car phone rang. In LA there are phones everywhere—rental cars, poolside lounges, and for some reason, always in bathrooms.

"Hi, Neil Blender here. What's shaking? . . . Oh. Oh, too bad. You sure? . . . Yeah, she's just here for the day. . . . OK. OK. I understand."

He gave me a look. Neil Blender always gave looks.

"Bad news. Cher can't make it today. She's taping her special. But if you can stay for the weekend, she'll meet us on Saturday."

"I told you, Neil, I've got this special thing I must do this weekend. My whole relationship depends on it. I thought you were driving Bree up to the wine country on Friday anyway."

"Well, I guess you have to decide what's more important. Making this project happen or hanging on to that guy. Choices. That's what it's all about, babe."

I thought: I've got you, babe, but I didn't say anything.

After a while, he said, "If it were me, you know I'd pick you over the black chick."

Bree must have told him. I wondered how much.

We drove to Century City and rode up an express elevator to the top of one of the tallest buildings, to the offices of Century's End Productions. A gorgeous blonde greeted Neil like an old friend. He gave her a respectable peck on the cheek, but added, "There's more where that comes from."

Tod Fuelle was about twenty-eight. He was wearing a baggy pink shirt and tight black slacks, and his hair was dyed jet black, greased back, and tied in a high ponytail. Although he had a large desk, he was seated on a rawhide couch across from two matching easy chairs. The entire office was decorated in a rancho motif. Chief Swift Running and Harry Gurvitz must be smiling down at this from the Happy Hunting Ground. Over in one corner was a wooden cart with wooden wheels. On it were piles and piles of manuscripts. I caught the title "Bullshit II" on the binding of one screenplay.

After Neil introduced us, Tod asked, "Can Serene get you something? Perrier? Diet Coke?"

"I'll have some coffee, Tod," Neil said.

"I'll have diet Coke," I added.

"Very good," Tod said, like the waiter he once was. "Well, I've looked at your treatment. . . ." and after a long, long pause, he said, "Interesting."

The blonde brought us the drinks. She was one of those women who walked on heels so high, and managed with nails so long, that her very functioning under such handicaps spoke of an unstoppable determination.

In a few minutes, Slow-go Rosenbloom came running into the room. "Oh, Laura, you look fabulous. And after all you've been through. I mean, the earthquake was enough, wasn't it?" He kissed me on the lips as if he were checking to see if I feared contamination.

He plunked himself on the couch next to Tod, and at Tod's urging he began. "So, Laura, you realize that Tod is very interested in this project, but there's some confusion over Dirk and Bree's compliance. Now, just to reiterate, you have no signed agreement with them?"

"That's right." .

Then Neil added, "And it is possible that they may refuse to cooperate. Bree is a very savvy attorney and may go after you if you proceed without her cooperation."

"Well, yes," I said. "I hadn't thought about it. She had originally encouraged me to go ahead with the screenplay I submitted to you, Slow-go, but that was a while back—before the breakup."

"And before Del Warfield," Slow-go added.

"Right." Tod lunged forward and began talking animatedly. "See, I see the whole story changing now. I see it as a story not about lifestyles or yuppies getting older and weirder but about how a marriage can be saved. I think relationship salvage is a hot subject these days. Divorce is just not appropriate in today's economy. Too risky. I think people are interested in a comedy about the staying-together lifestyle."

"Yes! Yes!" said Neil.

"I really think you're onto something," said Slow-go.

"Laura," Tod said, shooting his BB eyes my way, "what's

happening with Dirk and Bree? Are they going to get back together or what?"

"Well, I don't really know. On Friday we're all supposed to go to a relationship renewal weekend in Sonoma led by this rabbi who's into Zen Judaism."

Tod Fuelle burst out laughing. Neil and Slow-go did too. "Zen Judaism. I love it! I'm dying." Then he turned to Neil and said, "Are you writing this down?"

Neil started writing.

"And what's this I hear about them going back on Del Warfield?" Tod asked me.

"It's my understanding that a follow-up show has been scheduled in a few weeks," Neil answered for me.

Tod Fuelle suddenly stood up. We three stood up too. "So, this sounds very promising," he said. "Then—we'll be in touch."

On the way back to the airport, I asked Neil what it all meant. It was over so quickly.

"Oh, meetings are always like that. You figure out what it means in a couple months when the check does or doesn't come."

37

Life is like that. You really don't know what's going on until you get the payoff. And sometimes, you realize you had the payoff and didn't even know it.

I was thinking about Russ Nelman.

It was very foggy as we drove up toward the Valley of the Moon. Rod and Mai were surprisingly tense.

"You should have turned there."

"Mai, don't tell me how to drive."

"I'm just trying to save you from the big jam up in Vallejo.
You always forget about that."

"I've driven this road more often than you have."

"Well, if you don't make your move here, the other drivers
aren't going to let you in."

"We have plenty of time."

"Not if you keep driving this way."

I suppose they were thinking what I was thinking—something would happen this weekend and it might take a while
to realize the payoff.

I didn't really know what to expect, but I knew I would be
sharing a bed with Russ. One more time was really all I
needed. Then I could get on with my life's work, the semiotics
of Dirk and Bree.

By the time we turned off the highway and into Leafy Creek
Lane, it was dark. We went through the old iron gates, first
up the hill, then down to the restored dollhouse that was the
Inn. We each carried our bag and entered solemnly, like
soldiers arriving for boot camp. The clerk at the desk was
dressed in a long red velvet period gown.

"Hi, I'm Mina Snell. Welcome to the Inn at Leafy Creek.
Are you three here for the marriage renewal with Rabbi
Birnbaum?"

You three? She was so cool and nonjudgmental.

Rod and Mai went to their rooms. I entered ours appre-
hensively, but Russ wasn't there yet. What if he didn't show?
How embarrassing it would be to face the others. If he didn't
come by midnight, I would just walk down to the highway
and quietly hitch a ride home. And if I was picked up by a
maniac, who was left to care if I got killed?

I knew I shouldn't be thinking in that defeatist, negative
way. I kept remembering something Mai said about Cherry
Saunders: "She's the kind of person who tries to do something
positive every day, to work on things rather than complain-
ing." What could be said about me? "She's the kind of person
who tries to bitch and moan every day, to complain rather
than try."

See, I just couldn't stop.

There was no TV in the room. No radio. Just a four-poster bed, a marble washstand with a basin and a pitcher of water, an armoire, and a painting of a nude fat lady.

I sat down on the bed and leaned back casually. I wished I had brought something to read so it wouldn't look as if I were sitting there desperately waiting for him, as I was. I propped up the lacy pillows and put my feet up, but then I realized it would look stupid to have my shoes on, so I kicked them off. For a moment, I considered the effect of having Russ open the door and find me lying there stark naked. But what if the rabbi or Dirk came in? Or what if Russ walked in and rejected me? Sexual rejection was the worst. I pictured a letter from an editor beginning, *Thank you for letting us take a look at your article, "What Women Think About During Fellatio," but I'm afraid it isn't for* Working Mother.

Another reason not to undress: it was freezing. There was a little fireplace in the room, but I wasn't sure if I should light it.

I had actually gotten my hair done at a beauty shop—or a style center, as they say. I went out and bought a new dress— a very plain little black silk dress—that would make even a sow look good. I was definitely giving it the old college try. Of course in college, I had always catered to Larry, my old boyfriend, and his idea of a good time. Larry—for a good time try handcuffs.

I noticed a little folder leaning against the water pitcher, labeled "Laura and Russ." It had a picture of a heart that was half black and half white, like a yin/yang heart, and it said, "Welcome to the Love Game." Inside were a number of papers, including a weekend schedule. The welcoming dinner was to start in about half an hour with wine and cheese in the parlor. Maybe I could just slip out the back now. Maybe he really wasn't coming and I could spend the rest of my life figuring out whether I had finally gotten what I deserved. Maybe I really did deserve to be alone. But then, look at all the schmucks who are rewarded. It's enough to make you believe in an afterlife.

While I was wondering if I would get a better deal in heaven, Russ showed up. He just said, "Hi," and handed me a dozen red roses. I put them in the water pitcher and didn't even mention that I saw the guy by the highway selling them for two bucks a bunch. They didn't have to last forever, they just had to make it through the night.

He put his bag down and said, "Well. How have you been?"

"OK," I said. I wanted to jump him. Could he tell? I showed him the program and said, "Dinner's in half an hour. Here's the welcoming message. It says we're supposed to read this together."

Welcome to the Love Game
This is a weekend for mutual discovery and pleasure. While we set down no rules that cannot be broken, we do have some suggestions. One is that you try to refrain from lovemaking and intense discussion until at least after dinner. Two, that you make an effort to participate in games and rituals that may seem silly to you. Three, that you enter this experience as a quest for pleasure as much as for understanding.
Om. Shalom.

Russ sat next to me. "Good. I'm glad he's made that clear. So, aren't you going to ask me how *I've* been?"

"I did already."

"No you didn't. Listen, I do want to say something not too intense to you, Laura, which is that I missed you a lot."

Then he went to his bag and pulled out an extremely tiny portable TV. He set it up next to the bed, and there in the lovely century-old room was the familiar lipless face of Dan Rather saying, ". . . Contrara offered no explanation for the carnage other than the fact that he thought his wife was cheating on him. School officials say the school will remain closed as survivors meet with counselors. . . . Wall Street today was down sharply in record volume. . . ."

Russ smiled at me and took off his glasses. I didn't want to tell him about how things had not been going well between

Dan and me. So I said, "I can't believe you brought a TV.
That is so sweet. Do you know what it means to have Dan
Rather here?"

"Is that Dan Rather?" he said, squinting his eyes and trying
to see the tiny screen. "All I see are two breasts."

He leaned over and kissed me. I could taste the Scope on
his breath. He must have done it in the car. "Shelly said we
shouldn't until after dinner," I said. "I think we should try to
play by the rules."

"Laura, I really want you back. I don't think one indiscre-
tion the week of a major earthquake should be considered a
breach of our relationship."

"Then are you through with her?"

"I thought Shelly didn't want us to talk about anything
heavy till after dinner."

"I just want to know where things stand."

"Look, where things stand is, I want you very badly. You
know it's just about impossible for me to be here with you
and not want to undress you. All the way up here, I thought
of being with you."

And as he said this the eensy beensy spider was inching
up my leg, under my skirt, heading home. I stood up slowly,
without losing contact, and took off my dress. Oh yeah, I had
bought a new black lace bra and matching panties that morning too.

"Oh, you look so beautiful," he said. I let him take off my
new stuff. For a minute, don't ask me why—the mind is such
a trickster—I pictured Dirk in them.

Russ was on his best considerate-lover behavior. Slow
down? He could slow down. More pressure *there?* More pressure there. Stand up? Want to try it standing up?

I was leaning against the wall and I could hear voices in
the next room. It was Dirk and Bree. Neil Blender delivered
her on time and I made sure that Dirk had the gift, specially
made matching exercise suits. I could hear some laughter and
then it got very quiet. I imagined that they were kissing about
now. Maybe Dirk was getting into her underwear. Literally.

I didn't believe he'd never done that before the time Russ caught him in my bed. Yes, Dirk had removed Bree's bra and was wearing it as he touched her. I could actually hear Bree say, "Oh, that's so wild," as Russ held me. He was able to reach me as I bent against the wall and heard Dirk cry out, "God, Bunny, God."

Russ made sure I was coming first before he moved in for the kill. We were both too lost to see Dan Rather smirking his way across America to our little room of a hundred years ago, saying, "Have a good weekend."

"Yes, yes," said Bree.

We realized when we heard Dan say that we were going to be late for dinner, so we quickly put our clothes back on. Russ asked me why I was remaking the bed, and I explained, "In case Shelly comes in to check."

Shelly was standing down in the parlor, wearing what looked like a space suit, and his wife, Myra, was dressed in some similarly futuristic mini-dress. I couldn't tell if they were going for *Star Trek* or *The Jetsons*.

The wine was the local Leafy Creek label and I chose a nice Chardonnay. You could also have the Merlot. Mina Snell, in her Victorian gown, and Myra Birnbaum, in her space cadette dress, walked around the room serving warm herbed-cheese puffs. We chitchatted and drank, and then just before dinner, Shelly asked us to form a circle and join hands. I found myself in between Bree, who was wearing a white silk dress, and Dirk, who looked well-heeled in a powder-blue cashmere V-neck. Dirk took my hand and I turned to look at him. Dirk, who never smirked, had a silly little lopsided grin. Was it an I-know-what-you-just-did grin? I wondered if he had heard us while I was hearing them. Perhaps we were all basking in the same afterglow. It was as close to an orgy as it gets in a bed-and-breakfast.

Russ was across the room and had to hold hands with Mina and Mai. Rod looked extremely uncomfortable between the rabbi and Mr. Snell, who was dressed in an old-fashioned suit with a vest and a watch chain.

"Friends, lovers, and survivors," Shelly began. "I want everyone to close their eyes and take a very slow, very deep breath." I peeked and saw Russ peeking at me, and we exchanged conspiratorial smirks. "Now I want everyone to let go of the hands of those people next to you. Everyone take three more deep, deep breaths. One. Slowly, from the third shakra or the waist of your schmata. Two. From deep inside. Take another—three. Now let us stand very still. Let us hear the clock tick and think about love through all of time, from the couple who once built this house to those who will fly here by heliscooter in the next century. This is our theme: Love exists beyond time, beyond space, beyond rules. Now, I want all those people who had intercourse before dinner to open their eyes."

The last sentence startled me, and I opened my eyes to see everyone else standing there wide-eyed except for our hosts, the Snells. We all started laughing. Shelly had the loudest laugh I've ever heard. As he was guffawing he went around and hugged everyone. It was like that moment in a Jewish wedding after the groom smashes the wineglass with his foot—silence, then a kind of pandemonium of exhaling, sighing, and backslapping. The Snells finally opened their eyes and left the room.

We went into the little dining room and had dinner. First, pumpkin soup served in a pumpkin shell. Then a smoked lobster salad arranged on the plate like a little lobster. The main course was very thin slices of garlicky roast lamb, new potatoes seasoned with fresh rosemary, and a salad of dandelion greens, artichoke hearts, and slices of avocado. For dessert each couple got a tiny flan to share. It was molded like a heart, and one half was glazed in caramel and the other pure white—the yin/yang theme. Shelly insisted that we each drink no more than three glasses of wine, and everyone had to drink three large glasses of the Leafy Creek label water. We finished with some herbal tea, which Shelly said would help prevent hangover. Dirk, of course, drank only water.

After dinner, we were to go to our rooms and Shelly would

personally come up to tuck each of us in and have a brief
good-night chat. When we got to our room, we discovered
that someone had started a fire and left a bowl of fruit. The
roses were in a little glass vase and there was fresh water in
the pitcher.

I put on the purple silky nightgown I also bought that
morning. Russ just slept in his boxer shorts and T-shirt. We
got under the down comforter, and it was so cozy we were
almost asleep when Shelly Birnbaum came in. He was wearing
his pajamas and robe, but he also had on a prayer shawl and
a yarmulke.

He sat down on my side of the bed and hugged me good
night. "Laura, what do you most wish to get out of this
weekend?"

"I guess I want Russ to say that he will not see anyone else.
That he's sorry he cheated on me. That he loves me and wants
to marry me. And I want to see Dirk and Bree get back
together."

"It's good to know what you want." He hugged me again
and then got up and walked over to Russ's side. I think he
sensed that Russ was not into male hugging, and just asked
him what he wanted.

"I want Laura to come home. I want her to forgive me. I
want to make love to her several times. I want her to con-
centrate on someone other than Dirk or Bree."

Shelly patted his shoulder. "It's good that you both know
what you want. But sometimes getting what you want will
only make you want more. For this weekend, try to comfort
each other as if neither of you were part of the other's wanting.
Try to get some rest. Tomorrow we'll go on a picnic and you'll
get to talk about your wants for hours. But now, please cuddle
up to each other and relax."

He stood up next to the bed. "Breathe in very slowly and
breathe out very slowly. Good. In and out. In and out. Let
your feet float, your legs float, let your pelvis float, your chest
relax, your arms go limp, your neck go soft, and let your head
and mind just become space. Space . . ."

I don't know how long he stayed there. I was a goner. All
I can remember is part of a dream in which I was sent to
heaven. It looked a lot like the Jersey Shore.

In the morning, I wanted to talk about things before we
were in the group, but the schedule said we were to put on
comfortable clothes and come to breakfast first thing. I went
down the hall and took a quick shower. I ran into Dirk and
Bree walking quickly and determinedly in the matching pale
blue sweats.

"Hi," I said, and they didn't even answer. When they
walked past me, I saw that her sweatshirt had *Bunnynose*
printed on the back and his said *Wildthing*.

There was coffee and tea in the parlor, and Shelly said
anybody who wanted to could have a little to drink before we
did our morning exercises. I sat down next to Mai and said I
thought things were going really well. Mai said she thought
Shelly was very clever.

"Look," she went on. "He gets to have his weekend in the
country and play God and camp counselor. He ought to wear
a whistle instead of a mezuzah."

Mai did have an edge to her, and I was surprised that even
this weekend hadn't knocked it out of her.

"I'm sorry, Mai. My sarcasm's in the shop today. I'm in
love with the world."

"Well, if it works for you, great. But I've been to one too
many workshops for anything to do me any good—although
the second wine last night was a kick. Not that I would know
good wine from diet Coke."

"Shall we begin," Shelly called.

We followed him into the dining room, which had been
cleared out. There were mats all over the floor, and Shelly
told each of us to take a mat and do some stretches and some
yoga. That got us all relaxed, and then, when we were lying
there, he told us to begin to imagine things. "Imagine your
tension is a tiny army of soldiers living in your nose. I want
you to keep inhaling and exhaling deeply until the last soldier
marches out. . . . Now I want you to imagine you are survivors

of a war, a terrible war. Your village has been ravaged, your
loved ones have disappeared, and now the war is finally over,
and you are walking down the road of your ruined town.
Suddenly, just over the bridge at the edge of town, a figure
appears, walking in the mist. You run through the fog, through
the mist, toward the figure. When you get up close, you
realize it is your lover. This is the first time you both know
you have survived the war. Think of what you want to say to
your lover. . . ."

"You jerk, Dirk. Don't tell me the problem is my sexuality.
The problem is your sexuality." It was Bree. She stood up on
the mat next to Dirk, kicked him in the pants of his *Wildthing*
workout suit, and then stalked out of the room.

I saw Shelly nod to Myra, and she followed Bree up the
stairs. He said, "OK. Now is not the time to imagine. I want
each of you to follow me out on the path for a run. If anyone
has any problems like back pain or knee problems, please do
not run. Merely walk briskly. The path is marked, and if you
get lost, I'll find you. It's not necessary to keep pace with the
others. Just be sure to get your pulse up to about a hundred
and twenty. If you don't have a watch with a second hand,
just feel your pulse and see if it's got a good beat—somewhere
between reggae and bebop."

We followed him out the door, and pretty soon we were
going down a road thick with madrone and tan oak and live
oak. It ran along the creek, which was almost dry and appeared
to be filled with leaves. A little voice in my head said, "Hence
the name—Leafy Creek." We ran very slowly for about half
an hour. Since there were only two showers, we drew numbers when we got back. I was last.

While I was waiting, I went to Bree's room. I hadn't seen
Bree cry much in the past, but she was doing it now. "Dirk
claims I'm too rigid. He wants me to consider things I'm not
comfortable with."

"What kind of things?"

"Oh, I don't know, things he's seen in Richard Gere movies,
like taking a bath together. I think it's stupid. He wants me

to prove my love by experimenting with scents. He also wants
me to be supportive of his starting yet another business. I
just don't think that's fair."

"Do you think he's too demanding?"

"I just don't think I can trust him, especially with money.
He's like a child. And if I don't go along with everything he
wants, he'll leave me."

"Why would he do that?"

"Neil told me he thinks Dirk is just waiting to get his hands
on my inheritance, that Dirk as much as told him that."

This did not sound like the plan Neil and I had discussed
to get Dirk and Bree together. This sounded like the plan
Neil Blender had to get his share of Bree's inheritance. For
a smart woman, Bree Wellington was incredibly naive.

"But why would you trust Neil Blender?"

"Because he is devoted to pleasing me."

"Sexually?"

"In every way. He told me that he's always going to love
me, and that he'd wait for me regardless of whether or not
Dirk and I get back together. He says he'll never marry anyone
else, even if it means being a bachelor the rest of his life."

What a sacrifice, I thought. "Listen, Bree, I know for a fact
that Neil is as interested in writing about you and Dirk as I
am. As a matter of fact, we've been working together on this."

"Get out of here, Laura!" she screamed. "Get out!" From
the corner of my eye I noticed a vase in the room, and the
next time she yelled, "Out!" I beat it.

She had a right to be mad, but she should be as mad at
Neil Blender as she was at me. He's the one who's been
screwing with her head. She ought to scream at him, Dirk
ought to scream at me, and I ought to scream at . . . I guess
at myself. In fact, why isn't everybody walking around screaming all the time? I'd have to ask Shelly that. Somehow, I
thought he'd have an answer. He was a take-charge kind of
rabbi. As silly as he seemed, Shelly was there to fill a gap, to
perform a safe-psyche function, to lead the lost lambs of the
baby boom back to God. If he made us feel good, we'd let
him have his spiel.

When we all met down in the parlor again, Bree looked more composed. Mai looked good, but she seemed nervous, as if she was trying very hard to keep her mouth shut. She had spent some time on her hair and put on a little makeup, which was unusual for Mai. Rod looked incredibly uncomfortable, as if he was afraid of what would happen next. Bree and Dirk did not look at each other. Russ looked so fine.

Shelly held up three backpacks and explained that each was filled with a wonderful picnic lunch. He was going to drive us to a nearby state park, and each couple would be sent off on a specific hiking trail. We were to stay on the trail, walk for about an hour, find a nice spot for lunch, and walk back. We were to talk to one another about love—what it meant, what we were looking for, and how to reconcile the wishes we had explained to him last night. The game part of this exercise was that he was mixing up the couples. I would go with Dirk, Russ would go with Bree, Rod would go with Myra, and Shelly would go with Mai. The Snells had withdrawn from any further participation.

Well, this had to be the stupidest idea I'd ever heard. Bree looked amused, and grabbed her pack and walked over to Russ. To my horror, I realized that Russ looked absolutely delighted as he went out the door with Bree Wellington and her totally perfect legs.

We all got in the minivan and off we went into Shelly Birnbaum's wild blue yonder. It was the sabbath and I believe the rabbi was smirking.

38

The whole thing was too weird, like some kind of school field trip or something.

Shelly dropped off Dirk and me first at the Redwood Trail. There was a little sign that said "Mirror Lake, 2.3 Mi.," and we decided to head that way. Dirk, who looked as chagrined as I did and was in a really bad humor, extended his hand as if to say, "After you."

I said, "Oh, please lead the way."

I followed his heavy steps along the path, which was quite narrow with all the late-summer overgrowth, and dry from the lack of rain. I would have to get Dirk. He was quiet, and his anger gave him an aloofness I found extremely attractive. But—no. Uh-uh! That's the last complication we needed. Even I wasn't that stupid.

Besides, he didn't seem the least bit interested in me today. As far as his behavior went, I was just his wife's girlfriend. He was completely preoccupied with Bree. Finally, he said, "She's really being stubborn, isn't she?"

Dirk was marching so fast I nearly ran out of breath just trying to keep up with him. "We-e-ll. We're supposed to talk about love."

He started singing "Why Do Fools Fall in Love." I sang along, and when we were finished, I segued into "Love Me Do," which he segued into "Love Makes You Do Foolish Things." We continued our Vegas-lounge-act hike for about an hour. He stopped in the middle of "Can't Buy Me Love" and said, "How are you paying for this weekend?"

"You mean like VISA or check?"

"No, I mean, are you paying for yourself, or is Russ?"

"He paid for the two of us. Why?"

"Oh, it's just that Bree won't pay."

I thought that was a strange thing to say. Why should Bree pay? Dirk was into the second verse of "Love Potion Number Nine."

The lake turned out to be nothing but an algae-covered pond, so we turned on a little side trail and hiked up to the peak. It was windy and grassy, and we sat down to eat our lunch. There were Jarlsberg cheese sandwiches on baguette with spicy mustard. A small twist-top bottle of red wine, and another of water. There were also some beautiful apples, a bag of almonds, and two little madeleines. So far, the weekend

got four stars for food, three for ambience, and one for the
therapy.

I asked Dirk if he had seriously considered what would
happen if he and Bree split. He said it was very hard for him
to talk about it.

"I have a lot of paranoia about divorce because I see how
it affects other people, their children, and their lifestyle. I
can see what would happen if we got divorced now, and that
makes the possibility of it very threatening."

"I don't understand. Why is divorce still a possibility? It
seemed like you had patched it up. It sure looked like it last
night—and sounded like it."

"I knew you were listening."

"You did?"

"I know you. You're a snoop. I have to tell you, I could
hear you too." His laugh was a shade on the maniacal side.

I took a swig of the red wine. There were two plastic glasses
in the pack, but we seemed to have fallen into the intimacy
of a shared bottle.

"So what do you know about love?" I asked him, and he
immediately went into "I Know Something About Love." "It's
hard to talk about, isn't it?"

"Yeah. I don't get Shelly's game. You can hardly talk about
love with your lover, so why should you talk about it with a
stranger? Not that you're exactly a stranger, Laura."

"I sort of am. I've talked to you and Bree a lot about you
and Bree, but not about me. In a way, it is as if we *are*
strangers."

"Well, since knowlege between people is mutual, a back-
and-forth kind of thing, share a little bit of yourself with me.
It won't kill you. It won't break the rules of journalism—but
you've already broken those, haven't you? What is it you're
looking for with Russ? I know this is hard, but try."

"I think what I'm looking for in love is a family—you know,
mama, papa, sister, brother—a whole family in one person."

"Yeah, I suppose family is what Bree and I and Rachel
Whoopi had. It's important to me because my mother is gone

and my father is still working hard at his fur business, but we can't even talk about that without getting into a fight about the immorality of it. All Bree has is her mother, and her father back east. When we were a couple, it didn't matter so much if we were supportive of each other. When you have kids, you also want a co-conspirator, someone who'll back you up. Bree really didn't do that for me. For example, right now, I'm trying to start up a new business, I'm trying to raise capital, and instead of being supportive, she keeps berating me."

"But Dirk, you know that she'll eventually come around."

"With money?"

"I thought you meant emotional support."

"Money's what I need right now."

"I want a child," I said, surprising myself. "I didn't think I did until recently. I even used to be defensive about how it was basic to my identity to be without a kid. I don't know, it just changed. You know, my father died last week, when I was in Hawaii."

There, I'd finally said it. It was real. Dirk looked up and told me he had no idea I'd been going through that. "How are you dealing with your pain? You shouldn't hold it in."

"Yes, well, I've been trying to think of a way to keep his memory alive, and a child seems like the logical route. Now that I've decided I want one, I'm in a panic to get one. I'm like that. I put things off and then, boom—got to have it. It seems as if at the exact moment I realized this, Russ pulled away from me. God, why am I telling you this?"

"It's like that in a relationship. It's like dancing—you move forward and she moves back. I think you're telling me this because you feel a need to heal your relationship with Bree and me."

Something about that statement made me squirm and look at my watch. I saw that it was almost two o'clock. "Hey, we'd better start back. Didn't Shelly say he was coming at three?"

On the trail, we resumed our love song medley with "I Just Called to Say I Love You." As we passed the fake lake I said, "Oh yeah, don't forget . . ." and started in on "Sea of Love."

We were in the middle of "It Hurts to Be in Love" when I stopped singing and said it: "We're lost."

We had somehow veered off the trail and ended up on a paved road. We tried to backtrack, but couldn't seem to find where we had entered it. I guess neither of us had been paying attention. The road was in disrepair, and it wasn't clear whether any cars could drive on it.

We exchanged a number of theories about which way the sun would be in relation to which way we wanted to go, but neither of us was exactly a mountaineer. I began to suspect that this was some Birnbaum plot, part of the game, a Zen metaphor for love. It could even be the Love Wilderness Quest I had thought of subjecting Dirk and Bree to. But what's the point of sending people on a love quest who aren't interested in each other? The longer I spent on a date with Dirk the more I missed Russ.

"Look," I said, pointing to the next ridge. "A cabin."

As we walked toward it, it seemed to be farther and farther away. It took us almost thirty minutes to reach it. The cabin was a very rustic one-room job with a stone chimney. There was an old rusted-out Ford pickup with four very flat tires parked in front. At first, I thought the cabin was abandoned, but then I noticed there was a power line hooked up to it, and a huge satellite dish sat out back near what was once an outhouse. When we knocked at the door, an old man with an unkempt beard opened it. "Yeah?"

"I'm sorry," I said. "We seem to have gotten lost. We were on the trail from the lake and I guess we took a wrong turn. Can you direct us back?"

"You really are lost," the man said. "Come on in."

Inside, there was a TV tuned to *Lifestyles of the Rich and Famous*. The man sat down in front of it, breathing heavily. He motioned to two chairs at a little table—vintage fifties Formica, I noted, a collector's item. I considered for a moment the idea of opening a Harry Gurvitz Formica Museum. That would be easier than having a child.

The old man told us to have a seat. We moved the chairs

next to him as he picked up the remote and pressed pause.

I realized he had *Lifestyles of the Rich and Famous* on tape. He put the remote down next to him on a table covered with prescription pill bottles. "Could I ask you to get me a glass of water?" he said to me.

I went over to the sink and rinsed out a dirty glass I found there. Next to the sink there were more pill bottles, and a huge bottle of Maalox sat next to a bottle of Worcestershire sauce and another of A-1. I wondered what the man did when lost hikers weren't there to fetch him his water.

"My name's Scotty," he said. He took the glass of water and very slowly opened a pill bottle. The lid was held on with a rubber band so he didn't have to screw it back on. His hands were so shaky I thought all the pills were going to spill, but he managed to get just one out and popped it in his mouth like an M&M. "They call me Sonoma Scotty. I've lived here since 1959. They had to put the park around me 'cause I wasn't moving. My wife, she passed in '79 and I've lived here alone ever since."

"Well, I'm Laura Gurvitz." I had been using Gurvitz more and more since the Warfield Fiasco, especially around known TV viewers. "This is my friend Dirk Miller."

"Relative of Joaquin? I knew another Miller once could drink tequila like it was water. You wouldn't know a fellow named Tipsy Miller, would you?"

"No, I don't, but it's a common name," Dirk said politely. "Miller."

"Yeah, Tipsy Miller worked in my vineyard but he liked his liquor strong. I had a little vineyard. That's what I was going to do for my retirement, but that big grower come and offered me good money, cash money, and my wife—Rose, that was her name—Rose says to take it. And now she's gone. Go figure it out."

"Mr. . . . Scotty, do you have a phone?"

"No phone, but we got power in '75 when they laid out the park. I did a little work caretaking, but now I don't walk so good. They got a nurse, comes once a week and helps me

"No sauna either, I suppose."

"No. It's all antiquey."

"Ah-ha."

We rounded a curve and Dirk yelled out, "Right here!"

We walked down the road toward the Inn. We were both excited, exhilarated. I guess Shelly had known what he was doing all along—it's too hard to talk about love with someone you love.

The road divided and we went on the upper road, which was one-way downhill. Dirk was whistling a song I remembered: "*I found love on a two-way street and lost it on a lonely highway.*" I went into "California Dreaming."

When we walked into the parlor, everyone was standing there. Even Shelly had lost his cool. "Where were you? We were just about to call the park rangers. We all prayed for you."

"Just took a wrong trail—sorry," I said.

"OK, OK, let's stay calm," Shelly ordered, obviously just a step away from panic. "Let's all go upstairs and get ready for dinner, at six-thirty sharp. That leaves you some time to share what you learned today."

Russ and I went upstairs, and the first thing I said was, "How was Bree?"

"Oh, what an iceberg that woman is."

"Really?" I said, perhaps too gleefully.

"She's nice enough, but boy, what a barrage of anger—a lot of it directed at you. She seems to think you were plotting the whole divorce thing. I almost got the feeling that she was going to patch it up with Dirk just to spite you."

"Are you kidding?"

"I'm not."

"Did you tell her that I was plotting to *stop* the divorce?"

"I did not."

"Then what did you tell her about me?"

We both lay down on the bed and stretched out. It was good to be home. For some reason, I felt as at home in the Inn as I'd felt anywhere in a long time.

Russ was looking ahead with his hands clasped behind his head.

"I told her you were great in bed."

"You didn't!"

"I did. I could tell it really pissed her off. Bree Wellington is one of those women who don't want to get messed up."

I sat up on my knees next to him. I took both his hands and messed my hair up as much as I could. "Make it worse!" I said.

39

That night, dinner was a much less formal affair—a buffet of salads, cold cuts, and bread. All good quality, but no wine. After we'd had our fill, we took our chairs and made a circle for discussion.

When Shelly asked who'd like to start, Dirk stood up. "I think getting lost was a good metaphor for what happened to me in the Love Game. I think I have been lost for the past seven years."

"So what are you saying?" said Bree, also standing up. "Are you saying, after all I've put up with, that the marriage has been a waste?"

"Now, just a minute," Shelly interjected. "There is an obvious defensiveness and anger in your tone that is not in the spirit I had intended this weekend."

"Back off, Shelly, the game is over. This is real. Let them speak." Mai Blender, even when she was off duty, took a kind of cheerleader role for emotional touchdowns.

I was hoping that things were not going the way they seemed. Of course, I'd been more or less hoping that for the past thirty-seven years. Shelly was really no match for Bree

Wellington when she was on fire, or for Mai Blender when she knew what needed to be done.

Myra Birnbaum concurred. "I told you you'd be weak at this, Shelly," she said.

"Myra, this is a necessary part of the cycle. Let's see it through."

"OK, Bree," Dirk began. "I think we both know it's been bad between us for some time. I also think we were afraid to admit it. I think the survival of our relationship depended on neither of us talking about our pain and our real needs, and that's why I sought escape in my computer. But we have a child, and we can't just turn her off now that things aren't working out."

"Just when did I ever want to turn her off? You're getting us mixed up. You're the one who's always telling her to go away, that you have important computer business. Ha! More important than real business, which you can't manage to handle."

Shelly made one more valiant try. "Look, Bree, I think you need to pause here and consider the possibilities—"

Mai cut him off. "Shelly, she doesn't care what you think."

Rod responded. "Mai, stay out of it."

Myra defended her husband. "He's only trying to help."

This was not the dialogue I wanted Dirk and Bree to have. Was this supposed to happen? Maybe the rabbi really had things under control, but I think at that point, we all wanted to just quietly slip out of there. Since that was impossible, we tried to remain invisible. We were in the middle of something that should have been private, and the hardest part was trying to figure out what to do with our eyes. I did a quick shoe survey. Two pairs of heels, one pair of flats, one pair of sandals, one pair of men's dress cordovans, and three pairs of running shoes. Then I did a detailed study of the chandelier— crystal with frosted glass cups holding the light bulbs, designed to give the illusion of candles.

Bree continued, "I'm really curious about this 'we know it's bad between us.' When did *we* realize it?"

Why didn't Dirk just run away from this fight like a man? He, the veteran of so many therapy groups, looked at her as if the roomful of people didn't matter. The support group had become a kind of arena for psyche exhibitionism, and Dirk was an experienced gladiator. "We realized it when the love-making stopped."

"And why do you think it stopped, huh?"

"Well, honestly, I think it's pretty clear the problem is your sexuality. You just aren't interested."

"*My* sexuality? *My* sexuality? I am so sick of this," Bree said, looking around the room for some kind of support. None of us provided any, but she continued as if we had.

"That's really a laugh, isn't it? Ha! The problem is *you*, Dirk. You are the big, fat selfish problem."

"Bree, I don't want to go further down this road."

"No, you don't want to continue when challenged, and that's always been the problem. You just walk away from a fight, from a request, from anything that's too *stressful*. Too stressful—that's what you always say. Just like in business, Dirk. Things start to go wrong and you want me to bail you out, give you more and more of my money."

"You know, Bree, I thought it was *our* money. And things are not just starting to go wrong, you know that. Recovery peaked last year."

"Not true. Not true. Other recovery-based businesses are still expanding."

"But they do incest. Incest is still big, but we don't do incest. At Recovery, Inc., we were known for our work with cocaine. That's why our profits nose-dived. And I'm really glad you brought this up in front of everyone—that I'm a loser. Why don't you tell them just how much money I lost?"

"I only started this discussion to please you. You say I never please you."

I couldn't take much more of this. "Why don't we continue this discussion later?" I suggested.

Shelly was happy for the support. "A very good thought,

Laura. Others may want to speak." Dirk and Bree went on as if we hadn't said a word.

"If you wanted to please me, you would have responded to me this morning."

"I said I wasn't in the mood in the morning."

"Yeah, except when *are* you in the mood?"

"OK. OK," Shelly shouted, standing and holding up his hands. "I want everyone to go to their rooms."

"Who do you think you are, our daddy?" Mai said. "Let them finish."

"Mai, I told you to stay out of it!" Rod yelled.

"You can't tell me what to do, Rod."

Rod didn't say another word—he just stood glaring at Mai. Bree broke first and went upstairs. Mai followed her, and then so did Dirk. Rod walked out the front door. Russ and I were filing out quietly, when I heard Myra Birnbaum remark to the rabbi, "This is not good for the Jews."

"Myra," he said, "where is it written that success is good for the soul?"

Tying my livelihood to the Dirk and Bree equation was probably the stupidest thing I've ever done. I can't stand it when relationships are not going well—mine or anyone else's. I never could stand to slug it out with anyone. When things turned ugly, I'd just call it quits. Once you noticed the relationship was flawed, what good was it? I never got that thing about *working* on a relationship. It shouldn't be work. If it was no good, why not just move on? If other people wanted to work it out, fine. Hell is for other people.

When we got to the room, I said to Russ, "Well, that's the first I heard of Dirk and Bree having money trouble. I guess it's the end of an era. I thought their financial life was rosy."

"Maybe that's at the bottom of the problem," he said. "It's certainly not our problem." I could hear some slamming noises in the next room. I went over to the wall that divided us from Dirk and Bree.

After a while, Russ said, "Sex—that isn't our problem."

"Mm-hmm." I said.

"You know, the problem wasn't really that I was having an affair. I was having an affair because of the problem. The problem was your affair, your imaginary affair with Dirk and Bree."

"But an imaginary affair is not the same as a real one."

"Oh yeah? With you it's worse. The problem is that you just don't seem to want to involve yourself in my life or see me as a whole person. I was just the latest write-in candidate for the boyfriend slot."

I was trying to listen to him, but I was also straining to hear what was going on next door. They weren't slamming anymore and they weren't shouting. Were they reconciling?

Russ kept talking. "I'm at a crossroads now in my work and I have decisions to make, decisions that affect you if you're going to be a part of my life. I have the chance to become chief of surgery for the whole northern region. That means less operating and more being an operator. It also means— Are you listening to me?"

I had placed my ear on the wall. I could hear crying. Was it Bree or was it actually Dirk? One of them was sobbing and saying, "It just isn't there." It was Dirk. I'm sure it was Dirk. "OhmyGod, I think he's going to leave her."

I noticed Russ running around the room, throwing stuff into his bag. I held up my finger as if to say: Just a minute. I'm getting something important here.

"Goodbye, Laurie," he said loudly.

"What?" I asked, losing wall contact with Dirk and Bree.

"You haven't been listening to me at all. I don't get you, Laurie. I just don't get you. You don't want a life of your own. You didn't come here to work on our relationship, you just used me as a ticket, your entry into Dirk and Bree's relationship. It was bad enough when I thought that you were just using me for sex. Do you know what you called me when we were making love last night?"

"What?"

"Dirk." He walked to the door. "Keep the TV," he said, and left.

I froze in my place. There would be no public scenes for us, no forcing anyone to talk about it. It would just fade to black.

I tried to tell myself I didn't care. Why then did I feel as if I'd been kicked in the stomach? I felt angry at the world, and I had no one to blame but myself. I buried my head in the pillow. I didn't want Dirk and Bree to hear me cry.

Around nine o'clock, Mai came into our room. "We're driving back now. Shelly has given up and left. Where's Russ?"

"He left. I don't want to talk about it. Can I drive back with you?"

"Oh, of course you can, Laura," she said.

"Right now?" I asked.

"Yeah. Rod's getting his stuff."

"And Dirk and Bree?"

"They left about half an hour ago."

I hadn't even heard them go out. "Together?"

"Together," she said, "but in silence."

We rode home with just the radio for noise. "We're talking with Dr. Ronny Weeks about which comes first: economic recovery or psychological recession? Go ahead, caller. . . ."

I hardly moved the whole way home. I wondered if I was feeling sorry for myself or absorbing the tension between Rod and Mai, or just grieving for Dirk and Bree and the fall of the House of Yuppie.

It helped a little that I finally had my period when I got back to Berkeley. I mean, not that it's an excuse or anything, but if our hormones don't mean something, then how come they're even there?

I didn't really want to be pregnant anyway. Even if a baby was the best way to carry on the memory of Harry Gurvitz, I was not one of those women willing to go it alone.

When I got to the house, Russ wasn't there, so I packed up all my belongings and then sat on the porch for a while, staring out at the city and the bay. It seemed kind of funny that the Bay Bridge was still lit up. You could see the place where it fell in during the earthquake. A light was missing there.

I found a room at the International Hotel in Berkeley. I decided it was time to get back to where I once belonged—on track, back to my career. The first thing I did on Monday morning was call Slow-go Rosenbloom. "I suppose you know Neil has signed a deal with Tod," he said.

"What kind of deal?"

"To do the, you know, Dirk and Bree thing."

"Whoa, wait a minute. That was my deal, Slow-go."

"I know, and I would have loved to make that deal for you, but Neil held all the cards—including a statement of consent from Bree Wellington, Esquire."

"That bastard! He knew what he was doing all along. And you—you were in on it."

"No way was *I* in on anything, except to remind him that it would have to be a completely different script than yours. No one is stealing your script. His isn't even a romantic comedy. It's like a John Waters psychodrama. You couldn't have written this."

"Was it because Cher wanted me out?"

"What Cher? Cher was never involved in this project."

"But Neil told me Cher was interested."

"Honey, Neil's a bullshitter. It's a professional skill."

I was pissed, but not entirely surprised. I guess I must be a masochist or a hormone zombie, because the next thing I knew, I was on the phone with Neil Blender.

"Thanks for paying the repair bill so promptly," he said. "The car is now in good enough condition to sell. Look, I wanted you in on this project, but you weren't available—even for the meetings. Century's End is a big company. They can't afford to get involved with an unknown writer who can't even make it to meetings."

"Neil, you engineered those meetings for times when you knew I couldn't make it. You knew I was in Sonoma this weekend. You convinced Bree I couldn't be trusted, and you manipulated her into signing that consent. You used the LoveNet to play games with us all. Don't bullshit me—tell it to Cher."

"Oh, yeah, Tod hated the Cher idea. He thinks her career has peaked. She's not hot anymore."

He just couldn't stop—a man who believed his lies. Maybe that's what it takes to write screenplays. Maybe I didn't have that. Maybe it was time to just go back to waitressing.

"Look, I'd still like you in on this. Why don't I come up there in a few weeks—after Dirk and Bree do Del again."

"They're doing the follow-up?"

"Oh, I guess they didn't tell you, huh? Yeah, the Warfield show is coming out to San Francisco for sweeps week. They're doing a bunch of shows on things that got saved after the quake. You know, the people of the Marina who were able to save their stuff, the Bay Bridge reopening, San Francisco coming back to life, and Dirk and Bree, the couple who saved their marriage."

"Then they've worked it out?"

"Babe, they put it in writing."

All this gave me an idea, and I called my book agent immediately. Neil wasn't the only manipulator on earth. So he has the screenplay. So he'll get the Academy Award. So he has a mint-condition classic Mercedes. I still had something. Maybe not a life, but at least a proposal.

40

Chuck Chernoff was like a fatter, balder, sleazier Neil Blender, and the effect was exponential. "You must be Laura," he said. While his kiss was dry, his hug was like barely acquainted rape.

Once I had freed myself from his embrace, he said, "We're crazy, crazy about your book. When's it out?"

I didn't tell him that it hadn't even been written yet, that I had just faxed the proposal to my agent the day I called him two weeks ago and that the deal had just been offered two days ago. "It should be out by next fall."

"And the research has all been done? I mean, you can talk about these things knowingly?"

"Absolutely."

"Good, good. Well, we better get you to makeup," he said.

"Is that necessary?" I asked, not bothering to tell him that I had already gotten my hair done and had put on all the makeup I owned, including eye shadow. I doubted that the human face could absorb any more makeup.

"I know you'll want to look your best, and besides, our people can do wonders. It'll be almost as good as getting a face-lift."

Did that mean I needed one? I wanted to know, but he quickly ushered me into a room filled with mirrors and lights.

"Oh God, another one," a makeup woman yelled. "We'd better work fast."

In a minute, one person had my hair sopping wet and wrapped in huge electric rollers, and another who literally had a palette, was mixing colors and trying them on my face.

"No, no, still too white," she said, looking at me.

"I've had that problem all my life," I said.

"I'm sorry—what's your name?"

"Laura Gloriana."

"Look, Laura, we've only got a few minutes until airtime, so I have to ask you to keep absolutely quiet while I do you."

I've always been contrary. Shut up to me meant start talking, and talk meant clam up. So I bit my lip as she painted my face and curled my eyelashes and combed my hair. When she was all done spraying, she wheeled me around to face the mirror. I thought I was going to scream—I looked like a late-nineteenth-century Parisian hooker.

She took me by the hand and we rushed into the greenroom. I saw the remains of a buffet I had missed and lots of empty wine bottles. Everyone gathered around a monitor as the Del Warfield theme song came on. Dirk and Bree were there, and I thought for a minute they were going to laugh when they saw me with all that makeup and my hair in a huge pouf. But Bree gave me a let's-not-mess-each-other-up hug. Even with her makeup, or perhaps because of it, I noticed that she was beginning to get aging lines around her eyes. Dirk squeezed my hand while keeping his face turned toward Bree. When I went to kiss him, he turned the other cheek. It was the first time I had seen them since the showdown at Leafy Creek.

Bree started to speak. "Laura, it's too bad . . ."

A man near the monitor said, "Shh-h-h," as the announcer began. "Live from San Francisco, it's the Del Warfield show. Coming to you today from the Palace of Fine Arts theater in the earthquake-ravaged Marina District before an audience of actual earthquake survivors . . ." He paused, and the picture changed from scenes of earthquake-damaged structures to the faces of the audience as they applauded themselves.

"And now here's our host, ready to leave her heart in San Francisco—De-e-el Warfield." After lots of applause, the Del theme song segued into, "*San Francisco, open your Golden Gate.*" Del bounced onto the set wearing a dress covered with hearts and the hat used in *Beach Blanket Babylon* with the entire San Francisco skyline on it. The set was a cable car stop, complete with cable car and one of the actual drivers clanging on the bell. Del took off the hat and handed it to him, and he clanged more of the San Francisco song. She sat down on a bench under an artificial palm tree—obviously someone from out of town's idea of Northern California.

When the applause stopped, she said, "Oh, Oh," and applauded the audience. "*You* deserve the applause—you are all survivors, like this great city of yours."

They applauded some more.

"Have we got a show for you on this our Salute to the Saving of San Francisco Week. First, Richard Simmons is going to be here to tell us how the earthquake has affected dieting in the Bay Area, and then he's going to show us how to make quake and bake chicken . . ." She paused for laughter.

"Yes. Quake and bake. Then—and this is something I'm really excited about—we have as our very special guests . . . Dirk Miller and Bree Wellington. Some of you may have seen their appearance two months ago when they came on to talk about their caring divorce and Bree got so excited she beaned him with a vase. That's what happens when you're caring enough to send the very best . . ."

Laughter.

"Notice we have no vases on the set today. Smart, huh? Huh?"

Applause.

"And we have another special guest. Writer Laura Gloriana, who wrote a book about Dirk and Bree and now has a new book, based on extensive research into marriage and divorce. The book is called *Salvation: How to Get What You Need out of Marriage.* After that, we'll have fashion expert Marla Freedkin to tell us about postquake fashions. And finally, Mr. Tony Bennett will be here to sing his heart out. I bet you can't guess what he'll sing. Does this sound fabulous? Stay with us. A city is saved. Next, on the Del Warfield show."

After the theme song died down, I grabbed a bottle of white wine and took a swig of the dregs. Bree walked over and said, "Laura, I'm sorry about what happened to you."

"Yeah. I blew it with Russ. He was the best."

"Russ? No, I meant about Neil. I swear I didn't know he was going to cut you out entirely. I'm sorry I signed that thing. I called him and he told me he's coming to see you to work things out."

"Thanks," I said, and took another swig. To tell the truth, I had been so busy trying to find an angle to get on Del Warfield's talk show that I forgot one thing: I had nothing to say. I mean, it was a great career move, unless I made a complete ass out of myself. It could happen. Del Warfield and company made Neil Blender look like a Boy Scout in the manipulations department. If they could do it to Bree, think of what they could do to me.

Just then, Chuck Chernoff came along and yanked the bottle away from me. "Careful, you'll smear your makeup. Come on, we're going on the set."

I followed him, and Dirk and Bree followed me. We walked through a maze of wires and boards and computerized lights. I almost fell and broke my neck when my heel caught on a wire. Chuck Chernoff caught me just in time. "Careful, Lau-ra. Care. Full."

We got to the stage as Richard Simmons was spoon-feeding some crab-a-roni from a Crockpot into Del's big mouth. "Mmmm. Mmmm. And you say that's only two hundred calories?" she asked.

"For you, Del, I made it a hundred and fifty."

The audience applauded. When the camera turned to Richard, an assistant ran out and held a napkin for Del to spit the concoction in.

"Mmm. You see, with food like this you can start dieting again, San Francisco. Can't you? Can't you?"

Applause.

"Let's have a big hand for Richard Simmons. He makes me laugh. He makes me thin . . ."

Chuck Chernoff said to nobody in particular, "He makes me sick."

"In a minute, the latest trend in saving here in San Francisco—saving your marriage. We'll have Bree Wellington and Dirk Miller here to talk about how their marriage was saved. And we'll have an expert in salvation—Laura Gloriana—who just wrote a book about it. Coming up on what's hot and what's not: Marriage Salvage, on today's Del Warfield show."

"OK, now. *Now.*" Chuck Chernoff hustled us onto the stage. When I looked out at the audience, I kind of froze. I wasn't sure if I was supposed to bow or wave or what. But with the camera off during the commercial, everyone seemed to understand that time had ceased to exist, that reality was on pause; the audience chatted, ignoring what was happening onstage. Dirk and Bree were seated on the bench next to Del.

"Hi," said Del, giving them each a hug. "Great to see you again. I'm really glad you could come back and patch this up. We're nonviolent today, right?"

She was smaller than I thought she'd be—and sweatier. An assistant came out and dabbed her with a tissue.

Another bench was pulled up next to the one Del shared with Dirk and Bree. I was seated there, and then Chuck Chernoff slipped a microphone wire down my blouse. "Nothing personal," he said with a smile, and clipped the mike near my cleavage.

He ran back as the theme song returned. The audience was recalled to life and asked to applaud. "Oh, isn't this wonderful?" said Del. "I love San Francisco. America's favorite city is back!"

Applause.

"Now, also back are Dirk Miller and Bree Wellington, once described as 'the first known North American Yuppies.' Welcome back, Dirk and Bree."

Bree said, "Hi, Del."

"Good to be back," said Dirk.

"And here is the person who first described Dirk and Bree that way. Marital expert Laura Gloriana. Welcome, Laura."

I twitched out a smile and said, "Hi."

Del faced her audience. "Now, some of you may remember that a few months ago, Dirk and Bree were on the show to talk about their caring divorce, when the caring turned to deep passion. Chuck, you want to run that tape."

From where I was sitting, I couldn't see the monitors. I could only watch the audience, who sat like wide-eyed children staring up in wonder. I could hear Dirk saying, ". . . I was home with the baby trying to run a business, trying to raise a child, and even trying to make a decent dinner . . ."

And then Bree's voice: "Maria was watching the baby. You were fooling around on the computer. The Mobile Gourmet was making us dinner. And I gave up a thriving law practice for you . . ."

The real audience sat in silence, listening to the taped audience boo and hiss as Dirk said, "The baby and I were just an excuse for your own inadequacies."

The real audience let out a collective gasp as they watched the tape of Bree breaking Dirk's nose. I looked back at Dirk and Bree, who were able to see the tape, and Bunnynose turned to Wildthing and shrugged, as if to say, "Gosh, sorry."

"So, Bree, want to tell us what happened after that?" Del asked.

"Well, I think it was simply that Dirk and I had more feelings for each other than we knew what to do with. I want to take the opportunity to say publicly: Honey, I am sorry."

Applause. I could see Chuck make the gimme-gimme hand gesture to the audience.

"Of course I regretted my behavior, but it did bring the nail to a head."

"Uh-huh," said Del, as if Bree had said something intelligible. "And you, Dirk, you must have had a lot of anger after this."

"No, Del, not really anger. All anger is really self-anger, and I chose to act that out by lapsing back into substance abuse. When I finally saw what was happening, I took control of my life and my wife."

"Well, I wouldn't say you took control of me," Bree interjected.

"No. No, of course I didn't mean control. I mean I took control of myself and that empowered me, helped me to help you so we both could take control of the relationship."

"So, what was it that saved your marriage? Didn't the earthquake have something to do with it?"

"Well, not really," said Bree.

Del Warfield shot an angry look at Chuck Chernoff, who wrote something on a card. An off-camera assistant passed it to Del while the camera stayed on Bree.

She continued: "The main thing that saved our marriage was that we came to realize we weren't behaving like a family. We were behaving like a couple who had a child living with them—we weren't really ready to change our lifestyle in any way. I think we thought that once our daughter was born, we would just go on and pencil her in when we had time. The rest of the time she would be in some magic land called Childcare. We forgot to consider that she had a mind of her own, and denying that nearly destroyed us."

"But come now," said Del. "Don't you have some news about how the earthquake played a part in this?"

"Oh, I know what you mean, Del," Dirk said, smiling. "Bree is pregnant."

The audience applauded. I wanted to scream.

Dirk went on, "And we think it happened—the conception, that is—during the quake. One of the strangest things about our decision to split up is that it was kind of an aphrodisiac."

"How does that work?"

"Oh, you know, Del, each kiss may be the last. Combine that with an earthquake and you've got a real turn-on."

I thought back to that day in the tub. Dirk had just arrived after the earthquake. I left them quarreling, and he left Bree shortly after that. There was no way they made love that day. But what was the point in saying that? She was pregnant and I was not.

"Wow, so the earthquake has really brought this family together." Del looked at the audience. "Is that incredible or what? Huh? Huh?"

Applause. Cheers.

"Let me ask our other guest something: Laura Gloriana, author, journalist, marital expert, your new book is called *Salvation: How to Get What You Need out of Marriage*—and by the way, I loved it—but tell me, is it really necessary to have an earthquake to save a marriage?"

"Not really, Del," I said.

She was waiting for me to go on. I realized I had absolutely no idea what to say. "Uh-huh. Uh-huh," Del said, looking at me.

Finally, Del picked it up. "So, what do you think other couples can learn from Dirk and Bree's experience?"

"Well, I guess that when you've got the time and the money, you can mess things up and put them back together."

"Can I say something, Del?" said Dirk.

"Please do. Please do." When the camera turned to Dirk, Del looked at Chuck Chernoff, pointed to me, and shrugged. He sent her another note.

Dirk began, "I wouldn't say we just put things back together. I think we have had a real growth experience. It has not only resulted in a new life, but a new business life as well. I am now CEO for California Dreamin', Incorporated, a major supplier of California lifestyle products on the international market, and Bree and I are joining with Century's End to produce a movie based on our experience. If it helps other couples, it'll be worth it."

"And worth it to you?" said Del. "I hear you have signed a deal to have Miller-Wellington Productions as executive producers on the movie *Parenting, Kidding, and California Dreamin*, a story of a couple who give up the yuppie lifestyle and return to family values. Now, is that hot or not?"

Applause.

"OK. I think we have a few questions from our audience on saving a marriage or saving anything in an earthquake. Yes, the lady with the fake-jade earrings in the third row."

The camera turned to the audience. "Yes. I wanted to ask Laura Gloriana what she thinks the problem is in most marriages."

Del gave me a look that said move it or lose it. "Laura?"

"Well, I think the biggest problem is not waiting your turn. You might think of marriage as a kind of open stage and only one person at a time gets to do their act. The problem comes when someone hogs the mike or someone won't wait. You can't both be on at once. I think what happened to Dirk and Bree is that they didn't realize they had to let the other take a turn."

Of course, that's what happened to Russ and me. I forgot about his turn.

"That's not true," said Bree.

"She doesn't know what she's talking about," said Dirk. "Ask her about her own experience with marriage."

Del was delighted to go for my jugular. "Well, Laura, what is your own experience?"

"I've never been married," I said.

The audience laughed.

"I never wanted to be married," I added. "I never believed in the institution. It seemed to be all compromise, and it ruined your sex life."

There were a few hoots from the audience.

"It doesn't have to, Laura," said Bree. "It can be good if you work at it, and if your sex life isn't the center of your existence, it can also free you up for other things."

"See, well, that's my problem," I said. It was as if I had forgotten where I was. It was as if I was answering the same therapist who'd pissed me off years ago. "See, the reason I make my sex life the center of my life is because it's easier to get it on with new people. Once you have to start working on it, then it's work, and I already have one job."

A man in the front row clapped; a few other people hissed.

Then Del said, "So, you really don't have anything to save?"

"Well, not exactly. I did have a relationship with a great guy, but I blew it when I found out he wasn't perfect. He nearly was, but when it got to that point where we had to talk about it and work on it and worry about it, I just gave up. But I'm sorry now, really sorry. I feel so lonely—I can't work, I can't write my book, I don't even care about being cut out of the screenplay. I haven't been able to write a thing for *Lifestyle*, except a piece about a sleazy judge which they wouldn't print. All I really wish is that I had my boyfriend Russ back."

Then I looked right in the camera and said, "Russ, if you're watching, I want you to come back. I don't care about other women. I don't care if we get married. I just want you and me and the TV turned down low."

I realized the inappropriateness of my speech, not to mention the unfeministness of it. I shut up and looked down at my new dress—it was stripes and polka dots.

The room was dead silent. No one laughed or clapped or hissed. It seemed as if minutes passed, but it was only fifteen seconds—just like the earthquake. Then the Del Warfield theme song came on and Del said, "Now, we're going to hear from our good friends at Nightengale, the douche that can make you feel like June in December. We'll be back to hear what they're wearing in the West and—yes, he's going to be here—Tony Bennett, the man whose heart is always in San Francisco. Don't go 'way."

Del went over to Chuck and yelled, "You're the one who booked her on the show! If you ever humiliate me with a guest like that again, you're out of here. Next time, read her book more carefully."

"Del, it was a last-minute thing. We were supposed to get Sara Southward, but she's in detox."

I ripped off the mike. Dirk looked at me and said, "Listen, I am really sorry for you, and for the way this has gone."

"Sorry for me? At least I'm not a liar. I know you didn't get pregnant during the earthquake."

"True, we just found out yesterday, but that's not the point. No one will remember or count the months. Laura, look, I have great respect for you as a writer. I still want you in on this movie."

"Well, what did happen? What got the two of you back together? Was it Neil? Were you jealous of him?"

"Me? Jealous of Neil? You're joking. Besides, Neil's a businessman, a competitor who's succeeding in a competitive business in a difficult time. I admire him."

"Then what was it, Dirk? It's not because Bree was jealous of me?"

"You flatter yourself. Frankly, we couldn't get a divorce. I wasn't about to take less than seven hundred for the house— at one point, it was worth almost twice that. It's got four baths, separate au pair room, a wine cellar, spa. It sits on half an acre. You might say the real estate market is a modern love potion."

Now my wheels were spinning. I saw a new book—*The Fall of the House of Yuppie*—the story of how Dirk and Bree stayed together not for the children but for the property. He could sense that I was plotting something.

"This information is strictly off the record, Laura. You won't be writing about us until we work out mutually satisfactory terms. Bree has obtained a restraining order preventing you from writing about us till then. The times have changed. We can't afford to give our life away anymore. Talk it over with Neil—we've authorized him to make you an offer."

And so, he was outta there.

41

Down but not out, down but not out. That was my mantra as I drove through San Francisco, which was back to normal—that promised land we all are striving for. But what was normal? Too much traffic, too many insane people, too many homeless people, too many stupid people, too many goods for sale, too much concrete, too many ugly tall buildings, and an incredible number of elegant old houses. A naturally blessed location, a place riddled with faults.

I had no normal to go back to. We had never been normal in my family anyway. My parents were too old. I was an only child who had never learned to share. My sex life depended on constantly inventing my own pornography. My career depended on my exploiting that pornography. And by the way, what career? I had proposed a book I was incapable of writing, I'd had a major blowup with Sean Garrison over the Judge Corman piece, and I had a possible screenplay deal if I kissed Neil Blender's behind—and who knows what else?

Down but not out, I told myself as I drove across the newly reglued Bay Bridge. I was on the lower deck, and if it were possible to hold your breath long enough to drive across it, I would. Instead, I just held a button.

Mai told me I had to stop playing these negative tapes in my head. Mai had certainly bounced back. The day after the renewal, Rod left her. She went on a diet and enrolled in a weights-training program. She cut her long, long hair and had it styled in a shoulder-length bob. She bought a whole new wardrobe. She redid the house. It was as if she were going to wash every last trace of the sixties away. Ha, that'll be the day.

I told her to wake me when she starts investing in the stock market. She told me she already had a little inheritance that she had some guy manage. She had made him sell the South African gold stocks but had kept the IBM. "I'm not going to sell low," she said.

That's when she told me to stop selling myself short. I don't know—I mean, what did I have that made me any different from any other woman, except that I'm lucky in bed? Maybe I'm lucky because it's the one thing I have a positive attitude about. I suppose if I ever believed I could be good in a relationship, I could have one.

When the bridge was down but not out, I was looking at it one night from Russ Nelman's balcony, thinking that my really good quality was my doggedness—I could keep going. If a relationship didn't work out, I'd just pick myself up and go on to another. I hadn't even really thought that when you start to get older, you get a little tired of always moving.

I came off the bridge and let go of my button. An old song, "The Back Stabbers," was on, and I had to hit scan before the next "*What they do?*" I found Ron Walden, and Rabbi Shelly Birnbaum was on the show.

"Is there a God, and how does He know what's trivial? Go ahead, caller."

"Yeah, hi, Ron, this is Norm Fingerman, and by the way, I want to say I really love your show. Now, I have a question for the rabbi. If God let the Holocaust happen, then why would He help my plastering business succeed? I mean, you know, why bother?"

"Well, first of all, Mr. Fingerman, I don't think He just let it happen. God is not like a lucky charm. You can't just call on Him like He's a rabbit's foot."

"Thank you. Go ahead, next caller."

"Yeah, hi. I wanted to ask the rabbi what would be an appropriate Christmas present for a Jewish person?"

I got to the International Hotel just as they were lighting the tree in the lobby. I wondered if some Marxist or Buddhist or Moslem was going to organize a protest against it. I remembered the time they put the nativity scene in front of city hall in Teaneck, and Harry Gurvitz stood there for days in a blizzard dressed as Moses, carrying a sign that said, "Where's the menorah, already?" The man had nerve, he had gumption. He was the classic little man against the world. And at my best, I was like him. That's the book I should write. Not *The Fall of the House of Yuppie*. Not *Salvation: How to Save Your Stupid Marriage*. But *Harry Gurvitz: A Man and His Formica*. That's how I could memorialize him. Write about him, tell his stories.

The sounds of "Silent Night" were being piped into the lobby. "Christ our savior is bo-orn . . ." Where was an atheist when you needed one? I stopped to complain to Jeff who worked at the reception desk, and he told me a guy had come to see me and was waiting up in my room.

I walked up the stairs slowly, and made a little deal like those deals I always made when I was a kid and Harry and Lenore told me I couldn't have a scooter or something because it was dangerous. It was the original deal. If there was a God, it would be Russ. If there wasn't, it would be Neil Blender, and I would insist that I be given equal screen credit and at least Guild scale, and that we keep our relationship strictly professional. I needed a screen credit.

At least the Academy Award fantasy would still be kept alive, and having a fantasy is almost better than having a life. Only this time, it would be Rabbi Birnbaum who handed it to me, and I would say, "There are a lot of people I could thank, but let them get their own award." Then I'd hold the trophy up and say, "Laura, this is for you. You're a survivor and you deserve it."

Was calling myself a survivor offensive to Survivors?

I don't know. We live in confusing times. Maybe we'll look back on these past years as a golden age, and maybe we'll see them as a time when we were all on remote control. When I took stock of myself, I had to say that I had come through it all a more complete person. I could breathe, I had a pulse, and my internal bleeding was under control. My brain function may have actually improved as a result of what happened in the last few months. And I had heart. Maybe not miles and miles of it, but I could feel it beating. I opened the door to my room and definitely felt a little tremor. Either it was another aftershock or it was my heart.

Which way would it go? Would I shake it to the left or shake it to the right? Would I get a life or a lifestyle? Would I be outta there or into something? Would I be what's hot or what's not? These things may be trivial, but they were serious to me.

It turns out that yes, there is a God.

He smelled of Selsun. He had rinsed with Scope. And he was watching the Niners on my portable TV.